I0586645

Elvira

Wonders

Sanna Hines

FOR MY FATHER

CHAPTER ONE

People didn't move to Elvira. They moved away, generally in the middle of the night, after they'd pissed off some creature or run out of money.

A year ago, Elvira teetered one step away from ghost town. Now Josh stood in the moonlight looking at three upscale houses plunked down in a repurposed cornfield, their sod so new it still showed stripes. He didn't recognize the names on the mail boxes.

Things were changing in his tiny town.

All Josh knew about the place he and Archie, his ghost-hunting partner, were investigating tonight he learned from his girlfriend, Georgia. The homeowner, Bobbi Miller, arrived with a husband, took a nursing job at the nearest hospital, divorced the husband, and put up the house for sale. When she confessed fears of being watched and a bad presence in the basement, Georgia, her real estate agent, sent in Josh and Archie.

Bobbi opened the front screen door and approached Josh's position by Archie's van. A leggy, curvy blonde in jeans and tank top, she looked to be a year or two older than he was, maybe twenty-five or -six. "I heard a shout and then saw you running away," she said.

"Not running," Josh lied. "I, uh, I needed stuff from the van."

Bobbi's round blue eyes narrowed. "Something happened, didn't it? You saw him."

"I saw something by the bedroom window," Josh admitted. He left out the part about the menacing black silhouette.

"I *knew* he'd show up if I had a man in the house!" Bobbi crowed.

Josh shrugged. Panicked to escape, he dropped his camera. The only proof of the phenomenon was a lump on the head, self-inflicted, when he bashed into the master bedroom door.

Fortunately, Archie chose that moment to shove back the van's slider. "It's late. We should wrap things up." Archie flashed his winning smile at Bobbi with all the confidence of a guy who knew women liked his sandy good looks. If there'd been an ocean closer than a thousand miles away, he would have fit right in riding a surfboard.

Archie and Bobbi went into the house while Josh reached inside the van to grab a chilled soda can, which he held to his bruised forehead. He phoned Georgia. When she answered, he didn't bother with chitchat. "You can't sell this house. It's dangerous."

"How so?" From her tone, you'd have thought it was 2 p.m., not 2 a.m.

"In the basement, I felt like throwing up."

"Radon or bad wiring. I'll set out counters."

"The attic," Josh persisted, "has rustling noises."

"Could be bats or raccoons." Josh heard Georgia scribbling. "What else?"

"The bedroom. I got a whale of a bruise up there."

"Should you be telling *me* about your bedroom adventures?" Georgia purred.

"Damn it! You're not taking me seriously."

"I never do. That's why we get along so well."

Josh pictured Georgia smiling. Thinking about that smile and the luscious, red-haired babe behind it, he couldn't stay angry. "Hows about I come by your place for some TLC?"

"I'll be heading your way. A buyer is ready to make an offer on the house, but he wants a final walkthrough."

"Now?"

"He's a *newcomer*." Georgia's voice dropped to a confidential whisper. "You know we need to make them welcome. If we don't bring jobs back to Elvira, our town will dry up and blow away. The newcomers should help us attract tourists."

"This the guy with three wives?"

"He calls them 'sisters', so we'll leave it at that. Put Bobbi on the phone."

Josh frowned at the house. "She's inside. Call her direct, okay?"

Ten minutes later, Archie hadn't returned. Josh left the van to peer through the screen door. A shadow on the stairs slithered toward him. He backed away, and collided with someone. Turning, he found a stocky man in dark clothes.

Eying Josh, his expression unimpressed by what he saw, the new arrival said with a heavy Spanish accent, "I am here for Rrrroberta."

"She's probably still in the bedroom with Arch. They should be finishing up soon. I'm Josh Seldom," he said, sticking out his hand, "paranormal investigator."

The newcomer took it, fingers chilly as his gaze. "Enrique Molinero. Now, if you would let me enter?"

"Oh, sure. Go on in." Josh held open the door for the potential home buyer.

Molinero stalked across the floor of the cathedral-ceilinged hall. He bellowed, "Rrrroberta!" then something in Spanish, and bounded up the stairs, taking them two at a time.

Josh wrenched open the door to follow the newcomer, certain only things weren't right. A stream of staccato Spanish poured out from the master bedroom. Josh heard, "Screw you, Ricky!" before Archie flew through the door, thudded against the balcony railing, and floundered there, swinging his arms wildly to keep from pitching backward over it.

Jumping the last three steps, Josh caught Archie's shirt to yank him away from the rail. "What's happening?" Josh howled. Gasping, Arch pointed at the open doorway.

Inside the bedroom, Molinero had both hands on Bobbi's throat, choking her, shouting in her face. Her kick between his legs only made him yell louder and haul back a beefy fist. Josh plunged in to seize the attacker, who shot him a black look, then flicked him off with a nonchalant backhand.

Sent careening toward the door, Josh hit the edge, his head taking another whack in the same place as before. Vision clouding, he sank down, felt Archie rush by, then heard him grunt from a shove against the closet. Josh stumbled to his feet, feeling no real hope of stopping Molinero: That sucker wasn't going to be an easy take-down even with Archie's help.

The window screen exploded inward, clipping Molinero's right arm. Dropping Archie, he batted the crumpled mesh away, growling as a man in a black running suit stepped through the opening. Thirtyish, dark-haired and lanky, the man looked fit but no match for Molinero. Josh watched in astonishment as the new arrival cupped a hand, waggling the fingers, making the gesture meaning 'Come on!'

Head down, Molinero charged. His target stepped smoothly aside, caught Molinero's belt, and heaved him out the window. Josh heard a heavy thump, a yowl, and furious Spanish shouts.

The man in black said gently but urgently to Bobbi, "If you can manage it, *now* would be a good time to exclude him."

She scrambled to her feet and yelled from the window, "Go to hell, Ricky. You're not wanted here, you goatsucker. Don't come back!" Smirking with satisfaction, she crossed her arms, addressing her unexpected rescuer. "Who are you?"

"My name is Anton de Salis. I have an appointment to view your charming home. When I heard the commotion, I thought I might be of assistance. Have you been injured?" He had a curious accent, sort of British, sort of something else—Italian, maybe.

Bobbi fingered her throat. "Minor contusions. I'll be sore for a while." Looking closely at de Salis, she cringed. "You're one of them!"

De Salis shook his head. "I am not of the Mayan tribe. My people have different ways." He smiled, close-mouthed, at Bobbi.

A chorus of high-pitched, triumphant female shrieks rose up from below. Bobbi turned toward the window. De Salis blocked her view, saying, "My sisters prefer not to be interrupted when they are being persuasive. They will encourage the Mayan to depart quickly. It is best to leave them to it. May I?" He indicated the wooden shutters. Not waiting for an answer, he drew them closed and clicked the latch into place. "Fine quality," he remarked of the hardware.

Josh cast a glance at Archie, who looked as confused as Josh felt. Eyes darting from Bobbi to de Salis, Josh demanded, "Who *was* that? How did you get in a second-floor window? What's going on outside?"

"The ex," Bobbi spat out in answer to the first question. "He still thinks he owns me." She frowned at Josh. "But he shouldn't have been able to enter the house without an invitation."

Josh muttered, "My bad. I thought he was, well, *that* guy." Pointing to de Salis, he asked, "You're a...a...."

"Newcomer, yes," de Salis said evenly. "Are you troubled by the fact?"

"Hey, live and let live." Josh hoped the last part applied to the current situation. Werewolves, giants, fairies, and birds big as buses were old hat—hell, he'd grown up in Elvira—but vampires were new. He wasn't used to being so up close and personal with them yet.

Archie's head cocked right as he listened to the outdoor fracas, which ended with one loud scream. He asked, "Are those—whatever they are down there—*eating* the guy?"

"Merely reminding him of proper manners. Seems I've forgotten mine," de Salis noted. "This is a bad time for a walkthrough, I suppose."

"You still want to see my house?" Bobbi broke out in laughter punctuated by coughing. As de Salis patted her back, Georgia entered the room, her motorcycle helmet wedged under one leather-clad arm.

"Sorry," she said. "Couldn't get in sooner. There's a police cruiser blocking the driveway." Georgia wrinkled her nose and told Josh, "*Tom's* here."

"Not at Wolf Creek so close to the full moon? He must need money."

Shrugging, Georgia continued, "Cops earn plenty in this town. He'll have to hole up in his mother's basement if he cuts it too close." She put a bright smile on her face. "Looks like everyone's met. Are we ready for the tour?"

CHAPTER TWO

Three women stood waiting patiently before the screen door. After Georgia ushered them in, they made straight for Anton de Salis, forming a semi-circle around him, touching his arms and face, murmuring soft sounds of concern.

Normally, Josh didn't much notice what women wore, but three identical dresses in white, red and black with plunging necklines and fabric hugging each curve got his full attention. Short skirts. Tall heels. Josh sighed as the ladies passed him, one blonde as an angel, one with red curls an Irish dancer would have killed for, the last a tiny, doll-like woman with cropped black hair and china-blue eyes. They all had shapes that could stop traffic. Josh reminded himself to breathe.

"You can pick up your jaw now," Georgia whispered sweetly into his ear. "And remember, they're clients," she added.

"Not my clients," Josh hedged.

"If they buy this house you're investigating, they'll be your clients."

De Salis turned to the others. "Please, may I introduce Ioana, Trulia and Annina?"

"I'm delighted to meet you all," Georgia said. "We'll start with the top floor." She gestured toward the stairs. Josh noted happily how Georgia's backside, seemingly poured into her leather bike pants, held its own against the de Salis women.

Head atilt, Archie watched Bobbi retreat to the kitchen. He whispered to Josh, "Dayum. Five hot women in this house and none of them mine. Only thing waiting for me at home is Internet porn." He slapped Josh's shoulder. "Let's pack up our stuff."

A rap on the door made them turn. "Police!" Tom Hanrahan said unnecessarily. Josh had known Big Tommy since first grade, when the third-grader regularly pummeled him on the playground. A hulking bruiser even then—rumor said he had kin in Giantville—seventeen years later, Officer Hanrahan filled the doorway. He let himself into Bobbi Miller's house.

"Seldom," he said, as though Josh's name were a judgment, "and Ferguson. You nerds still playing Spook House?"

"They're working," Georgia replied, coming down the stairs, "like I am. Since you're working, too, maybe I could get some of the child support you owe me."

"I have expenses," Tom Hanrahan muttered, looking down at his size sixteen shoes.

"Put off your chest waxing until next month," Georgia suggested. "Benji's wearing flood pants. Oh, and he needs supplies for his experiments."

"What kid does experiments when he's four?" Tom huffed. "He should be playing with the Legos I gave him."

"He, um, vanished the Legos."

Tom frowned. "Vanished?"

"One of his experiments made them disappear."

"Look," Tom said, striding over to tower above Georgia. He wagged a sausage-sized forefinger in her face. "This is personal. I'm here on business. Where's the resident?"

Bobbi reappeared and introduced herself. Though she spoke evenly, Josh noticed her studying Tom, who restlessly tapped a foot. His coarse, blond hair draped over the uniform collar, his eyebrows were merging into a unibrow, and he needed a shave. Badly.

"I'm Officer Hanrahan. Your neighbors reported some kind of animal fight outside. I found broken bushes by the east side of the house. You been having any trouble with animals—large ones, glowing eyes?"

Bobbi blinked. "Animals? No."

Looking relieved, Tom eyed Bobbi with more than professional interest. Gaze returning to her top half, he asked, "I see bruises on your neck."

"My former husband came by." Bobbi stroked her throat.

"You could press charges."

Bobbi shook her head. "He's not coming back. And there won't be any more trouble. Thanks for looking in."

It took Tom a moment to realize he'd been dismissed. He stood there, scratching at his forearms and shifting from foot to foot until the sound of distant baying drifted in. "Gotta run," he said, brightening. He scrambled for the door.

"Hanrahan… Your ex, Georgia?" Bobbi asked. After Georgia's nod, she said, "He seemed, well, rather agitated for a police officer."

Georgia shrugged. "He's a Louie. Wolf Creek pack Alpha. It's getting near that time of the month."

That was such an old, old Elviran joke Josh winced. Bobbi didn't get it. "What's a louie?"

"*Loup garou*, fancy French term for werewolf," Georgia explained.

Bobbi stared at her. "You're kidding."

"Nope," Archie put in. "You should keep a wolfsbane bunch handy. We all do. Abby stocks them at her shop."

"Which shop?"

"Hirsute," Archie answered, pronouncing it *hair-suit*. "In front, she sells werewolf wear—you know, with Velcro seams and all—but she stocks herbs in back. Stores the wolfsbane vacuum-sealed so her shaggy customers won't complain."

Just then, the de Salises descended the staircase in single file. Georgia turned to them. "Can I answer any questions about the house?"

"It seems very comfortable, very suited to our needs," Anton replied. "The ladies wish to see this floor and the lower level, of course. Afterward, we'll be leaving. I'll contact you by phone in the morning."

"About the basement—" Josh began, mindful of his responsibilities as paranormal investigator.

"There's an unquiet spirit. Yes, we know. Some violence occurred in this location years ago," Anton said equably. "Such things do not trouble us. We are well able to look after ourselves."

"Ah," Josh said because he could think of nothing else to say.

As the vampire family continued their tour, Archie with Bobbi returned to the master bedroom to retrieve the camera Josh left there. Josh wound electric cords. When he was done, Georgia helped him carry equipment to the van.

She said anxiously, "I *hope* they make an offer. I'd be looking at three sales this month."

"What're the others?"

"De Salis bought Finny's Bar and the warehouse next door. He's turning them into a restaurant and nightclub."

"The Mayans are already up and running with their place. Two vampire clubs could be a little much for Elvira."

"De Salis thinks there's plenty of business opportunity. I guess he knows what he's talking about: He has clubs all over Europe. The difference is here he won't have to conceal the fact he and his people are vampires.

"And there'll be *lots* of tourists in Elvira, Josh, if Mayor Stedwell's plan works out. Half the town signed up to do bed & breakfast stints on weekends. Harry's motel will cater to the low-light crowd with blackout shades and snacks of hearty hemoglobin. For human blood, they'll have to visit the drugstore's drive-up window. It'll be pricey, though." Georgia paused. "That reminds me: Can't forget to donate blood next week."

Josh rubbed his nose. He didn't much like seeing blood of any kind, especially his own. He might just forget about the blood drive. "Harry's such a chicken. I'm amazed he wants the vamp trade at his motel."

Georgia chuckled. "He had this special neck brace made—looks like the kind you'd get after a bad crash, but it's lined with steel. Thinks it'll keep him healthy."

"Hope it works out for him," Josh muttered, shutting the van's rear doors. "The giants ever come around?"

"Yes. They'll be holding special events each weekend at the high school stadium. Even the fairies figured they could keep up with their war without too much interference after Stedwell offered them half the take on tour tickets and promised only two groups each day along the main path at Fern Cliffe."

"Which fairies, the Reds or the Greens?"

"Both. Their gift shops will be at opposite ends of the path."

"Did you know Stedwell's suckered Archie into leading thunderbird adventure tours?" Josh asked.

"No! Too crazy. They're dangerous."

"Archie figures those birds are big, but they can't lift a Hummer." Josh shook his head. "Personally, I'd rather sign on for water nymph tours—I mean, if I weren't with you," he put in hastily.

"No luck there. Gotta be a woman. A man couldn't keep his head on straight. We'd lose half the tourists," Georgia said with a smirk. "You might think about a ghost walk, though. You know all the hot spots."

"Good idea if I had the extra time. Well, I'm done here." Josh looked at the sky. "Not much night left."

"Ugh. I have to be out by seven to check my ads in the newspaper before the print deadline."

"Hardly any point in trying to sleep, then." Josh waggled his eyebrows. "Benji at your mom's?"

"Yes…" Georgia slid her arms under Josh's. Snuggled against him, she turned up her lovely face, soft skin peppered with freckles, lips parted invitingly. "Still want some TLC?"

"More than ever," Josh murmured.

He woke to a thump in the gut, two jabs to the ribcage and one eyelid yanked open. Josh was back in the playground with tow-headed, snub-nosed Tommy Hanrahan sitting on him, grinning, big teeth filling most of Josh's view. But no, the eyes weren't brown. They were Georgia's clear green, and they were full of curiosity not malice.

"Hi, Joswa," Georgia's son Benji chirped, releasing the eyelid to perch, face in hands, on Josh's chest, his skinny elbows etching divots into the pecs.

"Hey, Benj. Where'd you come from?" Josh turned his head, expecting to find Georgia's mother, Atlanta Beckett, standing in the doorway.

"Gramma dropped me off. She had to work. Aunt Vanny's at school. Mommy told Gramma you'd be here. We have all day to play!"

"I wish, kid." Josh gripped Benji by the armpits and hoisted him aloft. Squealing with glee, Benji's swinging feet kicked him in the groin before Josh twisted sideways. Benji toppled to the bed, bouncing and shouting, "Again! Do it again!"

Josh groaned and tried not to rub his nuts. He rubbed the lump on his head instead. Benji picked up on his anguish, if not the cause. "Joswa, did you have a nightmare?"

"Nightmare?"

"I always sleep with Mommy when I get one. Did you dream about the Big Bad Wolf?"

Thinking about Tommy Hanrahan, Josh said, "Maybe. What time is it?"

"Hungry time."

"What's the clock say?"

Benji rolled off the bed to stand by the dresser. "It says eight one O."

"Too early," Josh groaned. "Oh, well. I'm awake now. I'll make you pancakes—with chocolate chips if you have them. Then I've got to pull an engine at the garage."

Benji stuck out his lower lip. "But who'll take care of me?"

"I will. You'll help me. Ever pull a Hummer engine?"

"No!" Benji sputtered. "I'm four years old!"

"High time you learned." Josh grinned.

"A smiley face," Benji insisted, "on the pancakes."

"Sure thing, Benj. Go downstairs and grab the stuff we need. I have to get dressed and hit the can first."

As Benji headed toward the door, Josh remembered, "Wait. I need to ask you something." He took a deep breath. "How'd you feel if I was here all the time…lived here, I mean? I like your mama and you an awful lot."

Benji asked gravely, "Will you go to the cellar, growl, and break things?"

"No." Josh held the boy's gaze so he'd see the truth in those words.

"Will you stop me doing my 'speriments?"

"What 'speriments you doing these days, Benj?"

Benji shrugged, turning away, looking uncomfortable. "Fairy stuff," he whispered.

"Whoa, whoa! You're not trying to catch them, are you? They get really testy about that." *Damned testy.* Josh remembered another issue. "They ever try to talk you into going away with them?"

"No, I know the rules," Benji scoffed. "We meet by the horse pasture. They show me things, and I try to do them. I'm pretty good at it."

"You have the Gift," Josh felt a surge of nostalgia. He had fairy friends as a boy, like nearly everyone else in town. One old guy, Sedge by name, thought Josh had some talent, but it never panned out. When Josh hit puberty, his fairies drifted away. "Cool. Your mom good with this?"

"She says I'm lucky. Are you going to feed me now?"

"Real soon."

Georgia's pantry was bare—well, it was out chocolate chips, so Josh proposed breakfast in town at the Country Kitchen, assuring Benji they never ran out of smiley-face pancakes. While the boy gathered his things into a backpack, Josh wondered if Georgia fed the horses. Calling to Benji, he told him he was going to the barn.

Josh liked Georgia's horses. He'd ridden with her at the Beckett farm often enough when they were in school. Then her dad got sick and the Beckett family moved into town, except Georgia, who'd married Tom and stayed on the farm. While Tom was around, Georgia worried about the horses, boarding her bay geldings with a friend. Now Tom was gone, so Hank and Harley came home.

Crossing the flaking, green porch, Josh saw Hank grazing in the backyard. He walked over to catch Hank's halter before stroking his nose. "How'd you get out? Where's your buddy?" Harley, around the corner of the house, looked up, then trailed Josh and Hank as they ambled toward the pasture through soft, spring grass.

The electric fence was down, the gate section missing. *Odd.* Releasing Hank to inspect the damage, Josh saw the wire cut past the last insulator. He walked the fence line, looking for an explanation.

He found it. Laced to the dead thorn tree, a red-black mass no bigger than a newborn baby hung suspended, gruesome and gory. The head was smashed in. Wisps of gray hair mixed with gobs of brains spilling over a face, now crushed, unrecognizable. Wire wound from head to feet, the body naked and limp as a rag doll, every joint rounded as though each bone had been broken and only skin held the corpse together. The wings, unique to each fairy, were gone; only a scrap of cloth and a piece of copper chain maille identified the dead warrior as a Red.

Josh's eyes focused on the copper links. He remembered asking…

"Where did you get your metal shirt? It's pretty."

Sedge told him, "Each warrior makes his own. Comes from the heart, y' know, the pattern. Shows the warrior's spirit."

Seven-year-old Joshie said, "I like yours. It's nicer than any other fairy's."

"Thankee, laddie. Have ye been practicin' what I showed ye?"

Joshie hung his head. "I can't do it."

"Ye're young yet. Ye'll learn," Sedge soothed. "Have faith, and ye'll not fail."

I failed you, Sedge. Josh regarded the sad remains of his old friend.

Why? Hot anger shot through his veins, making his temples throb. *Why would anyone kill—torture—a fairy? How could anyone do this?*

Tears filled his eyes. He blinked furiously, but that didn't help. His cheeks were wet when an icy thought forced its way past grief: Fairies lived a long, long time. They never forgot; they never forgave.

There was going to be hell to pay.

CHAPTER THREE

Savannah Beckett slammed her locker door. "Well, that's it!" she told her BFF, Megan Shaw. They mirrored each other, both sporting black hair with crimson dip-dyes held in high pigtails, bright red mouths, pointed noses, and smoky eyes. Wearing identical black corsets and flares, they fell into a hug and sang, "No more school!"

"I can't believe it." Megan bent to hoist her backpack, now crammed with the accumulated junk of her last year in high school. "It's really, really *over*. Stupid of them to make us come in for an hour this morning, though."

Leaning against the locker bank, Vanny replied, "Yeah. Like we didn't already know we had to show up at six tonight to get our diplomas."

"Incoming," Megan whispered, nudging Vanny, who shoved off the lockers and shook out her pigtails.

"Morning, Miss Beckett, Miss Shaw," said the young science teacher in his deep, resonant voice.

"Morning, Mr. Snopes," Vanny and Megan replied in chorus. Hands on hips, Vanny produced a slow, enticing smile. Mr. Snopes held her gaze for a moment, graced her with a nod, then went on his way. The girls watched his supple backside disappear around the corner.

"Oh…" Megan moaned. "I love the way he calls us 'Miss'. Sounds so sophisticated." She stuck out her lower lip. "No more droolworthy Mr. Snopes."

Vanny shrugged. "He'll be around—and we won't be his students. I expect to see him at the club this summer."

Megan's eyes went wide. "You got the job."

"Uh huh. You're looking at The Feathered Serpent's newest employee. I'm the cover charge taker. The bouncer is Ricky, and he's a real fox."

"Is he…?"

"Of course. They all are except me."

"You're so brave, Vanny. What if they bite you?"

"The owner, Mr. Suarez, won't tolerate mingling among employees. Mingling—get it?"

"As in blood." Megan shivered. "But what about Benji? You're supposed to babysit him."

"During the days, stupid! Nights, I'll have better things to do."

"And look at," Megan added enviously. "Seriously, how cool is it to have guys come in you've never seen before?"

"Someone other than the twenty-six boys we've known since we were all in diapers, you mean." Vanny rubbed her hands together. "Way cool."

"And your mom's letting you work there?"

"She thinks I'll be running the night window at the drugstore."

Megan nodded, noting bitterly, "All I have planned for this summer is sweeping up at the hair salon. Same old, same old, though Mom put in a special booth for the newcomers."

"They need haircuts?"

"Sure. Hair and nails grow even after death," Megan said smugly. "Everyone knows that."

"I didn't, but I suppose they'd get kind of threadbare after a while if their hair didn't grow. Say, they don't show up in mirrors. How will they check their dos?"

"Mom worked it out. She put up an old movie projector screen and a spotlight. They'll get the silhouettes. Nails they can see for themselves."

"Slick." Vanny's phone started playing the *Addams Family* theme. Answering, she listened, then said, "Oh, okay. I'll be there."

"That was Josh," Vanny reported. "I have to get Benji and take him to breakfast. There's some trouble at the farm."

"What kind of trouble?"

"Dunno. Josh sounded freaked, though."

"I'm coming, too," Megan announced.

Josh moved fast. He put the horses in the barn, grabbed a clean saddle blanket to cover Sedge, called Georgia, who didn't answer, then her sister, Vanny. All the while, he'd been terrified Benji would come looking for him and find Sedge, but he intercepted the boy on the porch, took him inside and tried to break the news gently, giving Benji the idea Sedge died peacefully of old age.

Benji's concept of death was hazy, but he'd been told his grandfather "went home to God" last year. Josh put his foot down when Benji asked to see Sedge. Benji raged before frustration gave way to tears. Josh held the boy while he cried until Vanny appeared. Josh told her only that a fairy died, discouraging any questions with a warning shake of his head. Vanny scooped Benji into their special 'monkey baby' hold. Arms and legs wrapped around her, he allowed himself to be carried off. At last, Josh called the cops.

Unsurprised to find Tom off duty this morning, Josh explained the situation to his boss, Ed Brown. Josh had enough history with Chief Brown to be on a first-name basis.

"Fairies are always fighting," said Ed. "One of them offed another. Bag it, and bring it in. I'll drive it out to Fern Cliffe. It's a Red, you say?"

Josh counted to ten before answering. Half a dozen years older than Tom, Ed was only slightly more intelligent. "His name was Sedge, and he was Red Branch. But no, I'm not shoveling him into a garbage bag. We're looking at torture and murder, Ed."

"He had enemies. Maybe a slew of 'em."

"They don't KILL each other!" Josh howled, losing it. "Their fights are about embarrassing the other guy. No fairy did this."

"How do you know that?" Ed challenged. "You some fairy expert?

Like to go prancing in a tutu by moonlight?"

"Listen, you moron," Josh growled. "Someone wound Sedge in steel wire—*steel*. Steel's made from iron, and fairies don't touch iron. It burns them." Josh stopped, suddenly realizing how much Sedge suffered just from the binding, his whole body seared by contact with the wire. Josh cleared his throat, then went on.

"Maybe the creep likes torturing anything helpless. That'd include animals and children. Tom's *son* lives here."

Josh could hear Ed's sudden intake of breath. On a roll, Josh kept at it. "Could be the killer hates non-humans. There's a full moon tonight. He might be packing silver bullets to take out some overlarge wolves at the Creek compound when none of them has a man's brains to defend himself. Who knows what a psycho killer loose in Elvira will do next?"

"Sweet Jesus," Ed said, getting it. Finally.

When Mayor Stedwell showed up along with Ed, Josh let out a sigh of relief. A middle-aged African-American, Stedwell was a straight-up guy, and smart. Hired as village manager last spring then elected mayor in the fall, Maurice Stedwell's recruitment had been a last-ditch effort by residents to save their post office. Once a place lost its zip code—got consolidated into another town—it was gone, just a name on a road sign. Faced with their town's imminent demise, Elvira's two hundred thirty families anteed up a respectable salary and a bit more to fit out a decent office for their champion.

Mo Stedwell earned his money. First, he saved the post office with some fancy lawyering. Next, he shocked hell out of residents by proposing a plan so radical it took six months of hard arguing to sell. Elvira had more than good farmland and countless acres of picturesque forest: Elvira was unique, and it was time to start cashing in on that fact. Tourists would pay real money to see the fairies, giants, thunderbirds and nymphs. They'd be thrilled to walk among werewolves and vampires, to visit an active, ancient Egyptian community. There'd be jobs and prosperity in Elvira again.

Stedwell's clincher was to rebate his salary in exchange for a piece of the action from the 'Elvira Wonderland' he wanted to create. He bet big on success, and so, now, did most of the town.

Josh lifted the blanket from Sedge. Stedwell pursed his lips, saying, "Bad business. I'd be the last one in town to know what this means, but it couldn't come at a worse time for Elvira, what with the tourist season starting this weekend."

"Didn't do Sedge much good, either," Josh grumbled.

Stedwell winced. Motioning Ed to get on with collecting evidence, he took Josh aside. "I'm sorry for sounding insensitive. I'm still learning about the relationships Elvirans form with other species. You knew the victim?"

"We were friends when I was a child. He's Benji's friend now—*was* Benji's friend," Josh amended.

"How's the boy taking it?"

Josh shrugged. "He's four. He'll forget in a while. The fairies won't. Sedge's murder will start a war. All the Reds will join in; maybe the Greens, too. They squabble among themselves, but when push comes to shove, they've more in common with each other than with us humans."

Stedwell rubbed the back of his neck. "Any hope of stopping this war?"

"Finding Sedge's killer will help some. His armor— Ed, bring the evidence bags here."

Looking relieved to be called away from the gruesome task of unwinding wire from the corpse, Ed trudged over to the others. Josh pointed to the bag with the copper maille. "Only part of Sedge's shirt is here. Somebody took the rest. His wings and spear are missing, too. Whoever has those is the killer, or knows who is."

"I can't search every house in town," Ed said.

"But there's the pre-launch inspection," Stedwell remembered. "I'm supposed to do the rounds, make sure everything's up to snuff for opening day, especially at the B&Bs and shops. I'll keep my eyes open."

"I'm volunteering to lead ghost walk tours," Josh decided on the spot. "At least until the killer's found. Give me a list of places you aren't visiting, Mayor, and I'll knock on those doors, asking about paranormal experiences. I'll keep my eyes open, too."

"Thanks, but don't take chances. If you suspect anyone of this crime, wait for law enforcement." Stedwell glanced toward Ed, who pulled back his shoulders.

"I think you're barking up the wrong tree, Mayor. No offense," Ed added hastily. "We've always had fairies around Elvira. Came in covered wagons with the Irish, they say, then jumped ship when they heard about the prairies ahead. Didn't want to settle where there wasn't no forest.

"So why would an Elviran suddenly take to killing fairies? Could've been someone passing through—or the Gories. They'd love to see us sucking wind on this Elvira Wonderland thing."

Stedwell tapped a finger on his lips, then said, "Mayor Marshal has been supportive of our plans, but I suppose not everyone in Goreton agrees. I'll have a talk with Laura."

He turned to Josh. "One more thing: Do you know what fairy customs are concerning death? Will we violate any taboos by keeping the remains at the hospital morgue?"

"Ask Mrs. Withers. She's the only adult in town who claims to have the Gift."

The mayor squinted uncertainly. Josh explained that Mrs. Withers believed she could do fairy magic.

Raising an eyebrow, Stedwell asked, "Would you visit her? I don't know the woman. If I show up on her doorstep, she'll wonder why. I'd like to keep this..." Stedwell waved his hand at the crime scene, "quiet for a while, just until the coroner's gone over the body for clues. It'd help, I think, to have something concrete to tell the fairies when I take their comrade home. Perhaps you'll turn up some leads, as well."

"Crap!" Josh slapped his forehead. "I have to work today. The Hummer for the thunderbird tours is laid up in the garage."

"Put it off for a while. The tours won't start until next week. This matter takes precedence."

Checking in at the garage with his boss, Mike Mateer, Josh found the mayor had already called and convinced Mike to give him time off. That was a welcome surprise, but before Josh could start sniffing around, he needed food. He saw Georgia's motorcycle parked in front of the Country Kitchen, so he headed that way.

Peering across the room, he spotted her red hair, done up in a mass of braids bound with gold clips and blue beads. Josh slid onto a red vinyl chair across the table from her. "Somebody's remaking *Cleopatra* and you're angling for a part?"

Georgia laughed. She shook her head so the beads clattered. "I had to try the new Egyptian spa. The Egyptians have always been so mysterious. But now they've set up the spa for tourists, I couldn't resist giving it a try. I figured they do so well with the animal mummies, they'd have to be good with live people.

"And I felt like celebrating—de Salis bought the house! Now Bobbi's looking for a little place, a rent with option to buy." Closing her eyes, which were rimmed with black lines ending in triangles along her cheeks, Georgia reminisced, "The spa was wonderful: marble massage tables, acres of gauzy curtains, flute girls—"

"Wait a minute," Josh said. "I thought the priests were all men."

"They hired in from Goreton's marching band. The flute girls were costumed in black wigs and white robes. Very cute. And—"

She interrupted herself to stand, waving energetically at Benji, Vanny and Megan, who appeared outside the Country Kitchen's window. The girls were laden with packages; Benji looked bored out of his mind. Georgia went to hug her child, who pulled away, regarding her new look dubiously. She hugged him again, kissed his cheek, and spoke to the girls, who then walked on with Benji.

A subdued expression on her face, Georgia returned to the restaurant table. "What happened at the farm?"

Josh told her, omitting the worst details.

"I'll have to keep Benji in town with my mother," Georgia said. "I don't want him playing where some maniac might hurt him or my sister while she's watching him."

"Aren't you worried for yourself?"

"You'll keep me safe. Stay with me a while."

"As long as you want me," Josh promised.

Georgia left to reclaim her son, planning to take him to Giants' Park. Josh wondered if that was wise. Sure, Benji was big for his age, but the park challenged much older kids. Built during the Depression as a WPA project, the park meant money for the giants, so they'd done a good job. Giants were sticklers for contracts.

Problem was they built a park for giant-sized children. The swings were long; you could get going high and fast. The slide was ginormous. A kid falling off it....

Josh shook his head. He knew how Georgia would react to any criticism of her parenting: "He's *my* son, not yours!" And there'd be that flash of anger in her eyes, the memory of five years ago when he abandoned her senior year, his only aim in life getting into Cissy Rettger's pants. He'd figured to make his move at the graduation bash in Krueger's field, but there he'd discovered Cissy's sights were set on Archie. So, while Arch got lucky, Josh got drunk. Georgia hooked up with Tommy Hanrahan.

Well, that was the past. Josh paid his bill and stepped out into lemony, spring sunlight.

Elvira looks good, real good. Across the street, the movie theater finally replaced its John Wayne posters with new ones of a vampire saga. The pizza parlor's repainted plastic chef held a pie with red sauce, not sun-bleached pink. There was no difference in the stone-faced Wolves' Lodge, but Josh expected none. Some traditions would never change.

Walking up Main Street, Jose noted how Hirsute had added mannequins with Goth clothes and one looking like a Halloween vampire. From what Josh observed about the de Salis women, he figured they wouldn't be caught dead in those outfits.

With a grimace for his own stupid pun, he glanced into the corner drugstore, which had a cheesy fairy theme going. The figurines made in China looked nothing like real fairies.

Josh crossed the street. Standing before Benton's Hardware, he pursed his lips. In the window sat the same dusty toilets set there in 1962. Josh knew that for a fact. Behind the antique cash register hung a picture of young Walter Benton with a full head of hair posed proudly before those toilets at the store's grand opening.

Old, bald Walter Benton shuffled to the doorway. "Interested in toilets, are you?" Benton asked eagerly.

"I'm good for toilets," Josh assured him, noting critically, "This display's been here a while."

Benton hmphed. "Why mess with things when they're fine as they are? Just look at the newcomer club up the street. That Feathered Serpent should be in Disneyland. It'll bring noise and commotion, sure as shootin'."

A shadow fell on Benton's face. "Hi, fellers. Need somethin'?"

"Him," a gravelly voice rumbled. Josh whirled. In seconds, he was lifted under both armpits to stare into the scowling faces of two giants.

CHAPTER FOUR

"**P**ut me the hell down!" Josh yelled at the giant brothers, Humphrey and Christopher Thoon, who held him suspended between them. Both were blond and brown-eyed; they reminded Josh of super-sized Tommy Hanrahans. The Thoons were teenagers, not yet full grown, but they were pushing nine feet tall, Josh guessed, by the air space beneath his feet.

"You get the part for our truck yet?" Humph bellowed, squeezing Josh's left arm.

Josh flinched from pain in his arm and ears. Giants always talked too loud. "I'm *working* on it." He kicked out at Humph, who dodged the blow but gave Josh a hearty shaking in response.

"We need our truck for Saturday," Chris roared, clamping down on Josh's right shoulder. "There's a prize in the monster truck race."

"And if we win, Grid said she'd help us celebrate," Humph added.

"Both of you?"

The brothers shrugged, hoisting Josh half a foot higher. "We can share," they said together.

Giants were good at sharing; they had to be. Given the persistent shortage of female giants, a plucky giantess could latch onto several husbands. A girl was a better prize than money. Now faced with two anxious and horny young giants, Josh needed a plan. "Breaking my arms won't get your truck fixed. Let go of me!"

The brothers dropped Josh, who landed too hard on his left ankle. Hopping and swearing, he finally braced himself against the store window, glaring at the giants who stood waiting with crossed arms.

"Okay, okay," Josh said. "Deeble has a fuel pump. He has to fish it out of his junkyard. I'll get it, drive it out to Giantville, fix your truck, and you'll be all set."

"When?" Humph demanded.

"Uh…Thursday morning." Seeing the giants' eyebrows rise—they had only one apiece—Josh added, "You guys be there, too. I might need your muscle. Oh, and standard rates apply. I'll be working on my boss' time."

"Promise," Chris said.

Josh nodded solemnly. Giants took promises as seriously as contracts. They were the opposite of fairies in that regard.

"Say," he said, "do you know anyone in Giantville who has a grudge against fairies?"

"Who doesn't?" Humph said. "They're always trying to skin us on armor prices, the cheap little suckers." He spat on the sidewalk, leaving a sizable puddle. "Now, move."

Chris elbowed Humph. "Move, *please*," Humph amended as though trying out a new word. "We got some shopping to do inside."

Old man Benton, who'd been chuckling throughout this exchange, held open the hardware store door. "Come on in, boys. And you there, Joshua, look both ways before you cross the street. Mind the traffic."

Trying not to react like a sullen five-year-old, Josh limped across the empty street toward Village Hall. He'd completely spaced the giants' truck, but he had a few days for that one. Just now, he wanted the list Stedwell promised him. Though his cover was organizing a ghost hunt, he really hoped to ferret out clues to Sedge's murder.

When he reached the downstairs office window, Mrs. Wisniewski handed him a piece of paper. He sat on the concrete steps outside studying the places Stedwell didn't plan to visit. There were too many left for him to handle alone, especially with a punky ankle. He phoned Archie.

"'S up?" Archie mumbled.

"You still in bed?"

"Yeah. I was up most of the night."

"Me, too."

"With Georgia? I'll bet you were."

Josh let that pass. "Look, I need your help." After Josh explained what happened at the farm, Archie stayed silent for a moment. Then he swore. Finally, he said, "OK, so I'll help, but only till three thirty. I have work later. Shot the breeze with de Salis a while after you left. Said he wanted more construction crew at his club. I signed on to do electrical. Second shift's from four to midnight."

"You're working at night with *vamps*?"

"Nah. Just regular guys from town who need the cash, like me."

Josh arranged to meet Archie at Giants' Park half an hour later. Pondering where to start his detective work, he paced the village's grassy square. Like the rest of town, this part had been spruced up. Formerly a muddy field used mostly by dogs, the square now had sod, flowerbeds, trees in big pots, and quaint streetlamps with shiny black bases and frosted glass shades. The old bandstand was getting its second coat of white paint. Josh wondered how Stedwell managed to scrounge up money for all this, but the man had his ways. He surely did.

Georgia and Benji weren't in the park, so Josh perched on the low end of a seesaw no human kids ever worked as intended, planning his next move. The Baptist church on the corner was a non-starter: The town's pastors didn't believe in ghosts or thought they were demons. In either case, they considered ghost hunting foolhardy.

The director of the funeral home next to the church gave Josh the bum's rush. Normally sedate Kem Wati shrieked, "Are you crazy? My clients are *bereaved*. The last thing they need is to imagine is Aunt Harriet or Uncle Marv floating around in the draperies of this funeral home. And frankly," he added darkly before closing the door in Josh's face, "I don't want to think about that, either."

Josh mounted the steps of the massive Carnegie library constructed during Elvira's heyday. The librarian was the father of his high school classmate, Zachy Seagram. Red-haired and stocky, the elder Mr. Seagram resembled his son, but there the similarities ended. Zachy wasn't interested in books; he'd joined the Marines in search of action.

Seagram pumped Josh's hand enthusiastically. "A ghost walk tour—great idea! How about starting with a ghost hunt? If you find ghosts in the library—and you will, since the old cemetery's right behind this building—our patron numbers could go up dramatically." Smiling broadly, Seagram pointed toward a display table. "Couldn't think of a good way to attract the tourists. All I came up with were photos of the giants and fairies. I pulled all the relevant books in the library, too."

Josh asked, "Anyone been studying up on fairies?"

Seagram shook his head. "Not so far, but I'm hopeful. When did you say you'd investigate?"

"I'm not sure. I'll let you know."

Encouraged, Josh left the library to meet Archie in the park. There, he assigned Arch the northwest section of town, particularly the big houses facing the square. Josh went toward a more modest neighborhood. He wanted to find out what the Ryan boys had been up to lately.

The Ryan family seemed to have an endless supply of boys. Josh could name five, but there were younger ones coming up, too. When he approached the front door, he spotted two Ryan brothers lounging against a beater truck while another peered under the hood.

"Hey," Josh said, changing direction toward the driveway.

"Hey," Shane Ryan, the eighteen-year-old, answered. "You selling something?"

"Nope. I'm working on a tourist gig. Had any paranormal experiences?"

Shane asked, "You're not talking about drugs, are you?"

Josh shook his head. "Ghosts. Things that go bump in the night."

"We don't do our bumping in the night at home. Mostly, we do our bumping in Lola here." Rory, the sixteen-year-old, smirked while patting the hulk fondly. Dylan, a couple years younger, closed the hood and joined the others.

"When Lola's not running," Shane said, "our social life dries up."

Josh surveyed the truck. The sides and wheels were caked with mud. "You boys been taking Lola off road?"

Ryan shrugged. "It gets kind of rough down at the firebreak, you know?"

Josh knew. Sex, drugs and what passed for a road could all be rough at the strip of cleared forest that served as Elvira's lovers' lane. Personally, the firebreak creeped Josh out. If ever there were a place where a weird creature would sneak up on a luckless couple, it was the woods outside Elvira. "Let me have a look at Lola."

Shane handed him the keys. As he did, Josh noticed the telltale gold chain dangling from Shane's other pocket. "You've been invited to join the wolves?" Josh asked incredulously.

"Maybe." Shane grinned.

Josh considered this turn of fortune for the Ryans, who weren't among Elvira's elite. Only the best of the best became wolves. Though the new cubs wouldn't experience their first full moon until graduation, those keys to the lodge in town were prominently displayed for the last few months of high school. After graduation, the keys would open doors to pretty much any job in Elvira; they unlocked a lot of girls' knees, too.

Josh wasn't asked to join. He wondered, even now, what he would have done if he had been.

Wrestling the truck's dented driver's door open, Josh made a production number out of clearing away trash, eyes searching for anything that might have been Sedge's. He found nothing beyond the usual junk food wrappers, crushed cans, empty baggies, dirty socks, and one pristine schoolbook. Josh tried the ignition; the engine wouldn't turn over. He checked under the hood, found a loose connection and secured this with the screwdriver Rory provided. "Lola's back," he told the Ryan boys.

Leaving them crooning over their reanimated wheels, Josh was glad to find no grim evidence inside Lola. Wild as the Ryan boys were, he didn't think they were psychos who'd torture fairies.

But somebody in Elvira was. He had to keep looking.

When Josh tried to sneak past Ruthanne Quinn's house, she was on him like flypaper. "You took your sweet time coming here!" She rushed down her porch steps to wag a finger in his face. "You're planning ghost walks, and you didn't come to me first."

Hanging his head, Josh mumbled to Elvira's self-proclaimed psychic, "I didn't think you'd be..."—*useful*, he thought, but he said, "interested."

Hands on hips, Ruthanne declared, "That's your problem: You don't *think*. You don't have a properly organized mind. It didn't so much matter when you were just fooling around, but now that we have the eyes of America on us...Well! You definitely need me."

Josh looked down at the pint-sized brunette with the world-class ego. She'd been his childhood babysitter. Now pushing thirty, Ruthie's personality hadn't improved. "So *ask*," she prompted.

From inside the house, Ruthanne's crabby grandmother yelled, "Girl! I want my lunch."

"If I work up a ghost walk in town, I'll get back to you," Josh lied. *In a pig's eye.*

"You're thinking you won't," Ruthanne said angrily. "You're such a shit, Joshie." She turned on her heel, her braid swinging out like a lash at his face.

Two blocks south and one west, Josh came to the dead-end street with Elvira's most remarkable house. There wasn't a square angle to it. Under a wood-shake roof that poured down like cake batter, ivy covered the rounded walls. Every window had a half-moon top. The front door formed a circle of dark wood with green metal hinges reaching across it like straps. Statues of fairies filled the front yard. Come December, they'd all wear Santa hats.

The house might have looked charming but for the thousands of Christmas lights left up all year. With a resolved sigh, Josh picked his way over the moss-edged stones leading to Mrs. Sylvia Withers' house.

She answered the door, saying, "Goodness! Is that Joshua Seldom?"

"Yes, ma'am."

"It's been so long since I've seen you. Where have you been keeping yourself?"

"At Mike Mateer's garage. I'm a mechanic."

"Well, that explains it. My car never breaks down, so I don't need service. If you've come to see Silverbelle, I'm sorry, but she's not here. She graduated from Brown, did you know? Works as an aide to Mayor Marshal of Goreton now."

Silverbelle Withers, called Tink by everyone but her mother, had been a schoolyard bully second in ferocity only to Tommy Hanrahan until she abruptly turned girly-girl in the seventh grade. After a few years of pink ribbons, she'd switched over to Emo. Josh heard she'd gone off to college somewhere in the East. "No, ma'am. I've come to see you."

"Art lessons?" Mrs. Withers asked uncertainly. "I'm no longer giving those."

Josh shook his head. "I haven't done any art since you quit teaching."

"It saddened me when the schools stopped offering art and music education," Mrs. Withers said, waving Josh into her home, "but the alternative meant cutting the athletics budget. Obviously, the school board wouldn't do that."

Josh nodded, looking for a place to sit. Mrs. Withers' living room was as jumbled as her front yard. He spotted a corduroy armchair buried under books and a lot of foresty stuff—branches, leaves, and dried weeds. Computer equipment arced along one curved wall. Pointing at the screen with its picture of a sexy female Green fairy, Josh said, "Nice. Who is it?"

"Arrowroot. Beautiful, isn't she? But look at this one—he's my favorite." Mrs. Withers sat before her computer, clicking through files until she pulled up a picture of a Green warrior. "This is Reed. I adore the pattern in his wings." She turned back to Josh, saying, "Thank God for the Internet. I make my living selling fairy art now."

"Really?" Josh couldn't believe people would buy pictures of fairies.

Mrs. Withers smiled, and then rose to clear the armchair by shoving clutter on the floor. "Have a seat." She returned to her chair, swiveling to face him. "There's lots of interest in the wee folk—too much, if you ask me. This plan of the mayor's will be devastating to their way of life. They'll be exploited, commercialized...." She shuddered. "But you know about fairies. Are you still practicing fairy magic?"

"That's just for kids."

"Certainly not. I continue to learn from them."

Josh looked closely at Mrs. Withers then, finally understanding what had been tugging at the back of his mind: She looked the same as when she taught him in grade school. Maybe there was something to this business of the Gift.

Unlike her big-boned daughter, Mrs. Withers had a delicate face surrounded by bushy, brown hair, a thin figure and the perfectly straight posture Josh remembered from the classroom. She wore dark green, the color she always favored when she taught art classes, though today it was a sweat suit rather than a dress. "I've come to talk to you about the fairies," Josh confessed, realizing he couldn't learn what he needed to know unless he leveled with her.

He told her of Sedge's death. She listened in horror, hand to mouth. When he finished, she excused herself, coming back some minutes later with red-rimmed eyes. She said in a low voice, "Poor Sedge. So kind, such a dear. It's impossible to believe he's gone."

Her voice firmed when she said, "I can't understand how anyone could capture a fairy. They're more than able to protect themselves. There must be some charm, some spell...." She looked around her chaotic room. "I'll check through my books, but I've never run across anything to render fairies helpless."

"Can you think of anyone in town who hates fairies?"

Mrs. Withers held out her hands. "No. I mean, I suffered a lot of ridicule because I have the Gift, but people were skeptical, not angry. Most of that ended after Silverbelle put up the Christmas lights to prove we were an ordinary Elviran family."

She sighed, then added, "You must find Sedge's wings, armor and spear. He needs them to move on to the Otherworld—that's where fairies go after death. It's a place of feasting, heroic combat, and joyous sex." She eyed Josh severely, as though he were might titter like a little kid, before going on. "So, he needs to be whole. The fairies will accept no less."

"I'll do my best," Josh vowed.

"I'll help any way I can. There's nothing I won't do for the fairies," Mrs. Withers said fiercely. "Nothing!"

CHAPTER FIVE

Archie had some luck rounding up sites for a ghost walk: the old cemetery behind the library, and the lawyer's garden, where a guy hung himself long ago. ("They'll let us in for a cut of our gate, natch," Archie noted.) Since all the locations were close to the square, Josh concluded a tour might work, but they needed at least one more place. Archie suggested Village Hall, scene of Elvira's only notorious murder, a courtroom shooting. Josh went there to get Stedwell's okay.

While waiting in the mayor's outer office, Josh watched three men in black suits and close-fitting, blue skullcaps walk in. Two were middle-aged, one in his early twenties. The young guy stared at the mayor's assistant's computer like an Amish boy at a car show.

Curious because Egyptians rarely came into town, Josh set aside the new Elvira brochure he picked up (*Elvira—Little Town of Wonders*) and eavesdropped shamelessly while the first man in line asked to see Stedwell.

Nobody knew much about what the priests did at their temple by the river. They kept to themselves, just showing up at the grocery store once in a while to buy salt and toilet paper. Sure, the air got a little ripe in town when they held their big shindig each spring, but that only lasted a few days. They didn't cause trouble, and they paid their taxes on time, in gold.

As the story went, they worshipped Ptah, god of creation and rebirth; his wife, lion-headed Sekhmet, goddess of war and vengeance; and their son, Nefertem, god of perfume. When Napoleon's troops started destroying sacred places in Egypt and abusing the locals—particularly the men—the priests decided to leave. They crossed the ocean and then made for the Mississippi hoping to find another Nile. After getting sidetracked on a tributary of the great river, they spotted a black bull with a white blaze standing atop a cliff near what would become Elvira. They took it as a sign from Ptah, set up camp, and stayed.

They created a sizable temple complex over the years. The only thing about the Egyptians that bothered Josh was how they kept their community going with nothing but males.

Stedwell met with the priests for ten minutes or so, and then they left, frowning. The mayor waved Josh into his office.

"Problem?" Josh inquired, shaking the mayor's hand.

He smiled thinly and motioned Josh to a seat. "There have been thefts from their temple. Until the sacred symbols are returned, the priests warned me their gods will take vengeance on the town."

"Vengeance? Like how?"

Stedwell rubbed a hand over his brow. "We're in for, um, plagues."

Josh did a double take. "As in *The Ten Commandments*?"

"Let's hope we're spared the special effects. I'll have Chief Brown look into those thefts right away." Stedwell took a deep breath, then exhaled slowly, flexing his shoulders to release tension. "Now, what can I do for you?"

Josh reported Archie's success with the ghost walk and his own failure to find any link to Sedge's murder. Stedwell agreed to Village Hall as a tour site and reported the coroner found no external clues on Sedge's body. "I didn't ask for an autopsy."

"Don't," Josh warned. "The fairies wouldn't like that."

Stedwell nodded. "With the police shorthanded today, I can only urge you to continue working on the matter."

"I haven't much else to do except attend my girlfriend's sister's graduation tonight. How long can it take to graduate fifty kids?"

After the first hour, Josh remembered why he'd spaced off his own graduation, just five years earlier. He'd slept through most of it, only

35

waking when Zachy Seagram elbowed his ribs. Josh stayed awake tonight but wished he hadn't. The gymnasium felt steamy with the lemon-ginger smell of wolfsbane too strong, a little nauseating. He fanned himself with the graduation program.

Elvira High's principal, Mr. Sweat, started things off by urging graduates to be good citizens throughout their adult lives. He followed up with a list of everything the school needed but didn't have. Josh slumped in his seat. A lot of other people did, too, all of them acting like Sweaty sentenced them to Saturday detention.

At that point, Georgia took Benji to the bathroom. She missed the speech by the year's brainiac, who thanked every person he'd ever known and recited the many essential things he'd learned during high school. *Yeah, right. You learned to pop pimples and hunt up porn like the rest of us guys.*

When the valedictorian completed his epic tale, Georgia and Benji were still gone. Josh swiveled in his seat, looking for them. Mrs. Beckett tapped his arm. She whispered, "Benji's at the age when every public toilet is a wondrous place to explore." Chuckling, she added, "One day, you'll have children of your own. You'll see."

Josh squirmed. She was reminding him Benji wasn't his son but could have been if he hadn't wasted senior year on Cissy Rettger. "Yes, ma'am," he said. Mrs. Beckett was a real southern lady, soft-spoken, genteel, ever polite, always well turned out. She had her wolfsbane sprig neatly pinned to the crisp, pink lapel of her suit instead of dangling from her purse or shoved into a pocket. How she'd ended up with Georgia's hard-drinking, church-shirking, laughter-loving father, Josh couldn't guess, but Atlanta Beckett was no fool. She hadn't forgiven him for ditching Georgia in high school; she didn't think he deserved her daughter now.

Benji and Georgia returned just as the principal started calling up the graduates. When Georgia wriggled by his knees, beaded braids clattering, Josh admired the close up view of her backside, tonight in some sort of clingy, black fabric beneath a short, white jacket. Benji tucked in under Georgia's arm. She kissed the top of his head, and then smiled privately at Josh, warming him. Whether Mrs. Beckett knew it or not, he'd learned his lesson: Georgia was worth a dozen Cissys.

Mr. Sweat described each student's Elviran pedigree ("Able, Adam Clarence, son of David and Michelle Able, grandson of Gary and Carol Able and Robert and Patricia Bethune, great grandson of...") before listing everything the kid did since kindergarten. When it came to Beckett, Savannah Augusta, who had won a penmanship award in the fourth grade and a citation by her high school teacher, Mr. Snopes, for Excellence in Science, Mrs. Beckett dabbed at her eyes with a lace hanky.

Vanny looked pretty tonight. She'd cut back on the eye makeup— Josh suspected Mrs. Beckett had a hand in that decision. Her clone, Megan, seemed to have added to hers, but rigged out in an Egyptian hairstyle like Georgia's, the effect sort of worked. Josh noticed other women in the crowd had gone Egyptian for the night. That surprised him. Elvira was such an ordinary place.

A few of the graduating boys were missing. Murmurs accompanied each name Sweaty declared absent for the evening. Everyone knew why: The new wolf cubs had been publicly acknowledged, their status elevated and assured. Tonight would be their first full moon.

As Sweaty rambled on about McKay, Bryan Michael, some idiot's cell phone went off. Everyone else in the room roused at nearly the same time, searching for the person who hadn't turned off his phone *as instructed*. Outraged eyes raked the crowd.

The culprit turned out to be Ed Brown, who left his seat to go into the hall. A few minutes later, he returned, leaned over Josh and laid a heavy hand on his shoulder. "Seldom. Come with me."

Wondering how long it'd been since he'd replaced his truck's license tag, Josh asked, "Why?"

"Just come." Ed's furrowed brow signaled something worse than an expired sticker. With every face in the gym scrutinizing him as he slouched along in Ed's wake, Josh could feel his face flushing.

Ed didn't pause in the hallway but strode purposefully toward the outer doors. Josh dug in his heels. "Wait! Tell me what's going on."

"No time," Ed said over his shoulder. "We have to get to Wolf Creek."

"If it's a Louie problem, I can't do anything about it," Josh argued, now jogging to keep up.

"It's not." Ed stopped, turned, ran a hand through his hair, and exhaled a gusty breath. "It's more fairy shit. You're the fairy guy."

"*Thanks*," Josh said testily. "But I'm not 'the fairy guy'. All I know is what I learned as a kid—same as everyone else."

"Not me. I didn't mess with no fairies. So I need you, right?" Ed crossed his arms. "If you got any problems with that, I might remember how many unpaid parking tickets you've racked up."

Josh sighed. "Okay, but I have to tell Georgia I'm leaving."

"Miz Beckett can take her and Benji home. We've got to go *now*." Ed led the way to a white Escort. He jerked his chin at it. "There's mine." While Ed took off his sports jacket and laid it neatly folded on a back seat, Josh swiped at cookie crumbs on the passenger side. "Kids," Ed offered by way of explanation. He lobbed a rubber pacifier into the back. "Baby's down with an earache. That's why the wife isn't here to see my youngest brother, Ev, graduate."

Brown, Evan Andrew, a scrawny guy who smirked all the way to his diploma, had been short on accomplishments but long on Elviran ancestors. Josh pictured the first Browns wearing skins, living in caves, and fighting off the big birds with rocks.

"So the situation we got here," Ed said, looking around his headrest to back out of the parking space, "is another fairy stiff. Tink Withers found it near the wolf compound."

"Another one?" Josh asked, stricken. "Is it a Red, too?"

"How the hell should I know?" Ed huffed before he added reflectively, "Maybe not. I'm thinking Tink mentioned green. She was kind of babbling. Anyways, it was tore up pretty bad."

"Like Sedge?"

"Nah. Werewolf aced this one. You packin' wolfsbane?"

Josh nodded. "I'm not going inside the compound, though."

"Don't have to. Tink's parked by the bridge. She was on her way home from Goreton when she saw the thing. It must have gone a ways before it croaked."

Josh felt irked. "Look, do you have to be so crude about it? Fairies don't croak, they die."

"They ain't people," Ed said flatly. He turned north on the mile road.

"Neither are the Louies when there's a full moon," Josh shot back. His anger dissolved into a growing sense of alarm. *Another death—what did it mean?*

"You turn up any leads on the fairy killer with that ghost walk business of yours?" Ed inquired.

"No, though some people aren't happy about tourists coming to town."

"Anybody afraid of the vampires?"

Josh laughed. "Nope. Go figure."

"Elvira." Ed shook his head.

"Say, did you know Shane Ryan joined the wolves?"

"Not likely. His people aren't old-time Elvirans. Ryans arrived a couple decades ago. That's not long enough."

Pondering this angle, Josh noted, "The Browns have been here forever. Any of your kin in the pack?"

"My big brother, Earl, joined up back before we had the compound. In those days, the wolves went deep into the forest and ranged wherever they liked. Didn't get up to too much trouble—folks knew better than to go traipsing the woods on full moon nights. But this one time, Earl ran on past Goreton and got hisself shot by some city hunters with big bores. Guess they figured he was dead while he was healing. They took the pelt. When we found him, there wasn't much left of Earl to bury." Ed cleared his throat and then braked to a stop. "Well, there's the bridge. Look for Tink's car."

Josh peered left and right of the road. On both sides of the concrete bridge, sloping, grassy banks ended in massed willow shrubs edging the creek, which forked about fifty yards west around the forested island the wolves used for their retreat. The creek's rushing waters hemmed them in on two sides until the streamlets merged with Willow River, forming the island.

Beside him, Ed whistled softly. "Who knew Tink Withers had legs?"

From the shadows at the far side of the bridge, a great pair of legs stalked toward them, not running, but carving the distance with high-stepping strides. The legs ended at a black miniskirt topped by a jacket with wide sleeves; a band of hot pink in the middle left a lot of skin bare. The features were pleasing; the face shape, oval. Glossy, brown hair pulled back from the brow fell loose to the shoulders.

"That *can't* be Tink." Josh leaned forward to gawk at the approaching babe. He saw the dark, intense eyes and the unsmiling mouth. "She must have dropped a hundred pounds, been on a makeover show, had plastic surgery or...or...."

As she bent to peer into the driver's window, revealing more than a little cleavage, Josh slapped himself mentally. Ogling *Tink Withers*? What was he thinking?

Ed rolled down his window. "Let me in, Chief Brown." Tink reached for the handle of the rear door. "Howling has me spooked." She slid into the car, crushing Ed's sports jacket beneath her rump.

He said nothing, focusing instead on the sound now coming through the window, a chorus that began with high-pitched barking, then turned to short, sharp yips. One voice would start this before others joined in. From farther away came drawn out, mournful howls. Josh recalled every horror movie he'd seen.

Ed turned to face Tink. "This been going on a while?"

She nodded. "It started up after I called you." To Josh, she said, "Seldom? Why are you here?"

"He's the fairy guy," Ed explained.

The left side of Tink's mouth turned up. "Of course, he is."

"Nice to see you, too, Tink," Josh returned. "Where's the fairy?"

40

"By my Wrangler. I parked on the other side of the bridge, at the top of the dirt road that goes down to the Louies' parking spot." She pointed, adding, "When the howling started, I didn't feel safe in a convertible. I waited on the bridge."

"Good thinking," Ed said. He started the engine and drove the short distance to Tink's Jeep, pulling up beside it.

"I had time to kill before you arrived," Tink said. "I've already bagged what I could find of the Green fairy warrior."

Josh shifted in his seat to stare at her. "You tampered with a crime scene?"

"Crime scene! It's a fairy, not a person. It got too near a werewolf and paid the price." She shrugged. "Just one of those things, like road kill."

Ed glanced at Josh's glowering face, then laid a hand on his arm. "No point bickering. I'll come back tomorrow and have a closer look."

"Did you find the fairy's armor? His sword?" Josh persisted.

"The armor's there. One arm and a wing are missing. Oh, and its neck was broken. I didn't hunt for trinkets. If you think you can do better, go look for yourself."

"Okay, I will."

"Hold off," Ed said, staring pensively out the window. "Them wolves is pretty het up. Could be one of 'em's loose." He reached across Josh to open the glove box, extracting a flashlight and his service revolver.

Tink said, "A gun won't stop a werewolf."

"Fill 'em full of enough lead, and they'll drop," Ed told her. "While they're healing, they're no problem. Can't leave 'em to run anymore, what with the compound being so close to the road and all. Couple years back, Bucky Niemayer got squashed by an eighteen-wheeler. Sure he lived, but he'll never walk right again. The cubs are there tonight. Want some kid crippled for life? I can't take the chance."

"You're worried about the *werewolves*?" Josh asked.

"They're Elvirans," Ed reminded him, "same as any other. Still think we should look for a sword?"

"If we don't find it, the Greens will be pissed. On the other hand, if a Louie or two is out, that .38 of yours might not do the job."

Ed checked the chambers of his gun. "I could pick up the Remington in Elvira if it'd make you feel better."

"Oh, for Heaven's sake!" Tink snorted. "Josh has always been a wuss. He used to be terrified of *me*. I'll go with you."

"No, miss. You sit tight. I'll leave the motor running. If you hear yelling or shooting, drive away. Here, give me your keys. If we need your Jeep, we'll use it."

"What's that?" Tink pointed toward the place where the willows parted for the dirt road. "Looks like something bright by the big ash tree."

"Pretty close by," Ed remarked, "and open ground. We'll check it out. While we're there, I'll give a little look-see toward the foot bridge, make sure it's pulled up tight on the island side like its s'posed to be. Ready, Seldom?"

Josh reached for his door latch. He wondered why he agreed to something as stupid as helping a cop with more balls than brains protect werewolves while searching for a fairy sword. Maybe it was the Brown kid's toy that squeaked under his heel as he hauled himself out of the car. Or maybe it was Tink's scorn; she could still get under his skin after all these years. "Give me the flashlight," he said.

As soon as Josh and Ed stood beside the car, the wolves' howling cut off. The sudden silence felt more eerie and frightening than the noise. Treading through long grass, Josh thought he heard muffled growls, snarling, heavy bodies moving stealthily through the shrubs across the creek. His heart pounded, and his hands sweat.

"Point the light at the base of the tree," Ed whispered. "Something's there."

Josh estimated the distance between himself and the car. How fast could he run? Not fast enough.

But it wasn't a werewolf crouched, ready to spring. It was a big man's naked body, face down, blond hair reflecting the moonlight. Tom Hanrahan's left arm stretched out, slate gray and caked with blood.

CHAPTER SIX

Vanny sat at the cashier's desk inside The Feathered Serpent's entry hall. She knew she looked *hot*; she could see herself in the Serpent's only mirror, set opposite the desk so she could check on guests. Her new wine-red dress with corset worn inside, for once, pushed up her boobs and cinched her waist. She'd put up her hair, leaving only one dye tip dangling. Her makeup was dark and haunted: *perfect*.

Mr. Suarez, her boss, said she looked "just right." He'd even given her an ornate choker to wear on the job. Shiny, black crystals glittered at her throat and felt smooth beneath her fingertips. Vanny stroked them idly whenever there was a lull between customers, as there was now.

A lot of guests came in around eight-thirty—mostly men in large groups. They wore dark shirts and slacks, not too formal, often with a leather jacket. Handsome and exotic, the newcomers had wavy, black hair, thick lashes, and compelling eyes. Vanny forced herself to look away from those eyes. Mr. Suarez had warned, "Keep your mind on the money. Don't get caught by anyone's gaze."

When couples arrived, the men seemed a little edgy. The women weren't from Elvira, and they weren't vamps. After a while, Vanny understood why the men kept an arm firmly wrapped around their dates' shoulders or waists: With all the eye candy around, it could be hard for a girl to stay focused.

At first, Vanny worried someone from town would come in, only to tattle about her to her mother. But Elvirans weren't visiting the Serpent, which was the main reason why Vanny had been hired.

"Seeing you will teach them not to be afraid," Mr. Suarez told her during the interview. "I have put much money into this club. We must make it a place for your people as well as mine."

Though Vanny wanted Mr. Suarez to succeed—he really had spent a fortune on the place, what with all the carved stonework, the wall paintings of old Mayan scenes, elaborate lighting and the big, fancy stage where groups would play on weekends—she was glad Elvirans were staying away for now. She needed time to prove to her mother working at the Serpent was safe. The pay was better than anything else she could get in Elvira, and face it, the job was a whole lot more interesting than the night window at the drugstore.

Ricky, the bouncer, came in to chat for a while. Vanny liked looking at him, but when he talked to her, she found herself feeling a little lightheaded. She was relieved when Mr. Suarez interrupted the conversation, barking something in Spanish to Ricky, who leapt away from the desk with guilty speed. Mr. Suarez changed his tone to a mellower one, and the two of them went outside. When he returned, Vanny's boss told her, "Soon, we will be hosting some of your people. No charge for them tonight," and he smiled in a mysterious way before climbing the stairs to his office.

Vanny snapped to attention when Mr. Snopes appeared. He stared at her. "*Miss Beckett*?" he asked, as though she might be someone else.

"You can call me Savannah now I'm an adult," she urged, sucking in her gut so her boobs arched. "Are you alone, Eliot?"

He cocked his head, visibly taken aback by her use of his first name, but he said only, "Well, yes. I was dead curious about this place."

"We don't use the d-word in here," Vanny disclosed with a smile.

"The what? Oh!" Eliot laughed. He had a wonderful, deep-throated laugh that made Vanny's heart beat faster. She reached for his hand.

Startled, he flinched until she told him, "It's for the stamp, you know." Cradling his smooth, cool palm, she explained the three cover charge categories: *diners* were vamps, *dabblers* were casual human visitors, and *donors* didn't mind a little tippling. "Snacks get in free," Vanny finished, applying the dabbler symbol, a Mayan sun, to the back of Eliot's hand. "Tonight, there's no charge for anyone from Elvira."

Snopes shifted on his feet, peering anxiously toward the bar's double doors. "So, uh, I just go in? Is there anything I should know? Do I look all right?"

Vanny took in the navy jacket, the collarless ivory shirt, the hemp necklace and gray slacks. About to breathe, "You look *fine*," her attention was diverted by a dozen male voices coming from Elviran workmen lumbering into the Serpent.

"Free drinks!" Mr. Wisniewski crowed, waving a piece of red paper at Vanny. Others held up their tickets to prove they were entitled to freebies, too.

The bluster died by the bar entrance, where the men scuffed around, reluctant to go inside, until Ricky shoved through the crowd to seize a door handle. "Enter," he told Archie Ferguson, who stood closest to him, "and enjoy the hospitality of Fernando Suarez." But still the men hesitated until Ricky sneered, "You are afraid of a place where even a little girl is safe?" He swept a hand toward Vanny.

That settled it. Archie led the way, and the others followed. Vanny, bristling at being called a "little girl," shot Ricky a withering glance before she told Eliot, "Guess you should go on in."

"Will do," he said, and he left her.

Ricky clicked his tongue. "Do not be angry, *chica*. I spoke so only to make those men find their *cojones*. You are much woman—*muy bonita*." He bent close to her, his face inches away.

"Don't," she warned.

"A little kiss, nothing more," Ricky murmured.

"But Mr. Suarez said—"

"What he does not know will cause him no harm." Ricky held Vanny with his eyes. As he brushed her lips with his, Vanny sucked in her breath because she knew what was coming.

Ricky lurched away, pawing at his mouth, spitting out sharp Spanish words.

"I'm sorry," Vanny wailed. "I ate garlic mashed potatoes for dinner.

I didn't think." But she *had* thought—plenty—about how to stay out of trouble at a vampire club. She scarfed down two huge servings of potatoes. Listening to Ricky yell at her, she didn't feel so bad about tricking him.

What she hadn't expected was how angry he got. The lower part of his face swelled and took on a blue-purple tint in mottled patches. Ricky snarled and bared his fangs, eyes gone flat black and dangerous. For the first time at The Feathered Serpent, Vanny felt fear.

If three women, even more irate than Ricky, hadn't opened the outside door just then, Vanny would have panicked. The women shouted in a language she didn't recognize. Pointing toward the inner doors, one clearly wanted something from the bar area, but Ricky crossed his arms and shook his head.

The trio fixed their gazes on Vanny, and suddenly, she could deny them nothing. "Come in," she whispered, ignoring Ricky's growl.

In they came, single file, brunette, redhead and blonde, all dressed in white. To Vanny's amazement, Ricky edged away from them, backing toward the bar doors, which he yanked open to scuttle inside. The women dipped their heads pleasantly to Vanny as they passed her. They didn't reflect in the mirror.

Latin music playing in the main room cut off. Vanny could hear Ricky and the women arguing in different languages, everyone talking at once. Vanny had been banned from the bar area because of her age, but that didn't mean she couldn't crack one door a bit and peek in, did it?

Just as she reached it, she heard a thud against the other door, which swung open, and the blonde fell through, landing hard on her ass. Before Vanny could reach down to help her up, the redhead pulled the blonde to her feet, checking her over with a grim, tight-lipped expression. Both glared at Ricky, who smirked, shrugged, and went to the bar, where the bartender poured him a drink of some thick, dark liquid. Ricky tipped this back, downing it in one gulp.

The Elviran men sat at their tables gaping, faces unsure of how to react. The little brunette, who stood near Archie Ferguson, pointed to the door, and a few men, mostly the older guys, rose to go. Vanny's mind put the pieces together: The men came from the other vampire club, the one still under construction. Given tickets for free drinks by Ricky, they'd sneaked away from the job. The women wanted them back at work. Aha!

Vanny watched the brunette sashay—there was no word for the sexy way she moved—toward Ricky, who swiveled on his seat to face her down.

She slapped his swollen cheek.

Ricky roared and tried to grab the woman, who broad-jumped onto the bar, a slick trick in stilettos. When the bartender made a swipe for her ankle, she did a back flip to the floor. A couple of workmen stepped toward her, but she waved them off, neatly dodging Ricky's hurled drink glass at the same time. The redhead laughed.

A glass mug thrown by the bartender sailed past the redhead to smash against the wall next to Vanny, sending a shower of shards her way. She'd have taken cuts to the face if Eliot Snopes hadn't lunged at her, pulling her down and into the room. Sprawled on the floor, Vanny smiled at him in grateful shock even as more glasses whizzed by, cutting off escape through the leather doors. The Elviran men started lobbing beer bottles at the bartender.

Vamp guys with dates began shoving the girls under tables. Eliot said, "Quick. Do the same. Watch out for glass. The last thing you want to do is *bleed* in here." He lifted a tablecloth, gesturing frantically for Vanny to crawl inside the makeshift shelter before he joined her there.

Vanny wondered why Mr. Suarez didn't stop the brawl. A second later, she decided she didn't care. She'd rather be pressed up against Eliot Snopes than anywhere else in the world. She couldn't *wait* to tell Megan.

Megan marched glumly along the dirt road between rows of corn shoots toward Krueger's field, a patch of ground too infested with mustard weed to be useful for crops. Partiers and hunters used the place now. There were enough tree stands set up on the three forested sides of the field to reenact Gettysburg, come hunting season.

"Hurry up!" Nefer Wati hissed. "We'll miss everything." She slogged through the drainage ditch, getting mud all over her shoes. Megan picked her way across on stones. She didn't have as many pairs of shoes as Nefer.

Megan wished she hadn't agreed to go to the graduation bash with Nefer, a girl she didn't much like. Nefer judged people; no one was ever good enough. Half-Egyptian, she wanted everyone to believe Cleopatra was her ancestor.

My ass. Cleopatra had been a beauty and Nefer wasn't, yet she'd somehow managed to snag Shane Ryan as a boyfriend. According to Nefer, he was a "provisional wolf," whatever that meant. He'd been at graduation, but left afterward to go to the compound. With Vanny at work, Megan ended up with Nefer.

Nefer headed for the knot of people around the keg. Manning the tap, Mark Wisniewski offered her a beer. Nefer declined, surprising Megan. Nefer liked to drink, another thing she and Megan didn't have in common.

After some chattering, Nefer motioned Megan away from the crowd to settle on a hummock of grass at the forest's edge. "You have to try this," she said when Megan plunked down beside her. "It's great." Unclipping a water bottle from her belt, Nefer pried back the plastic lid, took a swig, and handed the bottle to Megan.

"What's in there?" Megan asked suspiciously.

"Wine, and a little something else."

"*What* else?"

"Blue lotus. Stuff my ancestors used to get high on. Makes you feel good, relaxed, but kind of horny, too."

"That's all I need," Megan moaned, "with nothing but dorks around."

"You could make out with me. I'm bi," Nefer revealed.

Megan tried to look impressed. Half her classmates already

announced they were bi. Only Bryan McKay decided he was simply gay—and he'd made such a big, Emo deal out of coming out that everyone got sick of it, wanting to strangle him or shout in his face, "You *told* us. Get over yourself." To Nefer, Megan said, "No offense, but I'd have to drink half a keg for that to sound interesting, and then I'd probably puke from the booze."

Nefer laughed. "Have some lotus wine anyway. It's a cool sensation."

Megan took a sip of the red wine. It tasted sour, but not bad. She watched couples drift off into the trees. Unattached girls tried to get the party going by doing a goofy moon dance. That fell apart because the dancers kept tripping over their own feet, so they wound up sitting in the dirt, smoking weed.

In the distance, Megan heard wolves baying. She drank more wine, finally asking Nefer, "You get this from your father?"

"Hell, no. After he left the temple, the others wouldn't have anything to do with him. I got the lotus from…well, never mind. It's none of your business. Why did you do up your hair Egyptian? Doesn't look right on you. And this—" Nefer fingered the hairclip at the back of Megan's head, "is a sacred symbol. It's not supposed to be a barrette."

Megan shrugged. "It's what the guy braiding my hair put there."

"A *guy* did your hair?"

"Yeah. Something wrong with that, too?"

"No, but—shh!" Nefer looked around. "Listen."

"All I hear is Adam Able and Jess Lesak doing the nasty in the bushes. God, does she have to be so loud?"

"Not that." Nefer made a face. "It's coming from there." She leaned forward, pointing at the moonlit field. "Kind of a rustling noise. And the *smell*. Eww. Pig shit is better."

Megan squinted. "I see some animals. Possums, coons or skunks," she guessed.

"Skunks?" Nefer jumped to her feet. "Look, there's another bunch …and another. How many of those things are out there?"

To Megan, the whole field suddenly seemed to be a wave surging for shore.

The tokers stood up, peered into the darkness, and started screeching. Someone yelled, "Rats!" Mark Wisniewski threw his arms around the keg.

"Over here," Nefer grabbed Megan's wrist and pulled her toward the trees. "I need a leg up." Nefer thrust a muddy heel at Megan's thigh and shoved off. Gripping a branch, Nefer swung a leg over it to lie with her arms and legs wrapped around the limb.

"Give me your hand," Megan called.

"No, you'll pull me down. Find another tree."

"You bitch!" Megan spat. "I hope the rats eat you."

The minute she said that, Megan's stomach dropped. Trees were no protection: Rats could climb. Other kids seemed to be remembering the same fact. They sprinted toward the farm road. Megan dashed after them.

Megan fell far behind the other runners, last in line, most vulnerable to the scrabbling of claws, the squeaks and the chittering sounds she heard closing in. Fear washed over her, drowning out all sensations but the pounding of her feet on dirt.

Something touched her back, then slid down to her waist. She screamed as her feet left the ground. Lifted onto a big, black horse, Megan didn't even have time to breathe before she was thrown hard against the rider's forearm holding her in place when the horse did an abrupt one eighty and launched into a canter directly toward the rats. Instantly, the column of rats split, forming two streams pouring into the cornfield and away from the path. As the horse slid to a stop, the rats were gone.

"What's happening?" Megan cried. She twisted to get a look at her rescuer. "Who...who are you?"

She stumbled on the words, tongue disconnected from brain by eyes struggling to take in the awesome perfection of the male face so near hers. Below blond hair combed back from the brow to arch casually toward shorter, darker sides, was a fine-boned, straight nose and upturned lips. The eyes were pale blue, almost luminous in the moonlight. All Megan could see of the rider's clothing was a white, collared sweater unzipped at the throat. He looked to be in his mid-twenties.

"Fadri de Salis," he said with an accent Megan couldn't place. "I am sorry to startle you, but I always wanted to try that move, snatching up the maiden in distress, I mean." He chuckled, and nudged the horse to turn, slowly and steadily this time, toward the top of the road. "Are you comfortable?"

"I'm…" Megan didn't know what she was except in some weird sort of dream. "I'd feel better straddling the horse instead of sprawling on the withers."

Fadri set her on her feet, then dismounted to boost Megan onto the horse's bare back. He swung up behind her, saying into her ear, "Better?"

"How can you be riding at night? No one rides at night. Horses get schizy after dark. What happened to the rats? Why were you at Krueger's Field? Where are you from? What—"

"Too many questions." Fadri groaned. "I will answer them all, but first, you must answer three of mine: May I ask your name?"

"Megan. Uh, Megan Shaw."

"Where is your home, Megan Shaw?"

"Thataway." She pointed east.

"Is it too far for the horse?"

"No, just about a mile from here."

"Then *thataway*—What a curious expression!" Fadri said, "is where we will go."

Maybe it was Nefer's wine or maybe it was something else, but Megan felt the contentment of a stroked cat. Pressed against the unknown Fadri de Salis, she could think of no place she'd rather be. Nothing this amazing had happened in her entire life. She couldn't *wait* to tell Vanny.

CHAPTER SEVEN

It was midnight before Josh and Georgia drove back to the Beckett farm, arriving with two vehicles, his truck retrieved from the high school lot and her bike. They checked on the horses before climbing the back steps, where Georgia headed for the porch swing rather than going into the house. "I'm too keyed up to sleep." She patted the faded cushion beside her.

Josh wasn't ready for sleep either; two nights in a row with Georgia were windfall bounty. Clearly, she wasn't thinking along the same lines when she said, "I don't want Tom to die from silver poisoning. Even if he's crappy about money, he's Benji's father."

Back at the creek, Josh called Georgia immediately after getting a blanket from Ed's trunk to cover Tom. Unconscious and barely breathing, Tom looked so bad Ed phoned Goreton Hospital. Elvira's clinic could handle routine problems, but crisis was way beyond their scope. Once the hospital made sure Tom was in man-form, they sent an ambulance. Gories refused to have anything to do with the wolves, a sore point between the towns. The ambulance arrived just before Georgia.

"I feel like I should have stayed at the hospital, waited longer," she said.

"With Tom's mother and sister scowling at you all the while. Jeez, talk about the big chill. Even the Thoon brothers would be scared of those two." Privately, Josh believed the massive Hanrahan women would fit right in at Giantville.

"They've been upset since I told Joellen I was divorcing Tom. She didn't care that wolf-Tom terrified Benji or could hurt her grandson. She kept saying, 'A boy should be with his father.'"

"Benji talked about the Big, Bad Wolf this morning," Josh recalled.

Georgia nodded. "Even though he was not quite three, he remembers when Tom transformed, here at the farm. It wasn't really Tom's fault; they kept him late at work. By the time he arrived, he was half-man, half-beast. I locked him in the root cellar.

"Benji picked up on my fear and started crying, but I couldn't stop to comfort him. I had to heap firewood on the doors. Tom howled, and Benji got hysterical. I still didn't believe the cellar doors would hold, so I grabbed my baby and drove into town. Luckily, Mom was there. Dad just had his second heart attack, and she'd more or less been living at the hospital, but she was home."

"Jesus," Josh breathed.

Georgia took him literally. "I think He helped us, but I couldn't let anything like that happen again."

"That was the end for Tom and you?" Josh asked carefully. Georgia never discussed her life with Tom. Josh had been in St. Louis learning auto mechanics during those years. With Georgia talking about her marriage now, he might get some of his questions answered.

"There wasn't a 'Tom and me' for a long time before the incident. I hung in there for Benji's sake."

"So...?"

"So, why would a fairy attack Tom with *silver*?" Georgia asked, once again dodging the issue. "Fairies know silver is deadly to werewolves."

"The sword couldn't have been pure silver or he'd have died. Too bad we didn't find the thing. My guess is the Greens added some silver to their swords *because* of the Louies. The Greens' territory is close to the compound."

Indignant, Georgia sputtered, "But that's...that's..."

"Self-defense."

Georgia calmed down a bit. "Okay, but if they're concerned enough to take precautions, why did the Green fairy—tell me his name again."

"Reed. I recognized his wing pattern from a picture on Mrs. Withers' computer. She's—she was—fond of him."

"Why did this Reed go near the compound on a full moon night—looking for trouble, planning to kill a wolf?"

Josh rubbed his face. "If so, we'd have a psycho fairy killer and a psycho killer fairy in Elvira."

"What's happening to our quiet, little town?" Georgia moaned. "This used to be place where nothing ever happened."

"Change, not all of it good. And speaking of change, Tink Withers doesn't look like herself."

"She lost weight and straightened her hair."

"Has to be more to it," Josh argued. "I mean she was the definition of troll."

"Tink always had decent features, but she slumped to appear smaller and wore the wrong clothes—ruffles and bows on a girl six feet tall? Even the Emo things suited her better. I'm glad she's looking good now."

"She wasn't so glad to see you."

"Guess she's still angry about my marrying Tom."

"Why?"

Georgia stared at him, astonished. "She began crushing on Tom in middle school. You didn't know?"

Josh snorted. "Tom's no Einstein, but he isn't blind, either. Go for Tink instead of you? I mean you, you're…." Josh threw out his hands, speechless.

Georgia smiled. Josh reached around her to massage her neck and shoulders. She leaned into his touch. "Mmm…that's *good*. Don't stop."

"Still feeling keyed up?" he asked as casually as he could.

"Not so much." She pulled his arms tightly around her, then shifted to kiss him until his blood raced.

In the morning, Josh left while Georgia showered—forced himself to leave, rather than start what they didn't have time to finish before work.

Stedwell wouldn't supply Josh with excuses for being late to the garage this morning, and Georgia wanted to contact Bobbi, who'd know about Tom's condition. Bobbi and Georgia had made a date to tour old Mrs. Lesak's house as soon as Bobbi finished her nursing shift at Goreton Hospital's ER.

Josh pictured the house, vacant since Mrs. Lesak moved to Florida. It had a nice, sunny look to it. Best of all, it was close to the apartment Josh shared with Archie in the loft of the old barn—"carriage house" his mother insisted on calling it—behind his parents' house.

Archie liked Bobbi. With any luck, he'd spend a lot of his time with her at the new place, maybe even move in.

"You want Archie out?" Georgia had asked Josh over a hastily sipped coffee. "I thought you guys were happy as roommates."

"Arch is great when you don't have to live with him. Since he did most of the work to fix up the space, I can't make him leave. Problem is he's a slob."

"Well, so are you," Georgia pointed out. "Last time I visited you, I could barely squeeze into the bathroom."

"I'm a different type of slob," Josh said loftily. "I leave clothes and stuff around. With Arch, it's food. I don't know how many times I've dropped my shirt on the floor, then picked it up later to find guacamole on the other side."

Georgia smiled. "I'll sound out Bobbi on the subject of Archie, see if she's interested. I'll let you know."

Georgia. Man! He loved that woman, Josh thought wistfully on the way into town. She teased him, but the teasing never went deep, never aimed to hurt. Most of the time, she made him feel a hundred feet tall, smarter, better. He had to stretch to live up to her image, but somehow, that felt good, too. He loved her, maybe he always had, but he couldn't tell her, not yet. If he didn't play it cool, he'd scare her away.

Sometimes, he slipped and tipped his hand, did something to signal more commitment than she could accept. When he assumed she'd see him after work, she'd tell him she had "plans." If he did something as simple as reaching for a heavy box she held, she'd wrestle it away, insisting she could do for herself. Move a chair in her living room, and she moved it back. Georgia could be brittle as burnt toast about her space, her independence, yet soft as butter in his hands when they made love. That's when it was hardest to pretend she was just another traveling companion on life's road; she was his *destination.*

Pulling into the garage parking area, Josh laughed at himself. Crap! He'd be writing her poetry next. But Georgia didn't like poetry; she liked beer and football. Josh figured himself for the luckiest guy on the planet.

"You actually gonna work today?" Mike inquired when Josh walked into the bay. "Think the mayor can scrape along without you?"

"Uh huh." Stedwell could take care of himself. Josh had a Hummer to fix.

The day went by. Josh felt grateful nothing surprising happened. Georgia called to tell him Tom was recovering. Josh smiled at the news, relieved little Benji wouldn't have to face his father's death; hell, that was hard at any age.

Wiping grease off his hands, Josh stood back from the Hummer, ready to give it a test drive. He called to Mike, "I'll go to Deeble's junkyard and get the part for the giants' truck." Mike lifted his head from under the hood of a Chevy, mumbling his approval.

The Hummer was a fortress on wheels. Josh felt like king of the road. As he rumbled over the tracks, past the grain elevator and the Dairy Queen, Josh wished Deeble's were farther away. He could have used another mile or ten behind the wheel. The sun was near setting. Maybe he'd cruise a back road after dark, open 'er up, see what she could do.

Josh parked in front of Deeble's. A celebrity from the '60s dropped in once, shot the breeze for a few minutes, and imprinted Deeble with everlasting awe. He'd put up a shrine to the guy out front, set amid rusting pipes and broken wheels. The automotive parts lay behind his office shack.

No one answered the bell on the dusty front desk, so Josh made his way around rubble toward the back door. Deeble liked to sift through his collection, sorting and re-sorting it, caressing each piece of junk. He was probably outside doing that now.

Josh found Deeble drawing a bead on two Red fairies poised with spears raised on the roof of the shed. As Josh watched, the old man racked his 12-gauge.

"Whoa, whoa. Put that down!" Josh yelled at the purple-faced Deeble.

"I'll get them thieving fairies, you mark my words!" Deeble squinted through his shotgun's sight.

Covering the distance between them in two bounds, Josh told the irate junkyard owner, "Mr. Deeble, if you don't cut it out, I'll have to deck you." As Deeble swore at him, Josh planted both hands on the gun's barrel, shoving it down. It wasn't hard to out-muscle Deeble, who had to be seventy-five or more.

"Them buggers rob me blind! Steal all the copper wire they can carry," Deeble raged.

Josh turned his head toward the fairies. "That true?"

They thumped the butts of their spears on the shed's metal roof. The closest one, a well-muscled young warrior, said, "Who be ye, then, to stick yer great nose in our war?"

"War?" Deeble bellowed, struggling with Josh again. "I'll show *you* war."

Josh said into his ear, "Look, you kill these fairies, and their whole clan will be after you, day and night."

Deeble stopped struggling. "I only got rock salt in the loads."

"Fairies are so little," Josh whispered, "even rock salt could kill them at close range. Just...just give me a minute."

Releasing the shotgun barrel warily, Josh watched Deeble shift from foot to foot and then shake his fist, but he didn't shoulder the weapon. Josh approached the fairies. He introduced himself and learned their names were Heron and Bream. Josh waved them closer. The bigger one, Heron, hovered near his head.

Josh argued, "Deeble's an old guy, a gaffer. Get him all riled up and maybe he'll have a heart attack. This place will be shut down. Is that what you want?"

"We're needin' copper," Heron insisted.

"Then *pay* him for it."

Heron shook his head.

"All right, make him a gift, like you do for your old folks who don't have enough. Leave it where he'll find it and not have to think it's charity."

Heron tilted his head, then flew back to confer with Bream. After some whispered debate, both returned to stand at the edge of the roof, Heron asking, "What sort of gift were ye thinkin' we should be makin'?"

"We'll work that out later, after Deeble's cooled off. I've a roll of wire at my place. You'll have to cut the copper free from the insulation, but if you want it, it's yours."

"An' why would you be offerin' such to us?" Heron asked warily.

"I want your promise not to hassle Deeble, at least for a few days. By then, we can figure out what gift would be right. Deal?"

Bream tugged at Heron's arm, his expression leery.

"I'll throw in as much beer as you can drink. That is, *if* you can handle human beer."

"'Tis naught to our poteen," Bream jeered.

"Then we're on," said Josh. "Oh, and take a gander at my wheels. Ever ride in a Hummer?"

After a calming word with Deeble, Josh piloted the Hummer toward Ruttenberg Road, where he could put pedal to the metal. Scanning open fields on both sides, he told the fairies to hang on before he floored it. The Hummer lumbered forward at a snail's pace. The fairies laughed. Sheepishly, Josh turned toward home. The sun had set, and he'd had a long day. He wanted a beer. So did the fairies.

Josh's passengers occupied themselves during the rest of the ride by challenging each other to leap across the gap between inward-facing bank seats—a modification Josh installed for the tourists—then land solidly on their feet without using their wings. The loser earned blistering scorn from the winner as well as ordinary blisters when he misjudged a leap and touched steel. Fairy humor was raw but funny. Josh hadn't known that. Sedge always kept it clean.

Sedge. Heron and Bream didn't know about Sedge. Should he tell them? Stedwell wouldn't have a clue what to say, and Mrs. Withers seemed tightest with the Greens. Who else could break the news to the Reds? With a heavy sigh, Josh resolved to do the job.

The Seldom homestead occupied five acres hugging Elvira's southernmost village limit. "A little bit country, a little bit rock & roll," his father called it. City-born Bob Seldom refused to live where he could "hear the neighbors flush their toilets." Though Josh's mother complained of the awful commute to her job at the elementary school where she taught second grade, her husband, a traveling salesman, laughed at the four minutes the drive took. He wasn't as cheerful about the kiddie toys that littered the backyard each spring when Josh's mother opened her daycare operation. Josh parked, and stepped out of the Hummer to move a big wheeler blocking the patch of asphalt leading to the garage. He told the fairies, "We're here."

"A grand place it is," Heron said after flying out the door, carefully avoiding the sheet metal.

Josh nodded. The house was okay, he guessed. A two-story, L-shaped white farmhouse, it had some gingerbread left over from the olden days. Though a good place to grow up, the house seemed a little empty after his brother and sister moved away. "We're going to the barn."

He whistled for Judy, the family dog. Dogs were funny around fairies, sometimes fearful, sometimes aggressive. In either case, Josh wanted to find Judy.

The black lab lay inside the barn, snoozing on a deflated plastic pool. She woke when Josh rummaged around, searching for the spool of wire. He stroked her head, grabbed a couple of toy teacups so the fairies could drink their beer, and then shut the door behind him.

Leading the fairies up the outside steps to his loft, Josh confessed,

"It's kind of a mess." After he opened the door, they agreed, describing his housekeeping skills with the same barbed wit he'd heard in the car. "All right, all right," Josh said, chagrined. He bent to clear the couch, picking up his favorite tee shirt, hoping there wouldn't be guacamole underneath.

Instead, he saw a red wing with purple-black iridescent patches, a pattern he knew all too well.

Dumbfounded, Josh's eyelids shot open while his companions' narrowed. He saw revulsion on those faces, the same emotion he'd feel if he walked into a stranger's place to find a severed arm. "I didn't know this was here!" Josh said in a rush. "I swear to God, I didn't!"

Bream and Heron backed away, Bream leveling a finger at Josh.

Quite suddenly, he couldn't move. He could breathe, he could blink, but that was it. Paralyzed, Josh watched the fairies fly up to his eye level.

"That's Sedge's wing," Heron hissed. "Have ye maimed him, then? Were ye plannin' more of the same wickedness by lurin' us here with yer copper and yer beer?"

"Speak truth!" Bream commanded. "Tell us of our Sedge."

Josh found he could talk. "Sedge is dead—murdered."

"The blaggard admits it!" Bream howled, lancing Josh's neck with his spear tip. Josh felt the cut, then a wet trickle of blood. Whatever they were going to do to him, he'd feel it—*all* of it.

Through the floorboards, Josh heard Judy barking, the sounds sharp and frantic. Midway through a bark, Judy's voice cut off, amplifying Josh's fear. Had the fairies killed his dog?

Heron and Bream drew away, their faces grim, their spears aimed at Josh's eyes. His mind struggled against unresponsive muscles and growing panic until Bream said, "Speak. Tell us—"

"To come in," a man's voice called from the staircase landing.

"Come in," Josh repeated. Watching Anton de Salis step into his loft, Josh found himself praying a vampire would save him.

CHAPTER EIGHT

"*A on scéal agat?*" de Salis asked the fairies, who gazed blankly at him. "Ah, you've forgotten your Irish. Pity," the vampire said.

"We're a tad busy fer blather," Heron huffed. He settled on the arm of the couch, taking a wide stance, spear held across his body with both hands. "An' who might ye be?"

"Anton de Salis. I've come to invite Mr. Seldom to the opening of my club this Thursday. We'll be hosting only Elvirans that evening, no tourists. It's a by-invitation-only affair."

"By Thursday, he'll be colder than a witch's teat," Bream declared. "We're after killin' him just now fer his villainy." He took a position next to Heron.

De Salis cleared a space for himself on the couch beside Sedge's wing, sat, plucked at his knees to release the tension on the fine wool of his navy trousers, and then laced his fingers together. "Carry on."

"Ye'll not be stoppin' us," Heron said.

"Wouldn't dream of it. I spent some time in County Sligo when fairies were rather more numerous than they are today, but I never witnessed an instance of fairy justice. What crime did he commit, by the way?"

"He slaughtered our kinsman!" Bream cried.

"The owner of this? May I?" De Salis gestured toward Sedge's wing. Taking the fairies' silence for assent, he lifted the wing to turn it slowly between thumb and forefinger, inspecting both sides before moving it closer to his face. He shut his eyes and breathed in deeply. After a moment, he said, "Curious."

Both fairies glowered at him.

"I am a vampire," said de Salis, "who draws on the life energy of humans. I have become expert in knowing precisely what they feel. It's...." He paused for reflection. "Rather like a chef who can tell the nature and quality of an unknown dish, pinpointing the ingredients and their origin from aroma and taste."

De Salis rose and approached Josh. Holding Sedge's wing before him, he reached a finger toward Josh's neck, saying, "I really shouldn't do this on a work night." Setting the fingertip red with Josh's blood against his tongue, de Salis tasted the sample.

He announced, "As I suspected, there's no guilt in the mix. This man is feeling alarm, frustration, anger, and a percentage or two of...*curiosity*." De Salis flashed an approving smile. "All in all, appropriate emotions for the situation, but he is not your killer. In fact," de Salis worked the sides of his mouth, "I am detecting sorrow. He mourns the loss of the wing's owner."

"Speak truth!" Bream aimed a finger at de Salis, who waved a hand before his face as though batting at flies.

"I know the countercharm to that one," de Salis said mildly. "The truth is I've no reason to lie. My people have been falsely accused so many times deceit disgusts me. If this man murdered your clansman, I'd say so. He did not. Release him."

When Bream opened his mouth to object, Heron muttered, "See to it." Looking resentful, Bream pointed at Josh, who unfroze.

Heron inquired of de Salis, "This knowin' of things.... Do ye ken what we're about? We fairies, I'm meanin'."

"I gather from your scents that you're not accustomed to taking life." De Salis looked at his watch. "I must go. There is still much to do at The Black Swan. You will join us, Josh—May I call you Josh? Oh, and the lovely Ms. Hanrahan, as well. I look forward to it. Delighted to meet you," he told the fairies. "Of course, you and your clan are always welcome at the club. *Buna saira*," he said over his shoulder as he left.

Heron and Bream sat down. Josh sat down. "Beer?" he asked.

The fairies didn't quite apologize ("Sure an' all, ye knew we were just after testin' ye," was Heron's explanation.), so Josh didn't quite let down his guard, resolving to nurse one beer in order to stay sharp. He worried about Judy, too. Though the fairies claimed to have done nothing to the dog, Josh checked her, relieved to find her unharmed. Maybe she'd picked up on his fear, or maybe de Salis' arrival set her to barking. As for why she'd stopped so suddenly, who knew?

When he returned to the loft, Josh found the fairies snooping through his bedroom and Archie's. He couldn't blame them; he'd spent yesterday nosing around half of Elvira. But when they started hinting Archie or Josh's parents might be killers, Josh knew it was time for tough love: He told Heron and Bream exactly what happened to Sedge. Their ruddy faces paled at the details; Josh pressed on relentlessly to make his point: "The murderer was someone sick in the head."

"A giant," Bream concluded. "They're ever after gettin' their armor cheapish, and they're a wild lot in their rages."

"Too few of them," Heron added. "Too many born of the same mothers dulls the wit of the tribe."

Could that be it? Might an inbred giant, infuriated by some trade dispute, crush a fairy as a knee-jerk reaction to frustration? "But the wire part bothers me," Josh said. "Seems too fiddly for their big hands, and I've never seen a giant anywhere near the Beckett farm. No giant footprints at the scene. What's the big deal about giants and armor anyway? They don't wear it."

"'Tis for weddin's and burial," Heron answered. "Tradition. Even the women must have breastplates and caps. Our Sedge was the best of the wire weavers."

Bream raised his miniature teacup. "To Sedge."

After a solemn toast, Heron and Bream reminisced about Sedge's skills as an artisan before going on to bawdier tales of his feats as drinker and lady's man. Josh hadn't known about those parts of Sedge's personality. It lifted his spirits to hear Sedge had a joyful life.

When the fairies started singing, Josh decided he should drive them to Fern Cliffe. He didn't want them flying drunk with the heavy spool of wire. Since he'd stuck with his plan to have only one beer, he was good to go.

Josh left them at the overlook, promising to return Sedge's remains as soon as the police would allow. He phoned Georgia and learned she'd brought Benji home, so Josh wouldn't be sharing her bed. Disappointed, Josh wished them both sweet dreams then returned to the loft where he nuked some leftover pizza, downed a few more beers, and fell asleep as soon as his head hit the pillow.

Stedwell called when Josh was getting in the Hummer on his way to work. "I need your help to take Sedge back to the Red fairies' village this morning."

"Look, Mayor, I can't afford more time off. I'll lose my job."

"You won't. Mr. Mateer will allow you to make up the hours this evening. Oh, but he said he'd—I'm quoting here—'can your ass' if you didn't return the Hummer. I'll pick you up at the garage."

Josh blew air through his lips. It was gonna be another one of those days.

Stedwell drove a silver Beemer. He'd arrived with it, so Elvirans couldn't complain he squandered their money, but more than a few envied his sweet steel. It still had new-car smell, Josh noticed as he climbed inside. Spotting a basket on a back seat, he asked, "Sedge in there?"

"Mr. Wati's caskets were too large. I asked him to prepare something suitable. What do you think?"

The basket was oval, roughly two and a half feet long. Made of tightly woven, fine bamboo, it had handles and a lid, all lacquered dark brown. "Looks nice," Josh decided, "sort of natural, the way fairies like things to be. Shit!" He slapped his forehead. "We have to go by my place. I have Sedge's wing."

That comment required a lengthy explanation, which Josh supplied as Stedwell drove him home. Josh left out the embarrassing part about being bound by magic, though he revealed de Salis helped convince the fairies of his innocence.

"Vampires have built-in lie detectors," Stedwell remarked when Josh returned to the car. "I learn something new every day. What will you do with the wing—give it to the fairies?"

"I'll put it with Sedge, where it belongs." Josh braced himself for another look at Sedge's mangled corpse. He opened the basket.

Sedge lay on a bed of red satin. His hair had been combed back to cover the skull damage and arranged at the sides around a curved wooden painting of his likeness set over the face area. His body shape looked nearly normal, as though the bones were intact. He wore a red shirt with the wide sleeves fairies favored, brown trousers and felt boots. The remnant of his copper chain maille had been placed at his feet.

Josh stared, amazed. "Mr. Wati did this? How did he make the picture, the clothes?

"I don't know. I just asked him to do his best."

Josh was nervous about moving Sedge's shoulder to slip the wing behind it. He didn't want to undo the undertaker's careful work. In the end, feeling sad, he laid Sedge's wing on his chest and shut the lid.

Stedwell wondered who could have put the wing in Josh's loft. They discussed possibilities on the way to Fern Cliffe. "Archie's been going to work at 3:45. I normally get home at 4:30, but I stayed late yesterday," Josh told him. "My mother's daycare kids leave at 5:00. After that, she does errands. Whoever left the wing must have shown up after 5:00. We don't lock the door, so there's no problem getting into the place."

"Report on this to Chief Brown. He should stay in the loop. Oh, and...." Stedwell paused. "This is delicate. Are you certain your roommate had nothing to do with the fairy's death?"

"*Archie?*" Josh wheezed. "He's no psycho. And besides, he did the ghost hunt with me that night. We even have witnesses: Bobbi Miller, Georgia, the de Salises, Tom Hanrahan."

"Tom's still in the hospital," Stedwell noted. "I've no idea what to tell the Green fairies about their man, Reed, but Mrs. Withers called to offer her assistance. She'll accompany me to their village when the coroner releases the body."

"How did she know Reed was dead?"

"Her daughter told her."

"Oh, yeah. Tink discovered the body. You know, I'll bet Mrs. Withers painted the picture of Sedge's face. She sells fairy art."

"That could be it. Well, we're here." Stedwell pulled into the overlook parking area. "Not half enough parking for the tourists. We'll have to do something about that." He went to open the trunk, removing a red flag. "We've worked out a signaling system with the fairies. When the Elviran flag is up, that means tourists are around. Flying this flag means we need to meet with the Red fairies."

Josh watched Stedwell raise the flag on a pole set up by the trees. He walked toward the edge of the rocky outcrop and peered over the side. "Got the gift shop up, I see." Studying the rounded walls and wood-shake roof, Josh added, "Sort of reminds me of the Withers' place."

"An architect friend in Chicago drew the plans. I hoped the fairies would put up little houses—you know, those miniature ones made of bark, moss and glass stones. The fairies had no idea of what I meant. We'll have to build those, too." Stedwell smiled ruefully. "I'd have thought they could whip up something with their 'magic'. Frankly, I think their claims of magical abilities are exaggerated."

"You don't have to believe in fairy magic," Josh told him, "but it'll go easier on you if you do."

"Why?"

"You won't be so shocked when it hits you."

Fairies appeared, flying up the overlook to surround Stedwell and Josh. They were all female, most of them young, a grouping that surprised Josh. Fairy women tended to avoid humans. He'd never seen so many at once.

"I'm Mo Stedwell," the mayor began. "This is Josh Seldom. We're here because—"

"We're knowin' why ye're here," an exquisitely pretty brunette fairy cut in. She flew forward, hovering with hands on hips. "It's me da ye're bringin' home—him that was slain by one of yer own."

"Yes," Stedwell admitted. "I'm very sorry for your loss."

The fairy lifted her chin. "Port him to our village," she commanded, turning a cold shoulder to the men while leading the rest of the troop away. Each fairy stared daggers at Stedwell and Josh as she passed.

Nonplused, Stedwell hesitated. Josh said, "Hurry. We'll lose them if we take too long. Then we'll never find the village."

"You don't know where it is?"

"Nobody does. It's invisible." Josh reached into the car for the basket.

Stedwell took hold of a basket handle. "Surely, you're joking."

Josh shrugged, grasping the other handle. "Let's go."

Climbing down the cliff was easier than Josh expected; the limestone slabs had been smoothed and leveled for tourists. He and Stedwell followed the path carved by ancient rivers through gullies, now softened by ferns. After a bit, the rocks parted to reveal a narrow valley where wildlife rustled around, hunting food. The air smelled good; the sunlight shone warm and bright, glinting off pale, young leaves. Josh would have enjoyed the hike if he weren't serving as pallbearer.

They came to a waterfall spilling down over a wide rock face into a deep, green pool. Josh pointed out a water wheel. Stedwell insisted the wheel was nothing but a stone. Josh let that pass. Not everyone could recognize fairyworks.

The fairies kept ahead of them, only showing themselves when they wanted the men to move faster, indicating their impatience with a beckoning hand. Then Josh and Stedwell spotted a fairy standing on a fallen tree. She told them to leave the path and enter a forest area floored with wildflowers. Here the trees were small—dogwoods with pink or white flowers, redbuds starting to purple. The trees gave way to a meadow. Josh and Stedwell stepped into it.

"Bear yer burden yet a ways to our summer gatherin' place yonder," Josh heard in his ear. He turned his head, finding the female who'd talked to them—Sedge's daughter—hovering there. About to ask her what she meant, he suddenly *saw* the village.

Ahead stood a structure made of grape or willow. Spring vines had yet to cover the entire tan-gray understructure. The branches forming walls and roof weren't pieced but grown into the shape of a two-story tower with a long, arching wing beside it.

To Josh's left stood a line of similar towers. Some of these stood more than two levels, if the horizontal braids of branches indicated floors. Dense near the ground, the structures held less material at their tops, producing a lighter, airier look. There were no roofs. Across from them on the other long side of the meadow, three large buildings shaped like igloos sheltered under the bent boughs of trees growing beside a stream.

The center of the village held the strangest constructions: flat-bottomed spheres or tapering cones with rounded tops. Sometimes the spheres had offshoots—other bulbous shapes that stuck out at haphazard angles from their sides.

Sedge's daughter flew toward the large, far building. As Josh followed her, he was aware of being watched. Fairy faces spied on them from the towers. One little boy, his wings barely sprouted, leaned far over the top edge of his home until his mother pulled him back.

Stedwell whispered to Josh, "The children are the cutest things I've ever seen."

Sedge's daughter whirled in mid-air, shaking a finger in Stedwell's face. "Don't be thinkin' to steal our wee ones or ye'll never leave here."

As Stedwell stammered his apologies, Josh wondered if he really appreciated how dangerous fairies could be. Stedwell kept silent after that, a good thing, in Josh's opinion.

They reached their destination. Sedge's daughter landed on the grass before the open-arched enclosure. Bending low to enter the space, Josh and Stedwell found inside the same group of female fairies that they'd seen at the overlook.

"Our menfolk are after doin' yer job, huntin' for Da's killer. I be

Moss," Sedge's daughter said. "These lot are Da's wives."

"All of them?" Josh blurted out.

"After me mum went off t'Otherworld, he were a great one for greenwood marriages," Moss remarked reminiscently, her hand stroking the basket. "They last but a year. Still an' all, they suited him." She drew in a long breath. "We'll see him now."

Josh hoped the undertaker's efforts would appease the fairies or give them comfort. He was wrong. The minute they lifted the lid from the basket, every fairy gasped.

"Where's his other wing, then?" Moss cried. "An' his copper shirt, his spear? What is he to do without them? We can't send him off until he's whole."

Stedwell said quietly, "We haven't located all his personal items yet."

"Well, see to it, sharpish! There'll be no peace fer any of yer kind before there's peace fer him. Now be gone." Moss clapped her hands.

"Funny," **Stedwell said,** standing beside his car at the overlook, "I don't remember walking back here."

"Sun's higher in the sky," Josh observed, "so I guess we did."

Stedwell squinted, asking, "Has your hair always been red?"

Josh pulled a few strands forward. They were orange. "No." He turned to Stedwell, announcing, "Mr. Mayor, your hair's red, too."

CHAPTER NINE

At 11:45, Megan was braiding Vanny's hair in her mother's salon office, "Sit up straight." She kneaded Vanny's shoulders brusquely. "I'll get the last parts all crooked."

"I'm so tired," Vanny groaned, slouching again in the desk chair. "Only slept three hour last night. Ouch! You're pulling too hard."

"Sorry. Almost done. Mom says we shouldn't miss out on the Egyptian trend. Even if I can't work in the salon until I get my license, there's nothing to stop me from setting up a braiding booth in the square when the tourists get here—all types of braids, not only Egyptian. I need practice."

"Just as long as I don't have to be your lab rat for every style," Vanny groused.

Megan held a hand mirror before her. "Like it?"

"There aren't any beads." Vanny turned her head left and right.

"We've ordered some online, but they're not in yet. Here." Megan set down the mirror to pick up a tissue-wrapped square. Tearing at the paper, she said, "I liked my barrette so well, I went back to the spa to buy another. You can wear it for now."

"Looks expensive. And what's this symbol? It's like an egg with a handle."

"That's an *ankh*. It means life or energy or love…something like that," Megan guessed. "And it didn't cost a lot. I don't know how they can afford to make and sell them, but they look really nice. Guess who's working in the gift shop—Shane Ryan's old girlfriend, Paige Marshal."

"The one who came over from Goreton to beat him up in the parking

71

lot at school after he dumped her for Nefer?"

"She didn't beat him up," Megan refuted while pinning the ankh to the back of Vanny's head. "She bitched him out and ripped his shirt. I saw the whole thing. Honestly! Some girls completely lose it over guys."

"I dunno. Sometimes you gotta do what you gotta do—like my kissing Eliot."

"WHAT?" Megan dug down with the comb, grating Vanny's scalp. While Vanny yelped, Megan spun the chair around. "*When*? Why didn't you tell me?"

Vanny grinned. "I wanted to see your face. Ha! You look like a fish on dry land, doing the o-o thing."

"Never mind about me. What did he do? Say? How did you ever have the nerve?"

"Well..." Vanny inspected her nails, drawing out the moment. "There we were, under the table while the fight went on at the club. I thought, *It's now or never*. I mean, he couldn't make the first move, could he? He's conditioned against it."

"Right, Miss Excellence in Science," Megan muttered. "So?"

"I tried to reach his mouth, but he turned his head when Mr. Suarez came in and started yelling for the fight to stop. I planted one on Eliot's cheek. After that, we crawled out from under the table. While we were dusting ourselves off, he said, 'No need to thank me. I'm just glad you weren't hurt.' When the Elviran guys skipped out, so did Eliot."

Megan leaned back against her mother's desk. "It didn't go well."

"Sure it did. He gave me this long look before he left. He'll be thinking about me," Vanny finished with confident nod.

"I wish I knew Fadri were thinking about me."

"Oh, yeah, the Mystery Man. Still have no clue where to find him?"

"I...I think I do." Megan's gaze lowered. Then, abruptly, she fixed Vanny with a hard stare. "Look, if I tell you something, you have to promise—*promise*—not to tell anyone."

Vanny drew back. "You're pregnant."

Megan rolled her eyes. "Be serious. This is important. Promise?"

"Okay. Do we have to pinky swear?"

"We haven't done that since third grade," Megan scoffed, "and this is a lot bigger than stealing candy from the drugstore." She paused, sighed, and then pursed her lips, finally confessing in a whisper, "He's a vampire."

"That's it—the Big Secret? Sheeit. We're falling over vampires in Elvira. I *work* with vampires, and IMO, they're not that nice—too pushy, too macho. I'll bet it's his looks. The only thing you didn't tell me about his face was how many nose hairs he has."

Megan bristled. "Just once, I want you to listen to *me*. I listened to you moan about Snopes for a whole year, and did I tease you?"

"No…"

"So, shut up and listen. This is a big deal for me. When was the last time I crushed on a guy?"

Vanny stroked her chin. "Kyle Lauder. Freshman year."

"Yeah, and then he moved away. It's been a long, long time, and this is—" Exasperated, Megan threw out her hands.

Vanny patted Megan's forearm. "I'm sorry, Megsy. Tell me." Folding her hands in her lap, Vanny waited.

"Last night, the salon was open late, but it was slow. By quarter to eight, Mom finished her appointments and started to close. Then three women walked in, all of them drop-dead gorgeous. They wanted cuts. Mom waved them into the chairs, but there was—"

"No reflection in the mirrors," Vanny finished.

Megan eyed her severely. "*Who's* telling this story?"

"You are," Vanny said contritely. "Go on."

"Well, you're right. Mom planned for vampires. I told you about the special booth with the screen and spotlight, right? It's in the supply area between here and the main room.

"Anyway, Mom showed them the setup, and they were stoked. They laughed at each other's silhouettes. All they wanted, really, was to get rid of split ends, but Mom thought they could use conditioning, and—"

Patience gone, Vanny revolved both wrists. "Get to the good part."

"They paid and left a huge tip. Then, they handed Mom *this*." Megan pulled a business card from her pocket, dangling it before Vanny's eyes. She read

The Black Swan, Fine Dining & Spirits
and **Cygnet**, Dancing (18+ welcome. No alcohol served.)
Anton de Salis, proprietor

"That Cygnet place sounds great," said Vanny. "Elvira has nowhere to dance or hang out if you're under twenty-one."

"You're missing the point. De Salis—that's *Fadri's* name. He has to be one of them."

"Well, there's your clue. Trot over to the new club and say hey."

Megan sighed. "I can't remember a thing he said to me on the ride home because of Nefer's crazy wine. Only sensations, like how the fields looked blue-white in the moonlight, how loud the frogs were, the feel of his arms around me...."

"So, go talk to him. What's he gonna do—bite you?"

"Well, yeah, maybe."

"If he wanted to do that, he had plenty of time when he took you home."

"Maybe he wasn't hungry, or is it thirsty? That's just it," Megan moaned, "I don't know enough about vampires. I feel so stupid. I don't even know basic stuff, like, well...." She paused. "When that vampire guy kissed you, were his lips cold?"

Vanny rubbed her mouth. "Yeah. They were."

"Do you think they're cold everywhere?"

"Doesn't seem to be a problem. They don't go around shivering."

"That's not what I meant. I meant *everywhere*." Megan pointed south.

Vanny snorted laughter, a burst that got Megan going. They begged each other to "Stop! Oh, *stop*..." when Megan's mother opened the door.

"We have visitors," Lisa Shaw announced.

Two Red fairies hovered in the doorway, one old and wrinkled; the other would have been a teenager in human years. Megan and Vanny gaped.

"They're looking for someone," Lisa went on. "Checking everyone's 'colors'."

"Spirit glow," the old one corrected. He studied Vanny, saying, "Um...dusty rose." Of Megan, he noted, "That one there's more yer cerise, I'd say."

"Gaffer?" the teenaged fairy inquired.

"Cherry colored."

"Ah." The young guy snickered. "Likely to a lucky feller about, then, eh?"

"Mind yer mouth, laddie," the grandfather muttered.

"Well, of course, they're pink," Lisa asserted. "They're young girls. And now you've seen everyone in the shop. If you don't mind, I'd like to get back to my customers."

The elder nodded. "Aye, as the sayin' goes, 'Keep yer shop, and yer shop'll keep ye.' Thankee, Missus. We'll fly."

So saying, both fairies headed for the salon's open front door. Megan watched them go, noticing that in the bright light by the entrance, her mother's hair looked strawberry blonde. Walking over to her, she asked, "When did you change your color?"

"The fairies said I'm green," Lisa disclosed, wrinkling her nose. "Guess that's better than gray."

"No, not that—your hair. It's different, but cool."

Lisa wedged in beside the mayor's wife to inspect herself in the mirror. Mrs. Stedwell tugged at her arm. "Lisa? I came in for a haircut. Why am I suddenly looking like Beyoncé?"

"I don't know, Nichelle." Lisa plucked at lengths of formerly black hair. "It's definitely auburn, maybe even a little lighter. I'd say—"

She was interrupted by a stampede of women, all with shades of red hair, rushing into the shop, the foremost of them battling for the two empty styling chairs, hands seizing armrests, hips butting off competitors like kids playing musical chairs. The winners—Mrs. Wisniewski and Mrs. Able—settled themselves triumphantly.

"I can't go home like this. My husband will think I've gone middle-aged crazy or taken a lover," Mrs. Wisniewski said.

"Dye me!" howled Mrs. Able. "I want my gray hair back."

Megan giggled. She'd never heard that one before.

Lisa asked the crowd, "Has everyone had home hair coloring go desperately wrong?" The chorus of denial was so loud, she covered her ears, but even that maneuver couldn't muffle the shrill cries of Nefer Wati, elbowing her way through the throng.

"This is an emergency," Nefer declared. "*Look* at my beautiful black hair. It's *purple*."

Lisa said clinically, "That's wine or burgundy, actually."

Hands on hips, Nefer declared, "I don't care what it's called. I want it fixed right now."

"Sorry, Nefer, but you'll have to wait your turn. As you can see, there are a few others ahead of you."

As though she'd first noticed the crowd, Nefer looked around. When her glance fell on Vanny and Megan, she accused, "You did *them*."

Everyone in the place gazed at the girls, who gazed at each other. Their hair was black, unchanged. They held up their hands and shrugged.

"Well, I don't want to wait," Nefer decided. "I'm going to the drugstore to buy some stuff and do my hair myself." Turning on her heel, she wedged a path to the door.

She made it two strides outside before stopping, staring, and scurrying back into the salon. "Rats! The street as far as Benton's Hardware is covered with rats, and they're coming this way."

"Nefer, if this is some sort of joke..." Lisa Shaw warned, stepping toward her.

"NO!" Nefer pulled the door shut and clicked the lock. "It's like Krueger's field. Megan, come over here and look."

The vanguard of rats arrived, dark shapes against the salon's frosted-glass door and window. Several of the rodents paused by the doorframe, sniffing and scratching experimentally, but these were pushed along when more rats arrived. They lined the base of the window, piling atop one another as a pyramid of writhing shapes arose.

Lisa shouted over the din of babbling customers, "Quiet! We need to keep our voices down, not excite them." She finished in a stage whisper, "Everyone back away from the window. Nichelle, call the police."

"I already have. Their line's busy."

"That's good. They know there's a problem. We'll have to wait for help." Lisa Shaw rubbed her chin. "Let's retreat to the office. We can hole up there if we have to. No pushing. I don't want anyone hurt. Megs, check the back door."

"Mom, I have an idea."

Sprinting through the office, she put her ear to the alley door and listened. Taking a deep breath, she opened it. "Don't do that!" her mother cried, but Megan was already in the alley, eyes scanning for rats, before she dashed to the corner, doing another check there. What she saw made her falter. The stream of rats spanned the intersection of Washington and Main, but they weren't turning down Washington where she was. Megan gathered her courage and raced to the door of the new Black Swan.

"Fadri de Salis," she flung at the red-haired workmen inside, who seemed unaware of the rat tsunami on Main Street. "Where is he?"

"Other door," Mr. Bethune said. "On Second, the Cygnet side."

"Thanks." Megan went out, turned the corner to Second, and ducked into the doorway under the sign of a young swan. She entered a broad, open space with a varnished wood floor and white walls. Semi-circular banks of dark wood held counter-style seating, and big, round tables were set between them. A glass case stood to one side of the dance floor, with a coffee bar behind it. At the far end of the room, a long console stood before a blank wall overlooked by smoked-glass windows.

"Fadri?" Megan called.

He didn't answer. She checked a cloakroom, shouted into the bathrooms, then stood wondering where else he might be. Spying another door near the coffee bar, Megan went to it and turned the knob.

She heard a growl, and watched a dark form rising from the far end of the small room. "What the hell?" came next.

Fadri's voice. Megan exhaled. "I *need* you."

Eyes adjusting to the dimness, she saw him sit up on a cot. Megan forgot what she was going to say. Drawing a hand through his tumbling, blond hair, Fadri de Salis presented an arresting sight, eyes gentle from sleep, broad shoulders, bare chest, one long leg extended beyond the sheet…

He tilted his head, eyebrows raised.

"I need your help," Megan explained. "There are rats are all over Main Street. They're piling up outside my mother's salon. You did something to them out in the field the other night. Can you do it again?"

"What time is it?" he asked groggily.

"Around noon. Oh! Can you go out in the sunlight?"

"With enough preparation. Hello, Megan Shaw."

"Hello, Fadri de Salis. Is this where you live?"

"This is where I sleep for a few days until my uncle's house is ready. The motel keeper is not to be borne. He continually urges *pig's* blood upon us." Fadri wrinkled his nose. "Calls it Swine Cooler. Smells vile."

"But don't you need—"

"I need to dress." He stroked the beard stubble on his face. "Need a shave, too, but no time for that if we're to attend to your rats. So…" He walked his fingers on air.

"Hurry," Megan urged, shutting the door.

Fadri emerged looking like an Australian cowboy, wearing jeans and boots, a long duster with the collar turned up and a broad-brimmed hat. Wraparound shades and leather gloves completed the outfit. He patted his pockets. "Ah, there's the key."

"Key?"

"We're driving."

"It's just around the block."

"At midday, we drive," Fadri said firmly. "Come." Outside, pointing toward a dark blue Mercedes with black-tinted windows parked in the glaring sun across the street, he apologized. "Forgive my poor manners, but I will not hold open your door just now." Fadri dashed to the driver's side and got in with Megan close behind him.

The drive was short-lived. As soon as they passed the Swan to turn onto Washington, they saw a torrent of water pouring down Main Street. A firefighter stood at the corner, hose in hand.

"They've opened the hydrants," Megan said. "They're washing away the rats."

"Your people have the situation under control. That is good, but we must now change direction. I can't cross running water."

Megan stared at him.

"An Egyptian curse," Fadri explained as he turned left into the alley, "to keep us from crossing the Nile, or so my uncle says."

"Stop here. This is the back door of the salon. I need to check on what's happening." When he did, Megan shifted in her seat to face the blond vampire. "You're *Egyptian*?"

"No, I am from Romansch."

"Where's that, like, Transylvania?"

"Switzerland."

"Switzerland," Megan repeated, shaking her head. She reached for the door latch. "Thank you."

"For what? I did nothing."

"You were willing to help. That counts for a lot in Elvira."

"Then…might I ask a favor of you? For *your* help?"

"Doing what?"

"Come by the club when you finish your work. My uncle expects me to program lights, music and images at Cygnet. You know better than I what will please your people."

"Do you mean Elvirans?" Megan watched him nod. "If you're going to stay here, they're your people, too." Fadri tossed his head, clearly surprised by the idea. Megan left the car but said through the open door, "If you want my advice, you're welcome to it."

"Until later, then, Megan Shaw, and let us hope the next time we meet, there will be no rats." He lifted his shades, winked, and drove off.

CHAPTER TEN

Mike Mateer stood in the bay door of the garage with a broom in one hand, a tire iron in the other. The new planter at the southwest corner of the lot lay on its side, soil and flowers missing. Josh got out of Mo Stedwell's car, stepping into a puddle that sloshed over the top of his shoe.

"When did you decide to get this place power-washed?" Josh asked Mike.

"I didn't. The firemen sprayed water everywhere when they blasted the rats."

"Rats?"

Mike described the tide of surfing rats that passed the garage. "Damnedest thing I ever saw. They weren't struggling, just riding along, calm as you please, until the water hit the low spot at the corner and angled toward the ditch across the street. That's where they hopped off and ran down the road. I figured they were heading for the grain elevator or the Dairy Queen, but no: They kept going until they reached the field by Deeble's where they disappeared in the corn. I've been waiting to see if they double back."

Josh groaned. "Deeble will think the fairies set rats on him."

Mo turned to Josh. "They didn't?"

"Nah. Fairies wouldn't use animals that way. I'm thinking rats could be one of those plagues the Egyptians predicted."

The mayor rubbed the back of his neck. "I assumed the priests were exaggerating."

"You thought the fairies were, too."

"What happened when you brought them the dead fairy?" Mike asked.

"They weren't entirely satisfied with our progress on the murder case," Stedwell began. "I'll be posting a statement on the town's website and putting up flyers in the square. It seems—"

"The Reds were pissed," Josh summarized. "They've cursed us with red hair until we find Sedge's killer and his belongings."

"Well, you two sure look goofy," Mike said.

Josh crooked a finger at him. "Take a gander at yourself in the Beemer's side mirror."

Mike set down the tools and squinted at his auburn buzz-cut, muttering "Sonuvabitch...." He looked up when Georgia turned into the garage driveway and parked the '59 Cadillac De Ville she inherited from her father. The Caddy stretched almost nineteen feet long, dwarfing Stedwell's BMW. Georgia only drove it when she chauffeured clients or took Benji some distance. Mike ran a covetous hand over the car's endless fins and obscenely long tail lights. "Sweet, sweet ass," he murmured. When Georgia stood beside him, he asked, "How's she running?"

"She's going great, Mike, but I need to talk to Josh. This is important, or I wouldn't keep him from his work. And could you, um, help Benji get a soda, please?" Georgia began rummaging through her purse for her wallet.

"The little man's credit is always good here." Mike waved away the cash. He opened the heavy rear door so Benji could get out.

The boy chirped happily, "Mr. Mike! You look funny."

Mike tousled Benji's blond head. "Yeah, I guess I do." He asked Georgia, "What kind of soda?"

"Anything without caffeine. Oh." Georgia looked closely at Mike, then Josh, then the mayor. "What's happened to your hair?"

"Punishment from the fairies," Josh said. "Hit everyone in Elvira."

"Why would red hair be a punishment?" Georgia asked innocently, but she sidled over to Josh with a wicked grin on her face. "I kind of like it on you. We could be twins."

"That'd be bad, Georgia, real bad," Josh reminded her.

Her tone changed after Benji gripped Mike's hand, tugging him toward the vending machines inside. "I'm glad you're here, Mayor Stedwell," Georgia said gravely. "There's been trouble about Tom."

"Not a turn for the worse, I hope."

"No, no. Tom's much better. He's awake and alert, sitting up and eating. I checked on that before I took Benji to see him. But when we got to the hospital, the Goreton police were there, and Mayor Marshal, too. Apparently, somebody told the Green fairies their warrior was dead, his body was in the morgue, and that Tom killed him.

"A bunch of them showed up at the hospital, demanding to know where Tom was. The security guard and desk clerk wouldn't give out the information, so the fairies rooted them."

"Rooted?"

"That's when they make the natural fibers in your clothes grow like ropes," Georgia explained. "So they did that to the guard's sleeve and pant cuffs until he couldn't move his hands or feet. The clerk's collar grew out to wind around her neck, scaring her pretty badly. She caved, and told them Tom's room number."

"You saw all this?" Josh asked.

Georgia shook her head. "I heard about it later from Ed Brown. He'd been visiting, and was leaving Tom's room when the fairies made it to the second floor. Ed asked them why they were there, and when they said, 'Revenge!' well, he couldn't let them past him. He blocked the door and pulled out his baton. That's when they rooted him.

"Ed's hand held the doorknob, so he was rooted *to* the door, making it harder for the fairies to get in. While they were working on that problem, an aide threatened them with setting off a fire extinguisher, basically holding them at bay until the cops and Mayor Marshal arrived."

Georgia shoved back her hair, and blew air through her lips. "I hope that guy gets a medal or something, and Mayor Marshal, too. From what Ed told me, Marshal did a great job of talking the fairies down. In the end, she convinced them to leave Tom alone, but they demanded the wolf compound be closed. Then they took their man from the morgue and carried him home. That's all I know." She looked toward Benji, who crossed the fuel pump aisle, holding his soda can with both hands.

"Daddy's arm is gray all the way to his tattoo," Benji reported, handing up the root beer for his mother to open. "And his fingernails are *blue*."

Georgia nodded. "Results of the silver poisoning, probably permanent. Tom's not too happy about that." Eyes on Benji, she added, "But he's going to be fine. Don't be scared."

"I'm not scared. I'm hungry."

"I know, and I'm sorry. I'll take you right home to feed you. It's just been—"

"One of those days," Benji said in a world-weary voice while he climbed into the car.

When Josh announced he needed to eat before starting work, Mike threw up his hands, but he didn't act angry, so Josh went to the Country Kitchen. There he met Archie.

"Hummer ready yet?" Archie asked.

"Yep. Test drove it and everything."

"Good. I want to take it out to try my tour route. Stedwell's office called to say the fairy walks were off for this weekend. We're doing the big bird run instead."

Josh nodded. Studying Archie's new appearance, he asked, "How're you handling the carrot top?"

"Jeez. This was all we needed, looking like each other, I mean. Half the people in this town already think we're gay because we live together."

"Yeah?"

"You don't keep up with the gossip, do you?"

"Not really," Josh admitted. "I'm socially challenged."

"Same here," Archie complained. "Haven't touched a woman in…

God, *way* too long."

"Strike out with Bobbi Miller?"

"She's friendly enough, but she's got issues left over from the ex, I think. Hafta go slow with her."

"I know how that is," Josh sympathized. "Take it slow with the Hummer, too. Don't beat it to death."

"Right, right," Archie agreed too quickly. Josh didn't hold out much hope for the Hummer's continuing health. If Archie turned it in later today, Josh could still repair whatever damage his lead-footed friend would inflict. "You'll get it back by four when you go to the club?"

Archie shook his head. "I'm off work for today. The Cygnet side is mostly finished. Came together fast because they gutted the old warehouse and put in everything new. Well," Archie signaled the waitress for his bill. "Gotta bounce. Oh, I almost forgot to tell you: I've booked us for a ghost hunt at the library tonight."

Josh frowned. "I'm behind at work. Why do we have to investigate tonight?"

"Old man Seagram's been blowing in my ear for two days. Couldn't leave you a message 'cause your voice mail box is full." Twisting his lip at Josh's guilty face, Archie went on, "Seagram says he needs time to work up a display for tourists about ghosts in the library if we find any. So, yeah, I said we would. It doesn't get dark until 8-8:30. You have until then. I'll spring for some burgers and bring them along. Show up at the library soon as you can."

By late afternoon, Megan had rehearsed at least a dozen lines to sound nonchalant, as though she'd just dropped in on Fadri instead of racing home to shower and change into her new clothes, a black flounce skirt and peasant blouse, emerald under-corset circling her middle. What came out of her mouth when she entered Cygnet was, "Wow...."

Snow fell. She held out her hands, but the snow was a trick of the lights. On one wall, white-capped mountains wreathed in clouds overlooked a deep valley. A close-up view of a skier doing a flip shared the space behind the coffee bar with ski tips sending up a cascade of rainbow flakes.

Fadri, at the console along the far end of the room, stood below a jewel-box, twilit city nestled against a mountain lake. As soon as he saw her, he said, "Ah, Megan Shaw," and the images disappeared.

"Aw," Megan complained. "The pictures were pretty."

He shrugged, waving her toward the console. "I am amusing myself, not doing my work," he confessed. "I miss the mountains of home, the places I know, the skiing."

"I've never seen real mountains," said Megan. Then it dawned on her, "How can you ski? Don't you get, um, sunburned?"

"But this is easy." Fadri snapped his fingers. "With balaclava, goggles, gloves and ski suit."

Megan grinned. "One day, I'd like to travel."

"You must do so. The world is a beautiful place, yet your town of Elvira is the most special."

Megan squinted at him. Fadri explained, "Here, I may enjoy the company of a lovely, young woman, and no one will say this is wrong. Never have I felt so free." He smiled, making Megan feel proud.

A moment later, Fadri shoved up the sleeves of his black cotton sweater, saying, "First, we test the lighting. Stand there, in the center of the room."

With new images of candles glowing from the walls and a spot lit area surrounded by a circle of stars, the room seemed both warmer and more mysterious. Megan heard the opening harpsichord strains of a song her mother liked, made popular by a film in the '90s.

Fadri stepped into the light and bowed. Holding out a cool hand, he took hers to stride alongside her. Confused, Megan followed gamely as he turned, gripped her waist and stepped forward with a long, graceful, reaching step. Megan faltered until she caught on to the dipping, swaying, rising motions that carried them through light and shadow, pivoting and sometimes slipping through each other's arms, amid the illusion of falling snow. Eyes fixed on her, Fadri waltzed Megan with a sinuous confidence that made the dance an intimate partnership. Megan's every sense tingled.

"That song was for me," Fadri told her as the music faded, "this, for you." He went to the console.

Megan nodded to the beat of familiar drums and guitars, a song she knew. She swayed and danced in a circle apart from Fadri, and yet not apart. His moves echoed hers, and he chimed in when she sang, "Yeah, I like you, and I feel so whoa ho woo!" Clapping at the end of this song, Megan heard Fadri say the music reminded him of a tune by The Rolling Stones. Not sure about that, Megan listened, found his choice a little too slow for her taste, but otherwise interesting.

And so they worked through dozens of songs, Fadri taking notes, striking through ones on his list that brought grimaces to Megan's face. They danced to a few, never a slow one like the first, but Megan found herself watching his hips far too often.

"Got any Fleetwood Mac?" someone asked.

Turning, Megan saw the Swan's contractors standing inside Cygnet's doorway.

Fadri asked Mr. McKay, "Are you done for the day?"

"Yup. Just waiting for your uncle to show up and approve."

"Well, then, which song would you like?"

Megan listened to the oldies, wondering why people thought they were so great. She tested out a few dance steps, but the rhythms were wrong. The men were pleased, though. They came into the room to watch the visuals, humming and tapping their feet. Country music was the next request; Megan grimaced. Fadri said to the men, "Try this."

A cartoon video came on along with a song about working men wishing they were rock stars. The beat was slow but compelling. Megan danced along idly while the Elviran guys smirked at the screen, one saying, "Oh, yeah, now that's what I'm *talkin'* about!" when a sexy woman pulled on a black stocking.

Watching the video, Megan heard her name called. She whirled toward the sound of her father's voice and saw him and two bowling buddies step into the club. They stared at the wall where the sexy stocking woman was now in split screen, all four images of her thonged ass strolling toward a door.

"Oh, hi," Megan called to her father. "Did you win the tournament?"

"It's time for you to go home," David Shaw told her.

"Home? Why?"

"No daughter of mine's gonna be dancing for men watching porn," he said, tight lipped.

"Aw, now, Dave, it wasn't like that," Mr. Lesak put in.

"You can butt out of this discussion anytime, Ron. I'm not talking to you." David strode across the floor, buddies flanking him. "Megan, get your purse. We're leaving."

"No, Dad. I'm helping Fadri. This is—"

"One of those creatures, I'll bet. Listen, mister—"

"De Salis." Fadri cut the music. "Welcome to Cygnet." He offered his hand.

Shaw did not take it. Gripping his bowling bag with both fists, he said, "Call yourself whatever you like, but you're all the same to me, you and those other freaks down the street. You've got one thing in mind: preying on Elvirans. Maybe you can fool young girls, buy off a few others with your money...." He shot an angry glance at the workmen. "But there're plenty of us who know the score. We'll stop you, shut you down—get our town back the way it should be."

Fadri squared his shoulders. "How will you 'shut us down'? Our permits are in order, and we know the entertainment business. We have operations in five countries—six, counting the States."

"If that's so, you have plenty other places to go," David concluded. "Elvira is a decent, God-fearing town. We don't want you here."

"Dad!"

He shoved a finger at her face. "I'm not gonna tell you again—get your stuff."

Megan shook her head. "I'm not ready to leave."

"Either come home now, or don't come home at all," David growled.

He turned on his heel and stalked off, his sidekicks glancing nervously at Megan before following in his wake. The other Elvirans took the cue and filed out in silence, leaving Megan alone with Fadri.

"Go after him," Fadri said, beginning to dial down the console controls.

"But he was *horrible*," Megan raged. "I'm so ashamed of what he said." She lowered her head, feeling mortified.

Fadri lifted her chin with a knuckle. "He's not the first to feel that way. At least, I know now that there is opposition in this town." He looked away, saying quietly, "And he is right. We do sustain ourselves on humans, not your blood, but your energy. Tonight, I took, perhaps, a minute of your life."

Megan drew back. "How?"

"Through touch. You felt a tingling while we danced?"

"Yes." Megan looked at her hands. "That was *feeding* on me?" Glaring at him, she stood outraged, demanding, "How dare you!"

Sky-blue eyes mournful, Fadri confessed, "An involuntary reaction, just as you gasp when you surface from water. I did not know my resources were so low. I stopped as soon as I could, but..." He held out his hands. "I *am* sorry."

"A minute of my life," Megan said slowly, "in exchange for tonight? A minute for a memory." She picked up her purse, began to walk away, and then dashed back, stretching on tiptoe to brush his mouth with hers, murmuring, "Even a minute and a half is a deal."

CHAPTER ELEVEN

Josh sat on the library steps, drumming fingers on a thigh, listening to his stomach rumble. He left work at 8. It was 8:30 now, and still no Archie, who didn't answer his phone and hadn't returned the Hummer as promised. *Where the hell was he?*

"Hi," said Ruthanne Quinn, startling Josh, so he jerked his head around. Climbing the stairs, she swiped at the top step with a tissue, inspected the spot for any remaining pigeon droppings, nodded, and then sat beside Josh.

"What are you doing here?" he asked.

"Checking on my book. I want to see if it's in yet."

"Library's closed."

"Since you're doing a ghost hunt, you can open the door. I brought sandwiches." Ruthanne searched through her tote. "Have a roast beef."

Refusing to rise to the bait and ask, "Oh, Ruthanne! However did you *know* about the ghost hunt?" Josh took the bribe, along with a can of ginger ale. He said only, "Archie has the key, and he's late."

"He had some trouble with the birds," Ruthanne reported between bites, "but he's been to your place to pick up his van. We won't have too long to wait."

Josh exhaled heavily. "Listen, Ruthie, you can cut the crap with me. The psychic shit is getting pretty deep."

"It doesn't matter what you think. The truth is I see live people when I want and hear dead ones when I don't, ever since the bridge—you know about that?"

Josh nodded. Though the bridge collapsed years ago, Elvirans still called the event 'The Tragedy'. Four people, including Ruthanne's parents, died. She'd been the only survivor. "Say," he asked, "have you ever tried your psychic thing with crime victims?"

"No!" Ruthanne recoiled. "Listen to murdered corpses telling me how they died? Eww."

Josh wondered next, "What about live people who can't remember what happened to them?"

"Such as?"

"Tom Hanrahan. He fought with a Green fairy during a full moon while he was in Louie mode. Doesn't remember how things went down."

Ruthanne said, "I don't see the past, but even if I could, I wouldn't waste my time on him. Asshat tried to steal my car."

"*Tom Hanrahan*?" Josh breathed, shocked.

"It was 'Tommy' Hanrahan back then. He was fifteen or so."

Intrigued, Josh wanted to know, "What happened?"

"The police caught him hot wiring the ignition. Ed Brown convinced me not to press charges. I was dating Ed at the time—"

"You and *Ed*?"

"He got around." Ruthanne smiled reminiscently. "'Course, that was before Jen Bethune nabbed him.

"Anyway, Ed argued that Tommy wouldn't be able to join the wolves with a police record, and that he'd make sure the kid learned his lesson. Ed kept his word. Tommy did our yard work all summer, with my grandmother bitching about every move he made. Oh, and he cleaned up the dog stuff in the village square, too."

"Really..." Josh drew out the word, enjoying the mental image of Tommy forced to shovel shit. "He told people he 'worked for the village'."

"Community service," Ruthanne clarified. She rose from the step. "Archie's here."

Josh craned his neck. He didn't see the van for another minute. Archie got out, waved, and went round to the back. Josh joined him there.

"Something's up with the piasas," Archie complained, using the local word for the birds.

"We're supposed to call them 'thunderbirds' so tourists will know what they are," Josh reminded him.

"They've always been *piasas* in Elvira. They're still called piasas on that sign in Alton. Hell, Marquette the explorer called them piasas. I'm not going to change," Archie declared. "But names aside, they're acting weirder than ever. Damned birds wouldn't leave me alone today. One landed on the Hummer roof and started hacking at the windshield with its beak. Claws tore into the seals," he noted. "I tried speeding up but couldn't shake it. Finally pulled under a ledge to get it off the roof. It came back to attack the Hummer's side."

"Holy shit!"

"Yeah, it was random there for a while, but I'm all right."

"I was thinking about the Hummer." Josh scowled. "How bad is it?"

Archie swiveled his wrist. "It runs. The doors open. Don't know about the windows."

"So, the bird tours are off."

Archie shook his head. "I'll stay across the river, farther away from their caves in the cliffs. Wish I could add Giantville to the tour since it's so close, but the giants don't want tourists there." He climbed into his van, bringing out only one duffle bag. "Let's do investigation lite tonight. Bobbi's taken two days off to pack up stuff at her house. She has to be out by Monday. Told her I'd drop in around midnight to help." Waggling his eyebrows, he added, "Who knows? I might get lucky." Archie shut the van doors, then pulled Josh aside, asking, "Why's Ruthanne here?"

"She wants into the Library. She brought sandwiches—roast beef on homemade bread." Josh and Archie looked at each other, tipped their heads resignedly, and said together, "Let's get started."

Ghost hunting with Ruthanne in tow was worse than Josh expected. First she pawed noisily through the shelf of new books beside the librarian's desk, then, not finding what she wanted, plopped her bag on the floor so soda cans inside clunked on the stone. Next, she dragged two heavy, screeching chairs to the display table, where she sprawled on one and propped her feet on the other.

"You're wasting your time there," Ruthanne called when Josh and Archie were doing a perimeter sweep of the main floor with the electromagnetic field detector and infrared thermometer. Chortling loud enough to hear across the room, she snapped on the table lamp.

Josh went to her, exasperated as much by the nagging feeling she was right as by the interruption. Neither he nor Archie sensed any activity, and their equipment registered normal levels. He forced himself to sound reasonable. "Look, after we go lights out, we don't turn them back on, okay?" Then he reached for the pull cord.

She stopped his hand. "There aren't any ghosts here or on the top floor, either. Only thing I hear in this place is coming from the kids' section below. There's an old biddy reading a story. Sounds like 'The Three Little Pigs'."

Archie plucked an electronic voice phenomenon meter and omni-directional mike from his duffle. "Want to try downstairs?"

"I'll join you in a minute." Shoving Ruthanne's hightops off the chair, Josh sat down. "Ruthie, you're being annoying, especially the giggling."

"I can't help it. You have no idea how silly you look, skulking around an empty room. It's hilarious."

"Glad to be entertaining," Josh groused, "but you're not helping. You should go."

"No way. Jeez, a night away from my grandmother is like a vacation for me. She's always picking at me for this or that, demanding service or attention. I can only write after she goes to sleep."

"Write?"

"Books. I'm Charmain Bliss, author."

"Never heard of you."

"Well, you're a guy. I write hot romances for women."

About to ask where she picked up her ideas, Josh remembered

Ruthanne saying she could see live people when she wanted. Squirming in his seat, he hoped she didn't drop in on him at night.

Ruthanne clapped her hands over her ears. "Damn. Wish they'd shut up." She waved toward the south wall. "It's like a county fair over there in the cemetery."

Josh took his EMF detector to the edge of the room, where he opened a window. "Huh. Needle jumped from 0.2 to a 5.0. Arch and I should do an EVP session outside. Too bad we promised Mr. Seagram a full investigation in here."

"I'll stay. If anything changes, I'll let you know," Ruthanne said. "Just don't promise to help them—the ghosts in the cemetery, I mean. They start making lists of jewelry they hid under floorboards, figurines that should have gone to Cousin Sal, hellos to grandkids...a whole lot of trivial shit, then they get pissed if you don't do everything they want. Boring."

"Seriously, you hear all that stuff?"

Ruthanne waved her hand. "Go out to meet the folks. I'll sit here and leaf through fairy books."

Josh retrieved Archie from the basement. They did a quick tour of the upper rooms, finding nothing but Ruthanne's smirk when they returned. Things were different in the cemetery, where they experienced a sense of heaviness while walking, felt the hair on their necks bristle, and saw, or thought they saw, shadow people. Then, with no warning, their equipment failed, fully charged batteries drained in an instant. The ghost hunt was over.

While they'd been investigating the cemetery, Bobbi left a message on Archie's phone, canceling their date. So, after dropping Ruthanne at her home, Josh and Archie went to their loft to review evidence together. Archie listened glumly for EVPs until he sat bolt upright, announcing, "Now, *this* is interesting." Josh reached for the headphones. He heard a female voice saying, "I'll blow your—"

"Chill," Josh said. "She's reading 'The Three Little Pigs.'"

"Oh." Archie slumped in his chair.

The sun shot straight into his bleary eyes when Josh went to work the next morning. He expected Mike to have a shit fit when he saw the Hummer's dents and scratches, but Mike was in good spirits, humming off key while he worked. "My wife thinks red hair is sexy." He made a face at the side mirror of a Fusion. "Can't figure it out, but I'm not complaining. No, siree, I'm not."

Josh remembered he scheduled a visit to the giants, but the part for their truck was still at the junkyard, so he drove to Deeble's, where an hour and a half passed before the old man found the fuel pump. Though Josh used the time to sound out Deeble on what he wanted from the fairies in trade for some copper ("A pair of those boots that make your legs feel young. Oh, and one of those bags that never runs out of food or drink. They'll do for starters."), he knew he'd be late—very late—for his meeting with the Thoon brothers.

Then Georgia called to say she had the day off, Benji had a playdate with friends, and did Josh want her to bring him some of her special potato salad for his lunch? Of course he did, and he asked her to come with him to Giantville. They'd picnic after he fixed the giants' truck.

Georgia looked good. She wore jeans and a sunny yellow blouse, tied at the waist. She smelled fantastic; a new perfume or something did a number on his senses. All he could think about was finding some private place, outside in the sun or maybe under the dappled shade of leaves, where they could *really* enjoy their time together.

As they neared the river, Georgia scanned for piasas, as every Elviran knew to do during the spring, when the big birds might be spotted cruising the waters like flying dinosaurs. During the summer and fall, piasas hunted across the river, feeding on deer or the giants' livestock. The giants took those losses in stride: The birds needed to eat, they said. Since adult giants were too large to be prey, piasas were less trouble to them than the fearful human settlers who'd chased them out of the Ohio Valley two centuries ago. After coming to Elvira, the giants protected piasas, and piasas preserved the giants' privacy. It worked out.

Josh crossed the bridge to head north along the river road, traveling past deep rifts in the rock left by glacial streams. The streams were long gone by the time the giants arrived to carve their homes into the canyon walls. The old part of Giantville, now used by young families, had a gate and a guard. Overhead, a network of cables protected children playing in the central park from any piasa that might think a juvenile giant looked like lunch.

The burly security guard stood roughly ten feet tall. Above shorts and a tee shirt, he wore a red, New York ball cap. He leaned down to Josh's open window.

"Giants fan?" Josh asked.

He grinned. "Damned straight. Who are you here to see?"

"The Thoon brothers. I'm Josh Seldom, mechanic."

"Okay. You're on the list. Go up the cliff road to New Town. Park in the co-op lot. I'll call ahead to tell them you're coming."

New Town sat on the rise behind the old city, overlooking the giants' farms and businesses. A residential section held sizable ranch homes built with boulder facades and rock-slab fences. The houses looked ordinary, except for their back walls, which were flat and blank, a style holdover from the days when the giants lived inside cliffs, Josh guessed. He pulled into the lot behind the building the giantesses used for their mail-order big & tall clothing business.

Chris and Humph Thoon were posing for pictures beside a black-and-blue truck labeled "Bruiser". The photographer was a blonde girl with a ginormous set of jugs. Two other teenaged boy giants lounged nearby.

"You broke your promise—kept us waiting," Humph rumbled ominously as soon as Josh climbed out of the Hummer. "Kept *Grid* waiting." He gestured toward the girl. "And Grid Finn doesn't *like* to be kept waiting."

To underscore that point, Grid shot Josh a dirty look and tossed her hair. The young bucks snapped to attention, moving to ring Josh.

Georgia flung open her door and stretched. "It's such a lovely day. I insisted Josh bring me along for the ride," and then she tossed *her* hair.

Giants understood henpecking. Their faces took on a knowing expression; their shoulders relaxed. Both Thoon boys turned their attention to the battered Hummer, inspecting it, and making snide remarks.

Josh set to work. Soon enough, he knew he'd made a fatal error: The pump didn't fit. He'd have to return to Elvira and make some calls to get the right one shipped in. The giants' truck couldn't be ready for Saturday's races, so the Thoons and their girlfriend would be disappointed. When giants were disappointed, they found something to crush.

It was time to get the hell out of Dodge.

Casually as he could, Josh pocketed his tools and strolled toward Georgia, telling her tersely that they had to leave, to get in the Hummer and start the engine. She raised an eyebrow, but didn't ask for an explanation. Once again, Josh realized how lucky he was to have Georgia, that rare gem of a woman who knew when to shut up.

Their timing was precise as trapeze artists. As soon as Josh locked the passenger door, he called, "Wrong part. Sorry. Have to order another," and they were off, Josh watching through the window as the angry giants shook their fists. He said to Georgia, "Step on it!"

Gritting her teeth, Georgia gunned the engine, sending the Hummer across the street (and the lawn of the field tiling company) straight toward the tree farm. "I'm making for the lake," she told Josh. "If they follow us, we can lose them on those twisty paths through the woods."

Swiveling to check for pursuit, Josh saw the giants pile into a customized Expedition with a raised roof. Intrigued by the design, he jolted back to the moment when the Hummer hit a pothole on the dirt road and his teeth clacked together.

"Sorry," Georgia muttered, "ruts are pretty deep. Buckle up."

Georgia was a decent wheelman, but Josh itched to take over, to push the Hummer harder than he figured she would. The Hummer wasn't nimble, but it could handle the rough ground better than the Expedition behind them weighed down, as it was, by five giants. Chris Thoon, at the wheel, apparently received unwanted driving instructions from Grid, whose mouth and hands moved a mile a minute. Chris looked like he was ready to bite a nail in half. Josh felt sorry for him until he remembered that *he* was the nail.

By the time Georgia and Josh left the tree farm to negotiate the trails around the lake, the Expedition lagged far behind them. Josh breathed a sigh of relief, but then Georgia reduced speed and the Hummer began swaying left and right, laboring over the terrain. "It's mucky here," she reported. "We're starting to dig in." A minute or two later, they were hopelessly stuck in mud.

Josh got out to push, but that did no good. Extracting the right wheel would take time, even with a shovel and board, which he didn't have. He kicked the tire savagely.

"We'll have to keep going on foot," Georgia said, "to the lake. I have a plan." She took Josh's hand, and they sprinted through an alder grove.

Behind them, the sound of the giants' truck motor stopped. Josh heard frustrated roars. The giants were stuck, too. That situation wouldn't improve their mood.

Near the lake, Josh said, "We're cut off."

"We need a distraction." Georgia added, "And we'll have one." She scrambled down the bank, but waved Josh back from the water's edge. There, she shouted, "Naiads, come forth."

Nothing happened.

"I know you're there," she groused.

Still nothing.

"Oh, *all right!* I'll do it formally. *Hemeti mew, sejem wi,*" Georgia intoned in a solemn voice, throwing up her arms.

Flat, calm water swirled into a whirlpool. A column at least four times Georgia's height rose, forming into a giant liquid woman draped in lilies. Hands on hips, the monster stared down with outraged eyes.

CHAPTER TWELVE

"**W**HO SUMMONS MEMPHIS NILUS?" boomed the colossus.

"Georgia Hanrahan Arsinoe-*sat*," Georgia countered bravely, standing her ground.

A huge smile spread across the water nymph's huge face. She shrank down to human proportions, turning positively chatty. "What a wonderful surprise. We rarely see relatives. I'm Memphis. You're the line of our sister Arsinoe?"

"My great-great grandmother," Georgia revealed.

Josh stared at his girl. *What?*

"Lost to us," the naiad said sadly, bowing her head, and Georgia did likewise. "Such a tragedy that she left our waters for the land—for a man."

"They were happy while they were together," Georgia told Memphis. "At least, that's the story I heard from my family. She died giving birth to my great grandfather."

"Give birth on land." Memphis' eyes narrowed. "Barbaric! Everyone knows the best place is underwater."

"Her baby thrived. His father took good care of him."

"The child didn't go to the temple?"

"Temple?"

"The Temple of Ptah-Sekhmet-Nefertum." Memphis waved across the lake where the top of the tallest pylon gateway could be seen beyond the trees. "All our males go there."

"So that's it!" Josh exclaimed, approaching from the bank to join the conversation. "*That's* how the Egyptians get new recruits."

Memphis snorted. "Hauled us all the way over here from Egypt, didn't they?" She smiled archly. "And not because they liked our singing. Wretched trip. Those *pithoi* jars reeked of olive oil. Well, that was long ago, ancient history now.

"Oh, I am so glad you've come to visit," Memphis said happily, addressing Georgia. "You have no idea how stale the gossip gets when you're cooped up with the same girls, year after year. I'm dying for some juicy, fresh tidbits. Dive in," she invited.

"Actually, Memphis, we're in a bit of a hurry. Josh and I—"

"Say no more." Memphis raised her hands. "What nymph isn't in a hurry? Pleasure must never wait." She waved Josh forward, studying him critically. "Could be larger, but if he's the one you want...." She shrugged. "Need a little help with allure, do you?"

"My sex appeal is *not* the problem," Georgia snapped. "There's a pack of giants on our tail. We need a powerful distraction."

"Well, why didn't you say so? Giants!" Memphis licked her liquid lips. "The men avoid us. They think we'll try to drown them, a scurrilous story invented by their females. Now, I ask you, why would we want to kill big, brawny men?" Grinning, Memphis added, "Let me tell the others." She disappeared into the lake.

"Georgia," said Josh, listening to trees cracking in the distance, "I don't think naiads can stop furious giants."

"Hush, they'll hear you," Georgia cautioned. "Wait. You'll see."

Memphis and six of her sisters, whom she introduced by name and as daughters of Nilus, river god of Egypt, emerged from the water. Their skin and hair were pale pastel. Each had a flower tucked behind one ear. Memphis, now lavender, somehow dropped forty pounds. The changes were easy to spot, since she wore little more than a few carefully placed lily pads.

She addressed the throng. "Ready, girls? We'll do Frolicking and Cavorting Routine Number 10."

"I don't remember that one," Polyxo complained.

"It'll come back to you. Just get into position." The naiads sprawled at water's edge. Turquoise Anippe splashed a bit of water experimentally at sky-blue Chione.

Memphis turned to Georgia. "You might, um, want to move off a bit with your man, there, once we get going."

"Let's go, Josh." Georgia grabbed his hand.

But the naiads began playing water games. They flicked crystal droplets at each other. They giggled or hummed. They were having so much fun, Josh felt happy watching them. The water sparkled deliciously. It would be so pleasant to take a dip, join in.

"Come on," Georgia urged again, tugging at him. "Giants, remember? Big, *angry* giants."

Josh ignored her. He had other things on his mind, like deciding which of the nymphs was the most beautiful. Memphis was okay, but the pink one—Caliande?—was *hot*. What was that shy, green Achiroe hiding? He peered around violet Argiope to find out. But why bother when Argiope was so...so... and the yellow Polyxo, well now, she had really great—

"MEMPHIS, GIVE IT A REST!" Georgia shouted.

Memphis waved one hand and the nymphs stopped what they were doing. They slouched back against the lakeshore looking bored.

"Aw, do we have to start over?" whined Anippe.

"That was just practice," Memphis said.

Josh turned to Georgia. He felt dazed, deflated.

"One more thing," Georgia told Memphis, "our truck is stuck in mud. Can you help us with that?"

The naiad plucked a lily leaf from the cluster across her hip. "Use this. It will stay dry no matter how much water there is."

After thanking her, Georgia promised, "We'll come back to visit another time," and she took off at a run. Josh followed numbly in her wake until they were safely within the alders. There his head cleared. When he looked at the nymphs again, he saw that they were not human-sized but larger, their proportions suited to giants. Still...

"Georgia, stop." He argued, "The nymphs will be hurt, squashed."

Shaking her head, Georgia told him, "Naiads can't be harmed as long as they're in their water."

"You really believe they can turn giants into love-struck imbeciles?"

Georgia smiled indulgently. "Four of the giants are male. When it comes to sex, you're all imbeciles. So, shall we keep standing here discussing naiads? Maybe we should include the giants in our conversation since they're so close."

Josh spun around. No more than fifty yards away, the giants were emerging from the trees, all the guys rushing straight for the naiads' rainbow array.

Grid ran to stand between them and the water, holding out her arms. "Don't go near them!" she bellowed. "They'll drown you."

Memphis rose from the water to tap Grid's shoulder. The giant girl turned to find herself face to face with the equally sizable lavender nymph. Howling, Grid shoved at Memphis, who dissolved, her lotus leaves drifting gently toward the water. Not so Grid, who reached too far forward, lost her balance, and landed in the lake with a massive splash. She surfaced, sputtering, one leaf dangling from the top of her head. Memphis re-formed and joined in the laughter erupting from naiads and giants alike.

"I'll bet that girl's never had serious competition," Georgia said. "It'll be character-building for her, but we shouldn't wait to see how this turns out."

"Just a minute. Looks like Grid's up to something."

The giantess' wet tee shirt recaptured the attention of her fan club, a fact not lost on Grid, whose scowl disappeared, replaced by a coy moue. She batted her eyelashes and reached a languorous hand toward Chris Thoon, who gallantly went to her aid.

Not to be outdone, the naiads redoubled their seductive efforts, voices rising in a song so compelling, Josh found himself taking a step toward the lake.

"Nuh uh," Georgia warned, setting her hands on his shoulders to turn him. "Cover your ears. We need to leave."

At first, Josh struggled to move his feet, fighting against the sensation of slogging through glue. The going got easier the farther from the lake he progressed until he hiked at normal speed. At that point, he uncovered his ears. The singing had stopped. The horsing around sounds he heard coming from the lake suggested a beach party.

Josh thought, *Eight chicks; four dudes. Not bad. Not bad at all.*

Memphis' lotus leaf, small as it was, dried the ground around the Hummer so Josh dug a trough with a broken tree branch and used it as a lever to free the stuck wheel. He left the leaf by the giants' Expedition as a gesture of good will—not that they'd need the help. Calm and unhurried, the giants could easily lift the vehicle, turn it around and go back to Giantville. Georgia and Josh went the other way, toward the Egyptian complex.

The Hummer ably handled the steep climb to the cliff that separated giant territory from the Egyptians. No bridge spanned the inlet supplying the naiads' lake. Josh would have to return to Elvira on the road through Giantville, but he wasn't worried. The Thoon brothers had surely forgotten about him. They were probably having the time of their lives.

So, when Georgia asked him to pause for a moment to take in the view of the temple, he did. "We rarely see it from this side," she noted, "just from across the river. It's awesome to realize how long it is. Now they're letting us inside the complex to visit their spa, do you think they'll offer tours of the temple?"

"Hard to tell. The Egyptians have always played their cards close to the chest. I never would have bet on them getting into the tourist business at all—or guessed they hooked up with naiads. Oh, and that reminds me: How come you never told me you were part naiad?"

"It's a family secret." Georgia looked down at her hands. "Naiads have no sexual hang-ups. That was shocking, back in the day. Also, my ancestors didn't want to let on we weren't entirely human."

Josh rubbed his chin. "You can't do what they do, can you—change color, shape?"

Georgia shook her head. "Nope. I'm only one-sixteenth naiad. What you see is what you get. That enough?"

"You know it is, lady," Josh husked, and he would have added a long, deep kiss plus other physical reassurances if Georgia's phone hadn't buzzed. From her end, the conversation consisted mostly of "uh-huhs" until she said, "Give me about…" she looked at her clock, "twenty minutes." Then she clicked off.

"I'm sorry, Josh. Our picnic's canceled. I have to get Benji. Kitty Broward says he's tired, cranky and ready to go home. He can't really play all day yet. But I'll see you tonight."

"Tonight?"

Georgia made a face. "Don't tell me you spaced off de Salis' club opening. It's so perfect that it's the same day as our anniversary."

Anniversary. Completely lost now, Josh said, "Of course, I didn't forget. It, uh, slipped my mind, what with being chased by giants and all. I'll pick you up at eight."

"I'll be in town at my mother's putting Benji to bed. I'll meet you at the club when he's settled."

After taking Georgia home, going to the garage and getting royally reamed by Mike for screwing up the giants' job, Josh finally figured out what Georgia meant by anniversary: They'd been together six months.

He'd lost touch with her during her marriage, a deliberate move on his part. It didn't seem right to cozy up to another guy's wife, even if the guy was a dick. But last Thanksgiving, when he came in from St. Louis and found himself listening half-heartedly to his mother's recap of Elviran gossip, Josh caught the part about Georgia and Tommy being quits. Josh called her then, and she sounded like the old Georgia, like no time passed since the days when they were close.

They met at Finny's Bar. Georgia told Josh only she and her son were living at the farm. Her parents and sister moved into town to be nearer the clinic when her father's heart started acting up. Josh offered his condolences on the death of her father. Georgia nodded sadly and didn't point out he'd missed the funeral.

Georgia enjoyed working in her mother's real estate business. She talked a lot about that, but not about Tommy. Josh knew better than to ask questions.

The sex they had that night was just for fun, nothing heavy, no strings attached. But the next day, Josh didn't feel like returning to St. Louis. He talked with Mike Mateer about working at his garage. Josh went to St. Louis then, packed up, and came back to Elvira. He told himself at the time he was sick of the city, but that was a lie. The truth was Georgia brought him home.

Josh soon learned Elvira wasn't the same town he left. Two factories providing most of the town's employment had closed. Farm prices were depressed. With money tight, people weren't buying anything they didn't need, so other businesses folded. It had always been hard for young people to find jobs in Elvira, but now there was little opportunity for experienced workers. The town was dying.

The only one with a plan to turn things around was the new mayor. By the end of November, he convinced most Elvirans to back his ideas for attracting tourists by telling the world about the fairies, giants, and piasas. The wolves didn't want publicity but weren't opposed to tourism. The Egyptians hadn't decided whether they'd deal with tourists or not.

Then Stedwell dropped the bomb: *Vampires* proposed opening clubs in town. Two different groups responded to the new Elviran website where Stedwell described the "Little Town of Wonders." Both vampire parties agreed to Stedwell's terms: Any injury to humans in Elvira would bring prosecution and immediate ejection of the offending group.

Elvirans talked of nothing but vampires through New Year. Were the risks too great? Could vampires be satisfied with donated blood? When the question of the club permits arose in January, approval squeaked by on one vote.

Thinking about all this at his loft, Josh cleaned up, and then wondered what a guy should wear to a vampire club. They dressed pretty well. He decided to unearth his sports jacket from the back of the closet. It was brown tweed, too heavy for the weather, but it was all he had.

When, miracle of miracles, he found a clean dress shirt, he went whole hog and added a tie. Slicking back his new red hair, Josh rolled his eyes. Georgia wouldn't recognize him. He barely recognized himself.

Josh stopped by the grocery store to pick up a red rose for Georgia, and then stood gripping it in his sweating hand, regarding The Black Swan. The old building gleamed with fresh white paint, trim in glossy black, and a front door of dark maroon. There was a flat sign with a picture of a black swan, and a wide marquee over the door with the club's name. The place seemed very Olde World.

The dark-haired de Salis woman stood in the doorway welcoming guests. A sizable crowd had gathered. People were sitting on benches outside, holding drinks or standing in groups. Josh belatedly thought about reservations, hoping he and Georgia wouldn't have to wait all night for a table.

Georgia appeared at sunset, staggering him once again with her sexy smile, her red dress, and the scent of her hair, loose around her face, just as he liked it. "You look great," Josh said, handing her the flower.

"So do you, carrot top." Georgia kissed him, and then slipped her hand into his. "Thank you for the rose."

The little vamp came to them, saying, "Good evening. Your table is ready," and waved them through the crowd.

"The place looks lovely, Annina," Georgia remarked as they bypassed the other customers, who glared as they went by.

"Thank you. We are well pleased." Annina crooked a finger at the redhead standing inside the doorway. "Trulia will seat you. Your server will be our cousin, Luca. He and the other cousins are newly arrived. Please forgive them if they fail to observe any of your customs."

"I'm sure that won't be a problem," Georgia assured her.

And it wasn't. After marveling at the rich décor inside the Swan, done in an astonishing combination of colors, from the plum ceiling to the cherry woods of tables, to the rosy peach draperies surrounding each booth, Josh and Georgia thoroughly enjoyed the atmosphere, the service and their steaks. When de Salis came by to greet them, noting that they were his special guests so there would be no charge for anything they ordered, Josh thought the evening could not be more perfect.

But then Ruthanne arrived, shoved into the booth beside Josh, and said, "Hi, Georgia. Josh, I'm glad you're here. Did you get my text? I found something interesting."

"I haven't looked."

"Well, I kept a hard copy." As she fished through her tote, Luca came to ask if she needed anything. To Josh and Georgia's vast surprise, Ruthanne ordered a drink and a calamari appetizer. "The place is so crowded," she explained. "I didn't expect that. Just thought I'd pop over for a minute. Got my grandmother to bed early by telling her the TV broke. You don't mind if I join you?" Not waiting for an answer, she handed Josh a piece of paper:

Come in the stillness,
Come in the night,
Come soon,
And know delight.
Beckoning, beckoning,
Left hand and right.
Come now,
Be mine to-night!

Josh did a double take. Why was Ruthanne coming on to *him*?

Ruthanne laughed. "Don't look at me that way. It's a spell for summoning fairies. I found it in a library book yesterday, but didn't think anything of it until I read the mayor's flyer about the dead fairy. Stedwell said to contact you or Mrs. Withers with any information, so I'm doing that. The book claimed fairies couldn't resist the spell; it has a hypnotizing effect. Anyone who wanted to kill a fairy would have to make him helpless first."

"Yeah," Josh reflected. "I've been thinking about that a lot. I'll ask Mrs. Withers if there's anything to this spell."

"She'll probably say no. She read the book some years ago. S. Withers was the last name on the checkout card."

Ruthanne added with a snort, "And don't flatter yourself. You thought I was hitting on you. No way. You're too young for me. Now, that guy...." Ruthanne pointed toward de Salis, who stood by the bar talking with blonde Ioana. "I need a drool bucket to look at him. Who is he? Is he married?"

"That's Anton de Salis. He's the owner of The Black Swan. Married? No, but he's sort of attached," Georgia said.

"Oh." Ruthanne slumped dejectedly. "He's gay."

Josh chuckled. "Not the problem. If anything, he has too many women. What?" he objected when Georgia elbowed him.

"He'd make a perfect romance novel hero," Ruthanne mused, propping her chin on her hands to gaze at de Salis. "I'll use him for my next book. I'm Charmain Bliss," she told Georgia.

"You're kidding!" Georgia shrieked. "I *love* Charmain Bliss books. I couldn't have made it through my marriage without them."

Josh squinted at her curiously. "Don't ask," Georgia said.

Ruthanne eyed them. "So you two are an item. That's *interesting*."

"Forget about dropping in on us for your research," Josh warned.

Georgia tilted her head. "Don't ask," Josh said.

"Well, I'm going to introduce myself to Mr. de Salis." Ruthanne popped a calamari into her mouth, munching meditatively. "I need an ice breaker. Should I order a Bloody Mary?"

"That'll do it," Josh said dryly. "He'll be impressed by your biting wit."

"Fangs a lot," Ruthanne returned. "Think I'll freshen up my lipstick first." She went off to the ladies' room.

Tucking into his chocolate torte, Josh forgot about Ruthanne. Georgia didn't. She rose from the table when dessert was done saying, "Ruthanne's been gone a long time. I'm going to check on her."

Minutes later, Georgia returned. "Josh, come quickly! Ruthanne's on the bathroom floor, and there are marks on her throat dripping blood."

CHAPTER THIRTEEN

Following Georgia, Josh stopped to buttonhole de Salis. "There's been an incident. This way."

They paused uncertainly before the ladies' room. De Salis knocked.

"Oh, for Heaven's sake," Georgia said with disgust, wrenching open the door. "Come in."

Ruthanne lay on the floor, eyes shut, head resting on her tote. Blood ran down the left side of her neck, staining the collar of her blue jean jacket and plaid blouse. Georgia knelt beside her to hold her limp hand.

De Salis froze when he saw Ruthanne. Then his face relaxed. "My people weren't involved. If they had been, she would look different. Lock the door, please."

"No," Georgia refused, eyes intent on de Salis. "We could be trapped in here."

"You're afraid of *me*?"

"Somebody attacked Ruthanne. We could be next."

"Fair enough, but I assure you I did not injure this woman, nor do I intend to harm either of you. Before we call the medics and police, I'd like to determine what happened—without interruption. This will take but a minute." He looked toward Josh, who turned the door latch, ignoring Georgia's wary frown.

De Salis knelt beside Ruthanne, slipping his hand behind her neck. "I sense even temperature among the cervical vertebrae, so there's no neck injury." Using both hands to feel along the sides of her face and around her skull, De Salis detected a bruise at the back of Ruthanne's head. "Someone struck her from behind."

"You're ignoring the obvious. She's been *bitten*," Georgia snarled.

"Perhaps. Those may be tooth marks." He dipped a finger in Ruthanne's blood.

"Stop that!" Georgia slapped at his hand. "Have you no shame?"

"I am NOT feeding on her," de Salis snapped. He laid his finger against his tongue.

"It's all right. He did that to me," Josh told Georgia.

"He *drank your blood*? When? Why?"

"Long story. Anton, what have you learned?"

De Salis sat back on his heels. "She was not fed upon, but someone wishes to make it appear so." He leaned forward to stroke Ruthanne's forehead, saying with bitterness, "Cowardly to use a woman this way." In a resigned tone, he told Josh, "Call the authorities."

"No...police," Ruthanne muttered, startling everyone. Her eyelids fluttered open. "Don't want Ed Brown here."

"How do you feel?" Georgia asked anxiously.

"Like hell. Monster headache. Somebody hit me." Ruthanne looked from Georgia to Josh to de Salis. Eyes opening wider, she said, "Oh, hi. I'm Ruthanne."

"I know," he said with a gentle smile.

"I want to sit up. Help me."

As de Salis raised her in his arms, some color came back to Ruthanne's cheeks. "You really are the perfect romantic hero. Amazing."

De Salis looked confused. "She may be concussed." He studied her pupils.

"Ruthie," said Josh, "there are puncture wounds on your neck. Do you remember what happened?"

When she felt her neck, her hand came away bloody. "Was I bitten? Am I a *dead*?"

"You are very much alive," Anton said.

"But will I be a vampire when the full moon is out or something?"

"No." He shook his head. "You have seen too many films."

"I read books," Ruthanne refuted. "I'm a reader and a writer."

"At this moment, you are a woman who needs medical attention. We must call for an ambulance."

"Oh no, you don't. I'm not going to the Elvira Clinic. If I need a tetanus shot, those oafs aren't going to do it. I might need a CAT scan, so we're going to Goreton Hospital, and you're going to take me," she informed de Salis.

"If that is your wish," he said, "but I really should not leave the club after this has happened. The Mayans, probably using humans under their control, are trying to force us from this town by making us seem guilty of crimes we did not commit. They may strike again."

"Look, I'm saving your bacon by not making a fuss," Ruthanne argued. "You could cut me a little slack and do what I want."

"Josh and I will take you to the hospital," Georgia offered.

"Don't tell me what to do! I get enough of that from my grandmother," Ruthanne said angrily. "*I'm* the victim, so I call the shots. I want to spend the next fifteen minutes on the road to Goreton, finding out all about vampires from Anton here. What kind of car do you drive?"

"A Mercedes."

"Excellent," Ruthanne purred.

"I don't like it," Georgia grumbled when she and Josh were outside the Swan strolling up Washington toward the village square. "I don't like leaving Ruthanne alone with de Salis one bit."

"Well, they've gone to Goreton, so there's nothing to do about it."

"We should have called the cops. What if de Salis lied when he told us a vampire didn't bite her?"

"He said he doesn't lie," Josh recalled.

Georgia snorted. "*That* could be a lie. And what's with his comment about his people not drinking blood? What kind of self-respecting vampire doesn't drink blood?"

"I don't *know*. I'm no vampire expert. But if I have to trust any of them, I'm picking him. He could have gone for my jugular and didn't."

Josh felt like biting his tongue after he said that, for next, he had to tell Georgia the whole, humiliating story of the fairy visit to his loft. He stalled until they reached the square, where she wouldn't be put off any longer. Sitting on a bench, Georgia listened, then hugged Josh fiercely, whispering, "Thank God nothing really bad happened to you. It's getting downright scary to live in Elvira. I've never felt this way before."

"I'd say that's exactly the feeling the person who attacked Ruthanne wanted to create."

"You believe it was one of us Elvirans?"

Josh reached an arm around Georgia's shoulder, pulling her close. "You saw how easy it is to bring out our fear of vampires. Until tonight, were you nervous about de Salis, even a little?"

"No," Georgia admitted. "I've always liked him. He's courteous... and charming," she added with an abashed smile.

"Easy on the eyes, too, judging by the reactions of the women in the club tonight." Hoping he sounded lighthearted, Josh asked, "You wouldn't, by any chance, have a crush on him?"

Georgia took Josh's face in her hands and planted a smoochy kiss on his mouth. "I'm good for crushes just now." Suddenly, she pulled away. "Oh! I left my rose behind."

"I'll get you another—six, even. One for each of the last few months."

"Make that seven. Think I'll keep you a while longer." Her face was radiant and hopeful.

"Georgia, I've been meaning to say...I uh, uh—" He stopped himself from blurting out the awful L-word that would ruin everything.

"You what?"

"Um, I think we should get going. There are people in the bandstand."

"So?"

"What I have in mind doesn't need spectators. Let's go to your house." He grinned and took Georgia's hand.

Inside the bandstand, Fadri told Megan, "It's not wise for us to meet like this. Your father—"

"Said not to go to Cygnet. He didn't tell me to stay away from the village square."

Fadri laughed. "A fine point. Are all women born lawyers?"

"Not me. I'm going to be a hair stylist like my mother. Always enjoyed the way people came into the shop acting depressed, then left clicking their heels after she'd made them look good."

"You look good, Megan Shaw," Fadri told her. "Very beautiful tonight." He reached toward her face.

Megan flinched. Fadri pulled back, raising both gloved hands for her inspection. "No mistakes."

"And what if I kiss you?" Megan wondered.

Fadri leaned against the bandstand wall. "There are times when I wish my mother didn't choose the vampire way for me. It can be so difficult."

"Your *mother* made you a vampire?" Megan asked, appalled. "Why would she do such a thing?"

"I lay dying. She gave up her life for me."

"You mean you, uh…"

"Drained her blood? No. Blood for us is like alcohol for you. It creates intoxication but does not sustain existence."

"I don't get it. How can you be a vampire and not crave blood?"

"I should begin at the beginning." Fadri paused, looking thoughtful. "My mother did not marry my father, who was a peasant her family could not accept. When I was nearly grown, she married Anton, becoming like him of her own free will. By human law, he is my stepfather, but I resented him for turning my mother and would not call him 'Father'. I settled on *uncle*, and so it has remained, even after I changed. We mark our relationships differently, according to trust—son, brother, nephew, cousin. We are one family.

"But at that time, I was still human. I went to war, was shot, and brought home to die. My mother would not let death have me. She gave me all her energy. I would have stopped her had I been conscious."

"That's so *sad*," Megan breathed.

"It was long ago. The pain is gone; only the memory remains. I fought with my countrymen against Napoleon."

"But that would make you..." Megan struggled with the mental arithmetic.

"Far too old for you," Fadri said.

"Well, don't tell my father. He thinks you're twenty-five, and that's bad enough. Oh, and that's another reason why I wanted to see you. My father and his group are up to something. They've been meeting at the house, going down to the basement and locking the door. I don't know what they're planning, but it can't be good."

"Thank you for the warning."

"Fadri, I'm really attracted to you, and I think you like me, too. I wish we could be like everyone else."

"I will never be like everyone else, Megan."

"But can I ever touch you without your doing, well, whatever it is you do to people?"

"Taking your energy, your life force." Fadri removed a glove. "Yes. I didn't need these tonight; they were for your reassurance. My energy is in balance." Reaching a fingertip toward the back of Megan's hand, he stroked it slowly. "Do you feel any tingling?"

"Not like when we were dancing." Megan studied her hand. "There's another kind of tingling." She looked at Fadri. "I have goose bumps."

"Probably from my cold fingers." Fadri rubbed his hands together. "We were so pleased when hot tubs were invented. Anton's new house, which we will occupy on Monday, has one."

"Really...." Megan smiled at the thoughts that sprang up in her mind.

"And to answer your question, if you kissed me tonight, I would have to return the kiss with many kisses," said Fadri, eyes gleaming. "I would like that. I would like that very much."

At The Feathered Serpent, Vanny sat at her desk, grinning with satisfaction. For the first time, people from Elvira were coming to the club. True, they were mostly men—after the fight, the place gained a reputation as a rough bar—but a few couples and even single women ventured in, one woman, in particular, looking so familiar Vanny felt sure she knew her, yet couldn't remember her name. The visitor smiled with prettily dimpled cheeks when Vanny stamped her hand. She had a confidence about her, a way of walking that invited attention.

"That one," said Vanny's new friend, Paco, who leaned against the desk watching the visitor enter the bar, "will make our men crazy." He held his fingertips to his lips and made a kissing sound.

"As if you cared about women," Vanny scoffed. Paco was gay, his preference setting him apart from many, but not all, of the regulars. He had his group, and Vanny liked them. In the days since she'd started at the Serpent, Vanny stopped worrying about working for vampires. She felt secure, in large part due to Paco and his friends. They treated her like a kid sister and enjoyed teaching her about vampire ways.

Paco had an impish face, light brown hair, and stood no taller than Vanny. He seemed to have a witty comment for every occasion. About the striking female visitor, he said, "She is like us, a peacock. We are always preening, always guarding our beauty. The smallest things— paper cuts, chapped lips, stubbed toes, *mi Dios*—are much trouble to repair. When you're dead, you must protect what is left."

Vanny remembered her trick on Ricky. His face stayed blue-gray for two nights afterward, and he avoided her ever since. "I thought you guys were supposed to heal super fast."

"That is those other *culeros*, the ones from Europe who lift up their noses at blood. Their wounds disappear, but they shake in fear of the sun." Paco struck a prissy pose, then covered his head with his hands, cowering. With a laugh, he went back to his lecturing. "There are some good things about undead life. It is easy to be brave, for death means nothing. The afterlife—this is it. No need to struggle for fame or to make your mark on the world. We make our marks—two of them—in our own, special way." Paco presented frontal and side views of his bright, shiny fangs. "These are impressive, no?

"Ah, but *chica*, I do miss coffee…rich and dark, the aroma making love to my nose. Coffee with Kahlua…Kahlua over ice cream…ice cream with *chocolate*. How fine it would be to taste something cold. Have a tall, cool one for me sometime." Paco shut his eyes in wistful reminiscence.

When he opened them, he winked. "As for cold, when you are in bed with one of us, don't complain about chilly feet. That is embarrassing. There are better things, *much* better things, to notice."

Vanny shook her head. "I don't want a vampire lover. I have my eye on someone else."

Paco nodded knowingly. "*El chulo con el culo bonito.*" When Vanny raised questioning eyes, he translated, "The foxy man with the pretty ass," and he added a throaty growl.

"How did you know?"

"Such a one I could not ignore. He was with you when *las brujas* made the fight but has not returned."

Vanny sighed. "I wish he'd come back. I haven't even seen him in days. I wonder—"

A scream from deep inside the club made Vanny jump to her feet. Paco leapt away from the desk to pull open the doors. "I see nothing but people rushing from tables, coming this way." As the first guests surged by, Paco called out, "*¿Qué pasa?*"

"What's happening?" Vanny shouted.

"Blood all over the women's john," called one fleeing guest.

"A woman's been killed!" cried another.

Vanny grabbed the cashbox from inside her desk. Even in a crisis, she knew Mr. Suarez wouldn't forgive her for losing his money. She tried to fight her way into the bar against the tide of outrushing Elvirans but didn't succeed until Paco bared his fangs to Ron Lesak, who backed away in fear. With Paco running interference, Vanny made it into the bar, skirting the center of the room to move more swiftly along the walls, heading for the hallway with the bathrooms.

A crowd of vampires gathered by the ladies' room. Vanny could sense their agitation, the tension in their muscles, the barely contained excitement in the way they jostled each other to peer inside the open door. For the first time, Vanny realized being human in a vampire club could be an advantage.

"Clear out," she commanded the Mayans. "Whatever's in there isn't Christmas dinner."

A few bristled, but most reacted like Peeping Toms caught in the act. Vanny pressed on. "Stop thinking with your stomachs. Get the hell outta the way. Somebody find Mr. Suarez."

"I am here," he announced.

The crowd parted for Vanny and her boss to get a clear view. There was no woman inside, alive or dead. All Vanny saw was a pool of blood, nearly black, one edge drawn out by a drag mark toward the partly opened awning window. Blood stained the wall and window frame.

Vanny handed the cashbox to Mr. Suarez and stepped into the room, where she checked the stalls but found nothing more. "I don't get it. This blood's not fresh. The window's too small for one person to squeeze through, let alone an attacker and victim. And couldn't you Mayans punch out a window if you wanted to leave that way? It doesn't add up."

Mr. Suarez barked at the vampires in sharp Spanish. They shook their heads. One gave an impassioned speech that resulted in Mr. Suarez scrutinizing each person in the group, head to toe. Afterward, he pursed his lips. He told Vanny, "None of my people can explain this. Jorgé reminded me to search for signs of feeding, but no one has feasted this night. Did any Mayan leave the club?"

"No. I was talking with Paco in the lobby, then there was the scream. Only Elvirans left."

"More of my people are with Ricky in the bar. I must speak with them. Paco, Jorgé—guard this door. *Chica*, guard Paco and Jorgé so they are not tempted to snack." Mr. Suarez turned on his heel. The others followed him, except for the two appointed guards.

Paco made a face at Mr. Suarez' back. "Fernando treats us as the newly awakened," he muttered, "savages, without control." He glanced into the bathroom. "We can see this without…without…." Paco blinked, turning away. "Jorgé and I will sit farther down the hall," he decided. "And we will guard you, *chica*, not the other way around."

The smell of blood was strong even to Vanny's nose. She joined Paco and Jorgé at the end of the hallway. "This is bad, isn't it?"

"*Muy malo.* Your people will tell us to leave this town."

"But why? There isn't any victim. The whole setup is fishy like…like a prank."

"And yet the story will grow and grow until it will be many people dead, men and women, bodies everywhere, all slain by Mayans. That is the way of fear."

Jorgé said angrily, "It is those others, the bloodless ones, the blue-eyed devils, who have done this. Tonight, they open their club. They want the town for their own."

Vanny frowned. "But I didn't let in any vampires I didn't recognize. I have the mirror, you know, to check on who's who."

"Someone working for them," Paco mused, "under their control."

"Well, that sucks," Vanny fumed. "We were here first."

"*We?*" Paco repeated.

"I'm with you guys on this one, dammit! There's no way I'm gonna let them run you out of town over something stupid like this—something you didn't do."

"Then you must talk with the police, who have arrived." Paco tapped his ear. "They will not trust Suarez, but they may believe you. It is good to have you on our side, *hermanita*."

CHAPTER FOURTEEN

On Friday morning, Josh helped Mike hang a "Welcome Visitors" banner above the garage bay door. There were a lot of signs along Main Street aimed at tourists coming to Elvira this weekend. The biggest banner spanned the entrance to the movie house parking lot, announcing "Taste of Elvira." That lot was already filled to capacity by the rides of people setting up booths on the village square.

"You get the Hummer all spiffed up?" Mike asked. "Shaw's coming by to paint the tour name on the sides."

Washing and detailing the Hummer served as Josh's penance for the rough use he put it through yesterday. Mike moaned about the piasa damage to the village's vehicle ("How the hell am I going to explain it to the mayor?") until Josh argued the claw and beak marks added some kick to the idea of adventure tours. Tourists could *see* big birds existed. That had to be worth something.

Across the street, David Shaw, who doubled as the town's printer and sign maker, worked with two giants to install their schedule of events on one of the posts supporting the Taste banner. The sign was bigger than Shaw, so the words were clear, even from a distance. The giants would be holding monster truck races, tractor pulls (with the giants doing the pulling), group tugs of war, and other feats of strength at the high school on Saturday and Sunday. What puzzled Josh was the symbol at the top of the sign, which looked like an egg in a silver cup. He wanted a closer look.

"I'll go ask Shaw when he'll be ready to paint the truck," Josh said.

"He'll get here when he gets here," said Mike. "What you can do is hike over to Village Hall and find out where the mayor wants the Hummer when it's done. I keep getting Stedwell's voice mail."

At the corner of Main and Washington, Josh saw Mrs. Stedwell leading a group of suits with name badges, probably tour company reps. The visitors stopped dead in their tracks, staring open-mouthed at Josh, who wondered if he'd left his fly open until he heard his name called by someone behind him. Turning, he watched Heron peel off from a troop of Reds who were jayflying across the street toward Benton's hardware store.

Heron asked, "Have ye learned what the old man will have fer his copper?" When Josh told him Deeble wanted a fairy bag and boots, Heron laughed. "Is that all? 'Tis easier than nickin' the wire. Where should we be leavin' the gifts?"

"Put them by his shrine to the movie star," Josh suggested, "or on the steps of his shack. Either way, he'll find them."

"Done." Heron fluttered his wings, preparing to move off.

"Wait. Have you learned anything about Sedge's death?"

"Not yet, but we're still asearchin'."

"When will you fix our hair color?"

"When we have our answers and *all* that belonged to Sedge." With hard pulls of his wings, Heron shot off to rejoin the other fairies.

Josh crossed the street and would have greeted Mrs. Stedwell, but she was fielding questions from her group. "Those were real fairies, weren't they?" a man asked. "The real, real deal," a woman said wonderingly, hand over her heart. "They actually *fly*. And me forgetting to take a picture!" Mrs. Stedwell stopped the woman from walking into the path of a truck while trying to photograph the fairies.

Josh hoped all the tourists weren't going to be so silly. Fairies? Meh. No big deal.

He spotted Stedwell on the steps of Village Hall, talking to Mayor Marshal from Goreton and Tink Withers. As he approached them, he heard Marshal ask Stedwell, "You're certain this business at the Mayan vampire club was some form of sabotage by their competitors?"

"The investigating officer concluded there were too many inconsistencies in the evidence to support the theory of a vampire attack. When our clinic's doctor tested the blood, he found only a tiny percentage to be human. The rest came from animal sources, similar to the types stolen from Harry's motel last night. Officer Hanrahan said—"

"Tom's back on duty?" Tink cut in.

"Light duty for now, but Goreton Hospital gave him a clean bill of health." Stedwell noticed Josh then and said, "Morning. What can I do for you?"

Josh reported on the Hummer's repairs. Stedwell told him to park behind Village Hall between the police station and the clinic. As Josh turned to leave, giants passed by with another sign.

Mayor Marshal asked the same question Josh pondered at the garage. "Can you tell me, Mo, what *is* that symbol on the giants' sign? Looks like an egg in a cup."

"It's a piasa egg, Laura. That's the grand prize for this season's champion. Whichever giant has the most points in their events wins it."

"Magnificent prize," said Marshal. "If it's viable, an egg would be worth a fortune to zoos and scientific institutes, I should think. Even if it isn't, it's an amazing collector's item."

"No giant would sell a piasa egg," Tink told her boss. "Back in high school, I wrote a paper on piasas. I interviewed giants, and did a lot of research on the subject. When the giants first came here, every adolescent boy had to steal an egg as a test of manhood. Since twelve- or thirteen-year-old giants aren't much bigger than human men, not all of them succeeded. There were deaths, so the giants abandoned the ritual, but the eggs still hold great significance for them."

"Taking the eggs couldn't have been good for the endangered thunderbirds either," Marshal noted.

"The practice wasn't as bad as it might seem. Piasas lay two or three eggs in a clutch. The first hatchling destroys the other eggs, so the number of piasas didn't decline due to the giants' egg napping. Those eggs wouldn't have produced more birds."

Josh felt impressed by Tink's knowledge, and he said so. She accepted his praise warily, as though he might be putting her on. Finally deciding he wasn't, she defrosted and nudged him, confiding, "Guess who's back in town? Cissy Rettger! I talked to her at her booth when Mayor Marshal and I were touring the square. She's the chef at The Black Swan. You should go say hello, catch up."

"Maybe I'll do that," Josh said, looking over the sea of booths. On the way back to work, he remembered that the last time he'd seen Cissy, she'd been wrapped around Archie. Did that matter anymore? And how weird was it for her to come back from Chicago to work for de Salis? *Small world.*

Georgia fed Josh dinner on Friday night, serving him fried chicken, spring leaf lettuce, and more of her terrific potato salad. Benji wasn't there.

"God, I love my kid." Georgia sighed. "I hate-hate-*hate* turning him over to Tom, especially when Tom tells me he has to work most of the weekend and won't have time for Benji." Georgia pounded her fist on the table in frustration.

"If Tom doesn't have time for him, why take Benji?"

"To please his mother. Joellen *insists* Tom assert his 'father's rights' every chance he gets." Georgia scowled, but added, "Benji doesn't mind being with her. I just miss him so much when I know he'll be gone all weekend." She leaned on her hands.

"You need some cheering up," Josh decided. "Extra hot fudge on a Dairy Queen sundae?"

There was a line at the DQ. Apparently, tourists had already arrived. Josh turned down Main Street, where more tourists were strolling the sidewalk. He suggested dessert or drinks at The Black Swan, but Georgia wrinkled her nose, looking down at her mini sweater, tank top and short skirt. "We're not dressed well enough, and besides...."

"Cissy Rettger's there. Look," said Josh, "I've been meaning to talk to you about her, about senior year."

"Oh, I was *so* mad at her," Georgia recalled. "She was playing you to get to Archie, and you couldn't see it."

"I thought you were mad at *me*. I ignored you, left you kind of in the lurch."

Now it was Georgia's turn to be surprised. "I didn't sit around pining, that's for sure. I had dates."

"With who?"

"Ernie Brown. He was sweet. I'm so sorry he died in that crash. Zachy Seagram—"

"*Zachy?*" Josh wheezed. "All he wanted from girls was—"

"The same thing all you guys wanted," Georgia finished with a wry smile.

"Want to try the Mayan place?" Josh asked. "They have live music tonight—well, if you can say a vampire band is 'live'."

Georgia shook her head. "I say we drive up to Goreton for some ice cream. Should be quiet there without the tourists."

On the road north, Josh noticed again the perfume that Georgia wore, the same as when they went to Giantville. It made him feel incredibly horny. He asked her about it.

"I'm not wearing perfume. But, oh! It's so hot." She unclipped the seatbelt and pulled off her sweater, then fanned her face with a hand. "I'm burning up, and I feel—"

Georgia swiveled abruptly to face Josh, who stole a look at her. Her eyes were wide, enormous, stricken. "Omygod—Rusalka Fever. It always hits this time of year." She held her stomach. "Pull over."

He did, expecting her to reach for the door handle and be sick. Instead, she made a low, growling sound, threw her arms around him, and kissed him with bruising passion, her body rubbing against his chest in a way that sent a jolt from his groin to the roots of his hair, then back down to his toes. Her fingers slid beneath his shirt, sparking more tidal reactions, then her hand moved south, and he nearly jumped. "What?" he choked out. "What's going on?"

"I need you," Georgia husked, tugging at his belt. "Can't wait…it's a naiad thing….must—"

"Whoa, whoa," Josh tried to say to remind her they were on the main road to Goreton where anyone might come along, but all he managed was a "woof" and a groan when her mouth convinced him neither of them were going to last for the long trip home.

But where?

"Hold on," he urged Georgia or himself; he didn't know which. Georgia took him literally. His foot stomped the gas pedal and tires spit gravel, the truck flying down the road toward the firebreak. Much as Josh hated the place, it was any port in a storm.

The tempest that was Georgia stretched luxuriantly, sated and becalmed. "I feel so *good*." She looked at Josh with lazy smile.

Josh turned his head toward the window, studying the condensation there. "I dunno. It's every guy's fantasy to have a hot woman jump his bones, but now that it's happened…"

"What?" Georgia asked, suddenly alert. "What?" she said anxiously, turning his face with a fingertip.

"It's…grrreat!" Josh howled, pounding his chest Tarzan-style, then grabbing her up in a bear hug. "You're great. Don't ever change."

Head tucked in against his neck, Georgia said, "I couldn't if I wanted to. Rusalka comes with the naiad genes." She pulled away, recalling, "I had no freaking idea what was happening to me when I turned eighteen and the Rusalka thing kicked in for the first time. There were no women in my father's line from his generation. No one remembered Rusalka Fever except a great aunt, who said when she saw Benji, 'Oh, a Rusalka baby. My first was one, too.'"

Josh was staggered by realization. "That's why you hooked up with Tom."

"Why else?" Georgia grumbled. "I didn't even like him, thought he was a jerk. But the two of us were on a collision course. Wolves always get a huge shot of testosterone around the full moon." Georgia shrugged. "Every woman with naiad blood—Oh, shit. Vanny! She's the right age now. She's been told about this, but the first time she'll be so dazed, she won't know what's happening. She could end up with someone like Tom. We have to get back to Elvira to stop her."

"Mr. Snopes—Eliot—I need you. *Right away."*

"Who is this?" his velvety voice asked.

"Vanny, I mean Savannah Beckett. I'm stranded outside the Serpent, Eliot. My car won't run, and I feel odd, light headed. I need a ride home."

"Miss Beckett, surely there's someone else available."

"I've tried everyone else."

He went silent, then said in a resigned tone, "Okay. It'll take me a few minutes. I have to get dressed."

"You've gone to bed already?" Vanny imagined Eliot, rising from the sheets, backlit by moonlight, smoothing his dark, rumpled hair. She shivered.

"Just relaxing. I'll be there soon as I can. Hold on."

He clicked off and Vanny made a low, growling sound deep in her throat. She went to the car, which she'd parked in front of her mother's real estate office. Getting inside, she pulled the hood release, then went out to unplug a fuse. Eliot knew diddlysquat about cars. He was so cute.

Vanny stood tapping a foot. *What was taking so long?*

The Kona blue Mustang passed her by, stopping half a block away. Vanny sprinted toward the driver's door. When Eliot got out, she threw her arms around him. "Thank you for rescuing me," she gushed. He looked so good—*smelled* so good—she didn't let go even when he protested, "Really, it's nothing," and tried to pry her arms loose from his neck.

A man around Eliot's age emerged from the passenger side. He leaned an elbow on the car's roof. "El?" he inquired.

"This is Miss Beckett, Jon. She's...." Eliot stared at Vanny's upturned, worshipful face. "She's, uh, not feeling well."

"I'm hot," Vanny explained.

"You look flushed." Finally succeeding in freeing himself from her embrace, Eliot placed both hands on Vanny's shoulders, turning her toward her car. "You're sure it won't run?"

"Dead as a doornail. Who's your friend?"

"Jonathan, my guest."

"He's staying with you at your *house*? For how long?"

"All weekend," Jonathan answered, "and part of next week."

"Couldn't you leave?"

Jonathan asked Eliot, "Is there something going on here I don't know about?"

"No, Jon. Miss Beckett—"

"Savannah!" she huffed. "You can use my first name. After all, we've kissed."

"*Savannah*," Eliot said frostily, "get into the car. I'm driving you home."

Jonathan said, "Let her talk. I'm interested in this kiss. Tell me more."

"Well, we were at the club, and—"

"Enough!" Eliot snapped. He pulled open the door. "Get in."

"No." Vanny shrugged loose from his hold. "You're not being nice. This isn't right at all. I'm going back to the club."

"Not when you're acting so strangely. Not with all those vampires there."

"Vampires? Is that one of them?" Jonathan pointed down Main Street. "'Cause if it is, he doesn't look friendly."

"Wow," said Vanny, watching the dark figure rushing toward them. He wasn't running. He was leaping or bounding—doing something that covered a lot of ground fast.

Eliot shouted, "Jon, get in the car. Miss Beckett—"

"*Savannah*."

Eliot gripped her arms, shoving her into the back seat. Vanny howled, "I don't want to leave. Let me go!"

Behind the wheel, Eliot clicked the automatic door locks and jammed the shift into drive. His Mustang leapt forward, but not fast enough. The vampire caught the edge of the deck spoiler, swung upward and landed on the trunk with a heavy thump.

Eliot swerved, his attention on the mirror. Jonathan shrieked.

Vanny stayed silent, captivated by the stunning male face peering through the window. She laid her hand against the glass longing to touch the vision beyond it.

The vampire held up a warning hand, then waved her back from the window. She shrank against Eliot's headrest, barely noticing the frantic chatter from the front seat. As Vanny watched, the vampire drove his fist through the sunroof. Little cubes of glass rained down, bouncing like summer hail when they hit the back seat.

Eliot jerked his head around, then pulled a hard right turn by the Baptist church. The vampire slid along the spoiler clutching the radio antenna to keep from falling off. At the next corner when Eliot turned again, the vampire curled his lip, raised his right knee and brought his heel down hard. The Mustang's trunk lid crumpled.

Jonathan cried, "He's going to kill us!"

"He's ruining my car!" Eliot wailed. "We have to get to the police station." Laying on the horn, Eliot squeezed his Mustang into the gap between police station and clinic, the car moving too fast to avoid clipping the rear corner of a Hummer parked there. The Mustang's airbags exploded.

Jumping off before impact, the vampire took the spoiler with him. He discarded it, then ripped open the door on Vanny's side and let it fall to the ground. "You're safe," he said, extending a hand. "Those men will not hurt you."

She stepped out, throwing her arms around his neck. "You're so wonderful," she purred.

"What the hell's going on out here?" Chief Brown demanded as he strode through the police station's back door. He stared at Vanny and the vampire, at Eliot and Jonathan fighting their airbags, at the Hummer, and then blinked into the headlights of Josh's truck.

Georgia and Josh reached Elvira in time to see Vanny get into a Mustang. They followed the car to the station, watching the whole, horrifying vampire incident on the way. Georgia threw open her door to rush to her sister's side. "Vanny! Are you all right?"

Vanny kept her eyes on the blond beside her. "I've just met, uh…"

"She's my sister," Georgia told the vampire. "I'm taking her home now. Ed, Vanny isn't well. If you have to talk with her, phone her. Josh, give me your keys."

"I can drive," he said.

Georgia shook her head. "Not this time."

Josh forked over the keys while Georgia hustled Vanny into his truck. He watched them drive off. Only then did he notice the Hummer. "Sonuvabitch," he moaned, going over to inspect the new mutilation.

Ed peered into the car. Josh recognized the science teacher at the wheel. His passenger clung to him, looking terrified. "Want to get out and tell me what happened?" Ed asked. Both men shook their heads.

"I was giving Miss Beckett a ride home," Snopes said through the window. "That…that newcomer attacked us. All I could think to do was come here." He added with downcast eyes, "Sorry about the Hummer."

Ed exhaled heavily. He turned to the vampire. "Anything to say?"

"Those men were abducting that girl. I stopped them."

"And you are…?"

"Fadri de Salis."

"Same last name as the guy who owns the club," Ed noted. He took Fadri de Salis aside, speaking confidentially, holding onto his elbow, then letting go abruptly, as though he'd thought better about touching him. "Look, I believe you when you say you were trying to help Vanny Beckett—"

"Actually, I thought she was Megan Shaw. They look very much alike."

"You know Megan?" Ed asked with an edge to his voice.

"We're…we've met."

Ed sniffed. "Megan and Vanny, they're both nice girls, right? And young. How old are you anyway—twenty-four…-five?"

"Older than twenty-one. Old enough, by the standards of your society, to make my own social decisions."

"All I'm sayin' is that if you're looking for fast action, you got the wrong idea about the girls."

Fadri bristled. "And what of those men? What were they doing forcing a nice girl to go with them against her will?"

"Way I see it, they weren't intending Vanny no harm. Those guys are fairies, for chrissake."

Fadri glanced over Ed's shoulder toward the pair in the car, who cringed. "Indeed? I had no idea fairies grew so large."

Ed said evenly, "There's a lot to learn about Elvira. You're a newcomer, so I'm not gonna nail your ass for this ruckus long as you pay for both vehicle repairs." He pointed at the vampire's gold Rolex watch. "I'm guessin' you're good for the money."

"And if I don't agree?"

Ed shrugged. "Seeing as you pretty much trashed that Mustang, I couldn't hold you by force, but the paperwork would be bad, real bad. When you get lawyers and judges involved, well, it costs a pretty penny. And jail wouldn't suit you, I don't expect, so offer to settle up with Snopes there—oh, and add an apology. That'd be neighborly."

Georgia was back. She pulled in beside Josh and left his truck. He told her what he'd heard, and then asked, "Will Vanny be all right?"

"Mom will take care of her, sit on her, if necessary. Poor Vanny… It's so hard when you're alone. Rusalka Fever lasts at least a day, sometimes more."

Georgia tucked her arm through his, running her tongue along her lower lip. "Don't plan on going anywhere for a while. I intend to keep you fully occupied, all night, tomorrow, and maybe Sunday."

"Yeah?" Josh said happily.

CHAPTER FIFTEEN

Megan and Lisa Shaw were driving toward the salon at 9 a.m. on Saturday, only to run into Elvira's first-ever traffic jam. Lisa made a detour to approach Elvira from the east. Crossing the train tracks and then turning onto Second, she headed for the alley behind the shop when Megan cried, "Mom, look!"

The white surface of the wall above the Cygnet sign showed wet, red paint. Lurid letters proclaimed: *Sin with Demons and Roast in Hell!!!*

Lisa braked to a stop and took a long breath before she said, "There was bound to be a backlash against the newcomers. You know how some people in town feel."

"B...but," Megan sputtered, "that's vandalism. It's ugly, and it's mean."

"Let's hope they get that painted over before too many tourists see it." Lisa set the car in motion again, only to stop when she turned the corner onto Washington. "Oh now, that...that's going too far."

The front of The Black Swan was splashed with red paint, the lower windows entirely covered by it. Before the door lay a ginger tomcat in a pool of blood. His throat had been torn away.

"Omygod," Megan breathed in horror. "That poor, poor cat! I'll bet Dad and his group did this."

"Megan, don't say that!" Lisa snapped. "Your father has been working on *legal* ways to make the vampires leave—zoning, public health and safety issues—that sort of thing. He and his friends aren't animal killers."

"Tell them they're wrong," Megan demanded. "Tell them everyone needs to get along. *Stop* them."

"I can't." Lisa thumped a frustrated hand against the steering wheel. "I don't agree with them, but they have strong feelings on the subject. They have a right to their opinions as long as they obey the law."

"Someone broke the law when he killed that cat."

"I know." Lisa shook her head. "We'll talk with the police, make sure they're aware of this."

"Something else is going on." Megan pointed across Main Street where a yellow police tape by the Wolves Lodge blocked access to the village square.

Lisa parked behind the salon and then went with Megan to the roadblock. Officer Hanrahan said irritably to a crowd of tourists, "Move along. Go one block north to Jefferson. View's better from there."

"What's up?" Megan asked when the street cleared.

"Green fairy protest," Tom told her. "They want the Wolf Creek compound shut down, so they've made a jungle of the square. Everything's covered in vines."

"My braiding booth!" Megan gasped. "It's closed?"

"They're all closed."

"Why are the fairies acting up now?" Lisa asked.

"A Green warrior died near the compound. The Green leaders will meet with the mayor and the wolves after Stedwell's done with the Egyptians. Until then, no one's getting in unless he's here to clear brush."

"Where's George Bush when we need him?" Lisa quipped.

"I'll cut brush," Megan volunteered.

"You ready to deal with rats? There were a lot of rats in town a couple days ago."

"We know," Lisa inserted. "They're back?"

Tom nodded. "Took to the jungle like ducks to water. Stedwell thinks the Egyptians might know something about the rats, so he's talking with a few of their priests." Tom checked his watch, then glanced toward Village Hall, noting, "One of the weekend rent-a-cops is supposed to relieve me so I can make the fairy meeting." He advised Megan, "Wait a while before volunteering for brush detail. Let's see what happens with the rats."

Lisa told Tom about the vandalism, then left to go to her salon. Megan wondered what to do next. She decided to wake Fadri, alert him to the mess at Cygnet and Swan, but by the time she returned to the Swan, a crew of Elvirans was already scraping the windows and hosing the walkway. Megan tried not to look at the garbage bag set in the alley. Around the corner, painters were blotting out the angry red lettering. Their ladders blocked Cygnet's door.

Megan hurried by, not wanting anyone to see her enter the club and report the visit to her father. Any of the people working outside could be on his side. Any of them could have painted the sign, then come back to earn money for cleaning it up.

Shocked by that thought, Megan barely noticed where her feet were taking her until she stood gaping at the thicket visible under the Taste of Elvira banner. Tourists jostled her on the sidewalk. She crossed the street and rounded the corner of Jefferson to get a better look at Elvira's new jungle.

It was hard to see past the crowd already assembled there. By hopping up and down, Megan made out a fencelike wall that reminded her of the thorn forest in the *Sleeping Beauty* movie. Frustrated by taller people blocking her view, Megan moved across the street onto the sloping lawn of the funeral home. From higher up, she could see vines swallowing Giants' Park, the booths, the bandstand—everything in the village square.

"Awesome, isn't it?" a man's voice said.

Megan found Nefer's father, the funeral director, standing beside her. "Oh hi, Mr. Wati," she said. "Yeah, it's random. Doesn't look like they've done much yet to clear up the jungle."

"When people try to cut it back, the fairies grow more vines. See there?" Mr. Wati pointed to a pair of Greens flying recon over Giants' Park. Megan spotted others at different points above the square.

"I'll bet the rats have been a problem, too. Officer Hanrahan said they'd overrun the place, and the smell is pretty bad."

Mr. Wati stroked his chin. "I was taught at the temple that rats were servants of great god Ptah. Ptah once saved a town from invaders with an army of rats. He sent the rats into the enemy's camp, where they chewed up the leather parts of weapons. In the morning, the enemies found no bowstrings or handles for their shields."

"That's a cool story," Megan said, "but I don't think these rats are so helpful. They ruined the graduation party and then swarmed Main Street on Wednesday."

"We can't know what Ptah intends." Mr. Wati smiled, looking closely at Megan. "Forgive me, but your hair ornament is the symbol of lion-headed goddess Sekhmet."

"I bought it at the temple," Megan said, fingering her barrette. "They've opened a spa and gift shop, did you know?"

Mr. Wati shook his head. "I have no contact with the temple any longer except for one young man, who is a relative."

"That's sort of sad," Megan said without thinking.

"Not for me. My wife and daughter are my great joys. Perhaps my relative will join us one day. But look," Mr. Wati interrupted himself, pointing. "The *hem-netjer* are performing a ritual. In the middle is the w*r khrp hmw*—the high priest, Great Leader of Craftsmen."

Megan watched three men raise their hands. One began shouting foreign words, his voice loud enough to carry across the distance. "What's he saying?"

Mr. Wati listened before telling Megan, "It is an invocation of Sekhmet, a prayer for deliverance."

A black cat climbed the steps of Village Hall. It curled around the speaker's legs, then sat at his feet. Soon, cats of every color and description were moving in, lining up next to each other, waiting patiently while more filed onto the stairs. The Egyptian priests stood motionless.

Megan thought she could have heard a pin drop if she hadn't been standing outside on grass. The crowd in the street went dead quiet, all chatter cut off. Fairies landed on high points of vine. Even the traffic noise from Main Street sounded muffled, far away. Megan's ears strained against the sudden silence, picking up subtler sounds, the scrabbling of claws, squeaks and chittering—sounds she knew too well.

As one, the cats on the steps leaned forward. A second later, they all looked toward the priest, who bowed. Then, like a wave of fur fury, they poured into the jungle.

Rats came flying out the opposite end of the square, terrifying spectators, who screamed and fled to the safety of the funeral parlor's lawn as the rodents raced down Jefferson toward Main. There was a squeal of brakes on Main when the first of them reached that point, mere seconds ahead of the cats. Stragglers weren't so lucky. Snatched up into sharp-toothed jaws or skewered by claws, the rats' frantic cries cut off when they were dragged under vines by relentless cats.

The battle sounds were eerie, horrifying but fascinating. As the rats' squeals died away, Mr. Wati said, "All praise to wondrous Sekhmet. Hers is the way of the cat, the lust for chase, hot blood in her mouth."

"Sekhmet is a *vampire*?" Megan asked, both eyebrows shooting up.

"Some have thought so, but to me she will always be the huntress for whom victory is paramount."

"Huh," Megan said, not sure what *paramount* meant. "Say, I saw a dead cat by the vampire club this morning. Somebody killed it."

"To kill a cat is sacrilege. The goddess will take vengeance on anyone destroying a life sacred to her."

"All right!" Megan punched air, imagining the cat murderer under an enormous lion's paw.

"There is a new development in the square." Mr. Wati pointed.

A dozen giants, male and female, standing in two rows on the street before Village Hall, lifted chainsaws, which looked absurdly small in their big hands. The saws roared into action as the giants pulled their cords and began cutting swathes through the vines, the first row taking the left side of the square, the second, handling the right. Watching them from the lawn, tourists cheered and clapped. Megan and Mr. Wati joined in.

Some of the fairies who'd taken to the air during the cat-rat battle dove at the brush-clearing giants, flying patterns around their heads to distract them. Others regrew vines or pointed at giants, obviously trying to root them. The rooting failed; one giant roared, "We're wearing *nylon*, you little bastards." The giant's grin spread wide as the fist he shook at the nearest fairy.

Despite the giants' efforts, fairy magic worked faster than chainsaws. Sweat broke out on the giants' faces, their chests and underarms. Looking furious now, they used chainsaws as weapons, feinting at the fairies, occasionally whipping vine sections at them. One giantess abandoned her saw, found a thick piece of vine, and held it like a baseball bat, defending the ground she'd cleared. She nearly scored a hit on the fairy taunting her.

Megan heard a Dixie horn. The Ryan brothers' truck squealed to a stop in front of the library. Guys piled out of the open truck bed; others erupted from the cab. It looked like all eight brothers were there. Shirtless and barefoot, wearing only running shorts, they began unloading water bottles, tossing them to one another in a chain reaching across the street. On the edge of the square, Shane made a stack of the bottles, then motioned his brothers back to the truck, where they all pulled out water guns.

Their guns weren't the stupid, cheap pistols Megan and Vanny played with when they were little. These were *huge*. Shane's stretched longer than his arm. The back end of Dylan's two-liter water bottle rested on his shoulder. Rory's resembled a cannon.

Of course. Megan started to snicker. Fairies couldn't fly with drenched wings. Soaked, they'd be forced to land. As pedestrians, fairies would be in a world of hurt where giants stomped.

The Ryans slipped into the square through a gap one giant managed to keep open. Seeing reinforcements arrive, the giants who gave up on chainsaws punched air. Those with saws running revved them. Shane yelled, "Attack!" and rushed at the fairies, who beat their wings double time to escape. His twenty-foot stream caught the last one in the ass.

After that, full-out war began, each Ryan boy picking a different target. When they ran out of water, they went back to the cache by the street.

Police near Village Hall looked confused, uncertain whether to stop the water fight or to let it go on. The men weren't Elvirans. Megan figured they were those rent-a-cops Tom Hanrahan mentioned. When one of them ventured toward the square, a giant planted his feet and crossed his arms, shaking his head. Faced with a guy twice his size, the cop backed off.

Shane hit a fairy dead on with a blast from his gun. The fairy went down, spiraling like a falling leaf onto the bandstand's roof. Spouting water from his mouth, he gripped the weathervane, looking dazed. A second fell into the vines still covering a booth. By the time a third waterlogged fairy sank into thicket, Ryans held the advantage.

Tom Hanrahan emerged from Village Hall, followed by two elderly Greens. Mayor Stedwell brought up the rear. Tom cupped his hands around his lips and bellowed, "Fairies declare a truce. Fight's done."

"Aw, Tom," said the giant who'd barred the cop from interfering, "we're just getting started."

"It's over, Argus. The fairies are clearing out."

With that, Greens hovering by the steps clapped their hands, and their airworthy comrades flocked to them. One of the Greens flew to Tom and whispered something into his ear. With another bellow, Tom told giants and Ryans, "Let the elders find the ones in the vines. They're not going to make trouble."

After the fairies collected their fallen, supporting the ones with sodden wings between them, they flew off. The brothers congratulated each other with high fives. Then a giant decided he could use a blast of cold water, so he stood cheerfully under the stream from Shane's gun. Other giants like that idea so much, they wanted to be sprayed down, too.

A woman near Megan asked her companion, "Think there's more?"

"Nah," the man answered. "Show's over, but it was pretty good, I gotta admit. And here I thought they were only doing boring tours in this town. Can't wait to see what they pull off tomorrow. Let's get something to eat."

Megan said goodbye to Mr. Wati, then went to the square to volunteer for clean-up duty. She spent an hour collecting vine sections and heaving them onto piles before she sat down for a breather, resting behind her liberated braiding booth. Maybe later she'd actually get to use it.

The noon sun felt hot. Megan dozed for a minute. She woke with a start when she heard voices on the other side of the booth.

"I know you were hoping to join us wolves, Shane, know that you've told people you are a wolf. It's not that simple. Your family—"

"Isn't good enough," Shane shot back. He said bitterly, "Ryans don't have the threads, the wheels, the coin. You think we're dirtbags."

"I was going to say you haven't been in Elvira long enough to understand the wolves. If your family isn't behind you...." Tom Hanrahan's voice paused. "There can be trouble."

"My brothers and I would do *anything* to join."

"Even lose the attitude, straighten up and fly right? Because that's what it takes. You can't be a wolf with a chip on your shoulder, looking for trouble or causing it. Today, you helped out, but other times, you came too close to the wrong side of the law."

"So?" said Shane. "I've never been caught at anything."

"*Yet*. Nobody gets away with dealing or stealing forever. Believe me, I know. Thought I was The Man back in high school, could do whatever I wanted. Then I got caught and had my nose rubbed in it, big time."

"Yeah?" Shane challenged. "What'd you do, bust into the candy machine in the school cafeteria?"

"Let's just say I tried grand theft auto before the game came out."

"I'm impressed."

"Don't be. I'd have been somebody's bitch in juvie if Ed Brown hadn't kicked my sorry ass around the block, made me see I had it all wrong. I didn't have a dad to get me squared up; he cleared out when I was a kid."

"My dad's nothing to shout about. He's a lousy truck driver," Shane sneered.

"He stuck around to take care of his family. That's what a real man does."

There was silence for a moment before Shane said, "None of the wolf stuff matters for me anymore. I graduated. I'm too old."

"You're not. There's a lower age limit—eighteen—but no upper one."

"I didn't know that," Shane said slowly. "Wow. Could make a difference."

"See that it does. You have potential. Don't screw up."

Megan rose from her crouch when the voices drifted off. So Shane wasn't a wolf? She rubbed her chin, wondering what that meant.

CHAPTER SIXTEEN

Megan lolled in the hot tub with Fadri, trailing kisses down his wetly glistening throat, feeling his hands squeeze her bare backside with increasing urgency beneath the bubbling water. He—

"I want my hair braided!" a shrill girl's voice cut into the daydream.

Megan blinked at the ten- or eleven-year-old who'd plopped down on the braiding stool. "*Now*," the kid told her mother.

The mother sighed, then asked, "How much?"

Naming her price, Megan added the clincher, "*And* you get a free souvenir from Elvira." She held up a cellophane wrapped, pink plastic comb, one of the many gimmicks her father sold to businesses in town over the last month. This comb had the Elvira village flag printed on it, along with the salon's name and phone number. It cost nothing, a freebie from Dad's suppliers, but every tourist so far liked it.

"All right," the mother agreed, digging in her purse for the cash. She cautioned her daughter, "Stay here, Olivia. Don't wander anywhere. I'm going over to the booth there to get the ice cream you want." To Megan, she said, "You'll look after her?"

"She'll be fine with me."

Olivia selected a style from the pictures Megan showed her. "So," Megan asked to make conversation, "do you like Elvira?"

The girl shrugged, forcing Megan to retrace a part. "I'm supposed to freak like a little kid when I see a fairy. At least, we didn't have to take the stupid bird tour. Mom said crash dummies shouldn't ride in that old, beat Hummer."

"What do you think of the giants?"

"Haven't seen those, but they're probably people on stilts, or robots, like those things at Disney World. What I want to see are the vampires."

Me, too. Megan looked at the sun, which was low in the sky. *Not long now*, she consoled herself.

"My dad's rich," Olivia went on. "He'd buy me a vampire if I wanted one. Dad says everyone has a price."

"I don't," Megan said, affronted.

"Sure you do. You're braiding my hair—and for cheap. We paid twice as much at the Renaissance Faire last summer."

Megan's fingers flew through the braiding. She returned Olivia to her mother with an unintended shove, watching the woman's face fall when the ice cream bar in her hand was loudly rejected. "I wanted cookie dough!" howled Olivia. "You eat this, and get me another."

After Olivia, Megan decided to shut up shop. The smell of food tantalized her all afternoon, but some of the booths were already closing. It was time for a personal Taste of Elvira.

Megan saw a crowd gathered near Jefferson. A news van was parked on the street. She hurried over to squeeze into a spot between spectators by the Swan's booth, where a reporter talked to a woman in a white chef's jacket. The reporter said, "Everyone wants to know: Is there anything *unusual* about food at a vampire restaurant?"

The chef leaned toward the reporter in a confidential way. "Oh, yes. We're *very* different." Then she smiled until dimples dented her cheeks. "We use only the freshest produce and seafood, locally sourced meats and dairy. We serve the best quality food in town."

Though Megan expected the reporter to look surprised or maybe even angry after being punked, he flashed a return smile and kept right on his line of questioning. "Surely, there's something exotic on the menu."

"Like duck blood soup or black sausage?" the chef inquired sweetly. "We're not offering those tonight, but if we get special requests from guests, we'll consider enlarging our menu."

The reporter turned to face the cameraman. "And so, there you have it, direct from Cecily Rettger, head chef of The Black Swan, Elvira's fine-dining vampire restaurant. This is Tim Bailey, bringing you all the news from 'The Little Town of Wonders'. Back to you, Keith." He made the throat-cut gesture. The cameraman lowered the lens and trudged toward his van.

Most of the crowd drifted away, but Megan and a few others stayed to hear how the chef would answer Tim Bailey's next question. "Off the record, aren't you afraid to work for creatures who might put *you* on their menu?"

"You sound like my family, only they're worried the demons will devour my soul rather than drink my blood."

"Demons?" Bailey asked.

"That's how they see the newcomers." The chef bent to pick something off the ground. Bailey watched, paying particularly close attention to her rear end.

The chef was pretty, if you liked the cheerleader type. All Rettger needed was blonde hair, which she might actually have beneath the fairy-red dye job.

Setting a cardboard box on the counter, the chef lifted the plastic-topped food display tray to place it inside. "I really have to be going. I've been relying on my *sous-chef* to do the prep, but I need to check his work."

"One more thing," said Bailey. "I've noticed most people in Elvira have red hair. Limited gene pool?"

"Latest fashion," the chef tossed out. "Come back and see us again for an update later in the summer, Tim, or stop by the Swan any time." She took her things and walked off, her stride jaunty, as though she knew Tim Bailey still watched her.

After the chef disappeared, Bailey noticed Megan. "Say, are you one of those Egyptians?" Megan shook her head, asking why he thought so. "It's your hair—and all those cats around you."

Megan looked down. Six cats, sitting serenely in a semi-circle, looked up at her. She'd have reached to pet them but for a flicker of movement seen from the corner of her eye. The cameraman jogged toward her and the reporter. He shouted, "Bailey! Cats—street's filled with them—coming this way."

Were the cats chasing the rats again? Megan didn't want to find out. She told Bailey, "Run!" and then took her own advice, racing toward Village Hall. There were big, strong doors on Village Hall. She'd be safe there.

When she reached the top step, Megan turned, curious to see what was happening behind her in the square. Uncountable cats' eyes stared back. Cats filled the space between booths from Jefferson to Washington, all of them sitting, all of them facing her. *What were they waiting for?*

In a moment, she knew. A gust of wind sent dust and debris from the street swirling into the air. Something slapped her face painlessly. Megan reached toward her cheek to pluck off a flower petal. Sapphire blue, long, and pointed at the tip, it smelled like bananas.

The scent was familiar. Every spring, when the Egyptians held their festival, the air in Elvira smelled of bananas, but never this strong, never this *rich*. Megan brought the petal close to her nose, breathing in the scent, savoring it.

The next burst of wind brought more petals, and the next even more, until the sky rained flowers. Megan wanted to cheer. Some people in the square *did* cheer. The musicians stuck their heads beyond the bandstand's posts to draw in long breaths before they scrambled to pick up their instruments and belt out a foot-tapping Blue Grass tune. For once, Megan didn't wrinkle her nose at the music she normally despised. It was right, just now. It was happy. Megan liked happy.

The cats liked happy, too. They stopped sitting like statues and bounded toward the street, the first ones there leaping up to bat at falling petals, nip them with their teeth and shake them. If the petal they were worrying floated away, they'd pounce, recapture it, and do a little cat dance. Those lucky enough to find a pile of flowers rolled in them. Even as more cats filled the already crowded street, they didn't snarl or fight. Fighting wasn't happy.

Megan scooped up flowers. Holding these in one hand, she arranged the petals to fan out like sunbeams in a kid's drawing. Suddenly, Megan realized they were blue lotus petals.

The air around her, the air everywhere she could see, turned blue, or maybe it was her eyes; Megan didn't know or care. Blue air was pretty. Blue was happy. Megan was happy.

She made her way down the steps, threading a path through cats, careful not to step on their tails or to trip over them, but otherwise unconcerned with anything they were doing. She wanted to see Fadri because seeing him would make her happy, and happy was good.

Fadri saved her from the rats. He looked gorgeous in the moonlight. He looked gorgeous at Cygnet and gorgeous in the bandstand. Fadri was gorgeous everywhere. Thinking about Fadri was good, but touching Fadri was better. Fadri touching her…Fadri kissing her…Fadri—

Traffic clogged Main Street. Megan stopped thinking about Fadri to avoid getting squashed. That didn't make her happy, but she did it anyway. It wasn't too hard to cross; the cars were creeping along, passengers holding out their hands to catch petals. Some of the drivers reached for petals, too. People on the sidewalk strolled arm in arm, laughing or kissing. Megan laughed because laughing felt good.

A group of women with white name badges stood peering into Benton's Hardware, all of them laughing. Two near the window giggled and pointed at the toilets. Another said, "Antiques!" Mr. Benton held open the door. The women flocked in. Mr. Benton looked happy.

Megan kicked up petals on the sidewalk as she walked toward Cygnet, watching the blue slivers twirl in the last of the day's light. Across the street from the Swan, she stopped. The building looked pretty, the damage gone, but people were coming out the door, lots of people. There was a burnt smell in the air Megan didn't like. The people who'd left the club and others waiting outside covered their noses. They stayed on the opposite side of the street, which was fine. Megan didn't want to talk to them. They didn't look happy.

A man dressed in a gray suit stormed out the club's front door to stalk down Washington. Next, waiters left the club and stood in a knot, talking angrily in a foreign language. Then Fadri came around the corner to join the waiters' group, and Megan's heart lurched. She dashed across the street.

Plucking at his arm, Megan drew Fadri away from the others, but let go when he turned a stony face toward her. "Megan," he said brusquely. "This is a bad time. I have to talk to the cousins."

"You're not happy," she wailed, stabbed by sorrow.

"The Mayans have played another trick on us, blocked the kitchen vent so the exhaust fan overheated. There was a fire; the restaurant filled with smoke. After what the Mayans have already done, this is too much. Anton has gone for the police."

"What are they doing?" Megan asked, pointing toward the waiters, who were now moving in a pack toward Benton's.

"Luca..." Fadri growled. "He leads the cousins. A hothead, he has not listened to Anton. They will fight the Mayans. I must stop them. You should leave." Fadri gripped Megan's elbow to propel her toward the alley. "Go to your mother's business or go home. There will be trouble in Elvira. I don't want you hurt."

"No." Megan shrugged loose from his hold. "I want to be with you."

Fadri's smile was reassuring as a kiss. "I'll call you after I've dealt with the cousins and the Mayans," he said, and then he sprinted away, his hair white beneath the streetlamp's glow.

Megan noticed the air's blue tint was gone. On the ground, lotus petals shriveled. She realized her giddiness had passed; she felt clear-headed and a little afraid. Ignoring Fadri's warning, Megan went after him.

A crowd chanting, "Fight, fight" blocked the street by The Feathered Serpent. That didn't stop Megan from seeing the action. When vampires jumped or threw each other, they soared higher than the heads of the bystanders. A pair went up with their hands around each other's throats. Snarling, a Mayan guy, thick-necked and wide-shouldered, leapt in from the Serpent's doorway.

Where was Fadri? Megan tried to muscle her way to the front of the crowd, but the first ring of spectators wasn't budging. Finally, she shoved a tourist hard, hissed, "I'm a vampire. I'll *bite* you if you don't move," and she slipped through.

Fadri was in the middle of things, grappling with the guy who'd jumped in from the sideline. Straining against each other, neither made progress until the Mayan punched Fadri's chest, sending him to the pavement. Fadri sprang up, left foot barely touching ground before a high kick brought his right foot into the side of the Mayan's head. The Mayan went down. Fadri swiped his hands, looking for someone else to play with.

He teamed up with the one he'd called Luca, and the two of them stood back to back, punching or kicking whoever came for them. They moved fast, legs sweeping low to drop an incoming attacker or stretching high in a side or back kick. Megan watched, mouth open, afraid no longer. Fadri was doing fine—better than fine. He looked wickedly lethal.

She jumped when a bullhorn boomed. "Stop!" Chief Brown's voice and then his body pushed past onlookers. Flanking him were Tom Hanrahan and the man in the gray suit, who had to be Anton de Salis. "Knock it off. Fight's DONE," Brown shouted.

A few of the fighters stopped, but not Fadri. He braced for a jab when de Salis waded in and grabbed his elbow. Surprised, Fadri looked over his shoulder. He took a punch to the gut before de Salis caught the opponent's wrist and twisted it, forcing him to his knees. When the Mayan struggled, de Salis pulled up on the arm. The Mayan glared but stopped moving.

Chief Brown hollered through his bullhorn again, and finally, all the fights broke off. Striding into the street, Brown said to Fadri, "Not you again," and jerked his thumb toward the sidewalk. Holding his midsection, Fadri straightened and grinned. Brown surveyed the scene. "No casualties. Tom, you get the Mayans cooled down. De Salis, move your people the hell away from here." He warned everyone, "I catch any of you newcomers fighting tonight, I'm runnin' you outta town. This ain't no boxing ring. This here's Main Street."

Spectators clapped and whooped. "Great show! Bravo!"

Chief Brown looked annoyed. He said, "Clear the street. There's music in the square. That's where you'll find entertainment."

As the crowd started to disperse, Megan heard a woman tell her companion, "Amazing what stuntmen can do these days. I hardly noticed the wires."

"Wires? There were wires?"

"Howard, you are so gullible. No one can move like that unless he's suspended by wires. Did you really think you were watching vampires?"

Tom Hanrahan tapped the woman on the shoulder. "This is Elvira. We don't use tricks. Everything here is real."

The woman nodded knowingly and winked. "Of course, it is." She linked arms with the man, chuckling softly as they walked away.

CHAPTER SEVENTEEN

On Sunday morning, Georgia lay curled up in bed behind Josh, one arm wrapping his waist. When he turned, she was stirring, all sleepy-eyed warm and smiling. Just as he reached for her, the doorbell rang.

"Who the hell is that?"

"Joellen's brought Benji home early," Georgia guessed. "Hurry and get dressed."

Josh pulled on his jeans and tee shirt. Hoisting a sundress over her head, Georgia declared, "I'm going to buy you a shirt that isn't navy blue."

"Hey, navy blue is what I do," Josh said.

"Do I look all right?" Georgia asked.

"You need to smooth your hair."

Georgia swiped a hand over her head as she and Josh hastened downstairs to the kitchen. Josh set to work making coffee while Georgia picked up her skirt from Friday night and threw it into the bathroom. She opened the door. "Ruthanne! Come in. How *are* you?"

"Fine, fine. The docs said I'd have a bruise for a while, but that's all. I knew you weren't busy, so I thought I'd stop by."

"Quick visit?" Josh suggested.

"I have an hour while my grandmother's in church." Ruthanne put the foil-wrapped plate she carried on the kitchen table. "No coffee yet?"

"I'm working on it," Josh said. "What's on your mind?"

"This." Ruthanne slapped a paper on the counter. "Oh, and I brought these for you, Georgia," she added, shoving the plate toward her.

Georgia unwrapped triple-layered, heart-shaped pastries. "They're beautiful. Mmm…fresh raspberries. You made these?"

"I like to cook; like to bake even more. Those are raspberry napoleons." Regarding the pastries fondly, Ruthanne sat at the table beside Georgia.

"So, what's this?" Josh asked, waving the paper. "Looks like a photocopy of a library checkout card."

"It's from the fairy book. The name before S. Withers is Emil Katschke, Georgia's neighbor."

"My former neighbor," Georgia said. "You remember Emil passed away last winter?"

"Do I ever. Chattiest one yet. They can't seem to shut up right after they die, and he was the worst of the bunch." Ruthanne shrugged. "For a while, they're really interested in what's going on, you know?"

"No, I don't 'know'," Georgia said, frowning. "You talk to dead people?"

"No freaking way! They talk to me, or rather, I hear them talking. Katschke was really pissed about the museum."

"Oh, that," Georgia said dismissively. "His daughter thought he'd put the provision in the will about turning his house into a museum because he was old and, well, senile. There's nothing special about the house. It doesn't have any important history."

"That's not how he saw it. Katschke complained he did everything legally, set up a foundation, put aside money for upkeep, then his family dropped the ball. They were supposed to make the place into a museum so he could stay there as a ghost."

"He left the house to himself?" Josh asked, handing Georgia a cup of coffee.

"That was the plan," Ruthanne confirmed as Josh filled a cup for her. "He always figured he'd come back as a ghost."

"Ruthanne," Georgia said, throwing out a hand, "that house is holding up the sale of the land. A number of farmers have looked over the property, but once they learn controls for the water system are off limits because they're in the house, they argue they can't keep cattle with no water. Without cattle, they don't need the pastures. Even selling the fields is a problem: Farm vehicles would have to use the house driveway. This whole business of a 'museum' is a pain in the ass, and with all due respect, there's no way anyone can prove what you're saying is true."

"But there is. Josh can do it with his equipment. He can prove Katschke's ghost is there. Katschke might go for the idea of having a 'curator' in the house, really just a tenant who'd leave things alone. The family would get rent, and the farmers could get access to the water. Everyone would be satisfied."

"Who'd want to live with a ghost?" Georgia asked.

"The newcomers," Josh answered. "De Salis didn't care about the spirit in Bobbi's house when he looked it over. There're a bunch of new guys at the club, those waiters. They can't all stay with de Salis. The Katschke house might suit them."

"Right," Ruthanne agreed. "The real reason why I got interested in Katschke and his house is I think he might know who killed the Red fairy.

"I talked with Mrs. Withers. She didn't remember the spell or the book, but she told me the fairy was killed near your horse pasture, Georgia. Now, the pasture's behind this house, so nobody on the road could see what happened, but Katschke's place has a clear view across the field. If he was wafting around that night, maybe he saw the murder. Since he read the fairy book, he might understand how things went down."

Josh said, "There's a weird sort of logic to your ideas, I admit, but too many *maybes*. Even if you're right, and Katschke's spirit is hanging around, the most we've ever scored on our ghost hunting equipment is a word here and there. That's a far cry from a conversation."

"No problem." Ruthanne helped herself to a napoleon. "I'll be there, and I hear everything. I'll leave it to you two to make arrangements."

Somewhere in the house, Georgia's phone rang, and she bustled off to find it. Assuming the ghost hunt matter settled, Ruthanne asked Josh what he thought of Elvira's opening day, and when he told her he'd missed the festivities, she filled him in.

"Sounds like the whole thing went bust," Josh remarked.

"Not at all. Comments on the village website were highly positive. People believed everything was staged. They just couldn't figure out how we did all the 'special effects'."

Georgia came back. "Vanny's on her way over, needs to talk to me."

"Is she all right?" Josh asked.

"Back to normal." Georgia smiled at him. "And so am I. Guess the fever's passed."

"You were sick?" Ruthanne looked worried.

"Flare up of a chronic condition, nothing contagious. Josh took great care of me. He's the best," Georgia said, squeezing his shoulder.

"My pleasure." Josh meant every word. He patted her hand.

Ruthanne took the hint and cleared out, followed soon after by Josh, who figured the sisters deserved some private time together. Before he left, Georgia drew in close, stroked his chest and said, "Josh, I...I—" She lowered her head, looking away.

"What?" he asked gently. "I shouldn't leave?"

"No, that's okay. I want to say, uh, well..." She gazed up at him, surprising Josh with the sparkle in her eyes when she said, "You really are the best."

He drove into town whistling. The day was warm; it'd be hot by noon. Josh rolled down the window, hanging an elbow outside. Cruising toward Elvira, he felt at peace with the world. When he spotted Archie gassing the Hummer at the garage, Josh pulled in.

"Hey, bro, glad to see you've come up for air," Archie called cheerfully. "Georgia over the flu or whatever?"

"She's fine," Josh wished he could tell Archie how fine, but he wasn't going there. "How were the thunderbird—" Archie's frown made him switch back to the normal Elviran term. "I mean the piasa tours?"

"Meh. Couldn't get near any birds. Spotted one on Saturday morning way up river. The tourists weren't impressed. Doesn't help that the

Hummer's all busted up," Archie observed. "Think you can get out some of the dents by next weekend?"

"Some, but there's no saving that quarter panel. It'll have to be replaced. I'll see what I can find on Monday."

"Monday's Bobbi's birthday *and* she's selling her house. I've asked her out for a celebration, but I don't have a gift. What the hell do women want?"

"I bought Georgia a necklace for her birthday. She liked it well enough, I guess. She wears it."

Archie hung up the pump. "Jewelry. Huh. Didn't think of that." He rubbed his chin. "Say, Egyptian stuff's popular. Want to go to the temple and help me pick something?"

Josh could think of no reason to refuse. "Sure."

They set out in the Hummer, which had irritating, new rattles, Josh noted. He'd have to fix those on Monday, but this was Sunday, a day off. Lolling in the passenger seat, he let the world slide by, enjoying the drive with Archie in companionable silence until they approached the bridge nearest the Egyptian complex.

Josh had seen the temple a thousand times, but he'd never paid much attention to the colorful paintings of the three gods. After the plagues of rats, cats and perfume, he studied the Egyptians' gods with new interest. First came Ptah in his blue helmet, his scepter ending in an upright bar with four cross pieces. Next to him stood his wife, lion-headed Sekhmet with a sun disk and cobra crown, and Nefertem, their son, a young man in a golden tunic, his long, black hair capped by two tall lotus leaves. A lower course showed a line of small, worshipful priests.

The towering entrance gate in the brick wall stood open and unguarded—a first, in Josh's experience. He looked around curiously as Archie pulled into a parking lot before two obviously new buildings. The bigger one must be the spa. Next to it stood a square, flat-topped structure labeled unimaginatively 'Gift Shop.'

Josh spotted a yellow bus from Goreton High School in the lot. The driver sat behind the wheel checking his phone. Inside the shop, Josh and

Archie found a dozen men and women inspecting shelves filled with goods for sale: coffee mugs, wooden boxes with inlaid mother of pearl, statues, bowls, plaques, vases and jars. Painted papyrus hung above the shelves. The back wall held three niches, one for each god. In the Ptah area, there were bulls, scepters and bronze rats. Sekhmet's display featured lions and cats, while Nefertem's held crystal flowers and perfume bottles, some of these large enough to house a genie or two. Archie went off to look at the decorated bottles.

Mayor Marshal of Goreton talked to the girl by the cash register. Marshal recognized Josh and hailed him, saying, "It's Mr. Seldom, isn't it?"

"Yes, ma'am. Nice to see you again."

"Have you met my niece, Paige?" Marshal gestured toward the clerk, who reminded Josh of Tink—well, Tink as she was now, tall and slender with sleek brown hair. Josh stuck out his hand, and Paige shook it.

The real Tink, who'd been leafing through books on the wall beside the desk, turned and said, "Watch it, Laura. Josh will probably try to horn in on our tour. He's always up to something."

Mayor Marshal regarded Josh, and then asked, "Would you like to join us? We've arranged a temple tour for Goreton village council members. We'll be holding an Egyptian festival later in the summer."

"Why an Egyptian festival?"

"We're a bit envious of Elvira's success with the tourists," Marshal confessed. "Decided we should do something for our town. Since Elvira's not promoting the Egyptians actively, we saw an opportunity."

"We thought they didn't want a lot of tourists here," Josh said in his town's defense.

Marshal smiled. "It's taken some persuasion, but the high priest is willing to consider other options now."

A priest in the standard black suit and blue skullcap stepped into the shop. He looked like the young guy Josh saw in Stedwell's office when the priests came by to warn the mayor of plagues. Introducing himself as Geb, the priest told the mayor he would be their guide, and asked her group to assemble outside. Marshal urged the shoppers to finish up. As they paid for their purchases, Josh went over to Archie, who still hadn't selected a gift for Bobbi.

When the last of the Goreton council members left, Josh told Archie to get a move on or they'd miss the tour, but Archie wouldn't be hurried. "It has to be the right thing," he insisted. "Bobbi's special. I want to give her something for her birthday she'll really like."

"There's jewelry in the front case," Josh informed him, but Archie twisted his lips.

"Paige," said Geb, "bring out the lotus necklace."

Her gasp made Archie turn his head. The Egyptian beckoned him with a crooked finger to the front of the shop. "You aren't from Goreton?"

"No. We're from Elvira."

"And you need a gift for a woman of Elvira?"

"Yes…" Archie said cautiously, clearly wondering why Geb asked.

"Then this," Geb declared, opening the velvet box Paige held in both hands, "is what you should give a special woman."

Josh gazed at the golden lotus pendant suspended from a string of dark blue beads. The necklace looked expensive, too expensive for Archie's penny-pinching ways. So, he watched with surprise when Archie ran a covetous finger over the metal, then the beads. Archie was actually considering the thing.

"The beads are lapis lazuli," Geb pointed out. "They're matched for color and pyrite content. See how they all have the same golden sheen?"

Archie checked the price tag, and drew back, coming to his senses. He shook his head, saying, "I can't afford it."

"I offer it to you at half the marked price, a good bargain, a steal," Geb said.

"Why? Is it broken or something?"

"It is flawless, a gift for a queen, one of our best pieces, which is why I want it worn by a woman of Elvira rather than a tourist, who will take it far away. Gracing the throat of a lovely Elviran, it will catch the eyes of many, and they will come here to buy our art. Call it advertising."

"I don't know…" Archie muttered, but he didn't take his eyes off the necklace.

"Stay here with Paige a while. Reflect on the offer: You will find nothing better for the price. Just now, I must escort the Goreton council members."

Josh pulled Archie aside after Geb left. "Get something else," he whispered. "Let's go on the tour."

"No. I want this, but I don't know if I should buy it. I—Aw, go ahead without me. I need to think about this. I'll meet you at the Hummer."

Josh left Archie warring with his wallet. He went outside and walked up to the group, which stood listening to Geb lecture.

"Across from us, you see the garden where we grow food for our table. Our workshops are there—" Geb waved at a long, low building, one of three set in a squared U shape. "Next to the workshops are the places where we sleep and eat. Beyond the trees, there are fields of hay and grain for the cattle we keep in the pasture beside the temple. We breed for bulls, always hoping one will bear the marks of the divine Apis bull, but none have been born in our community since it began."

"When was that?" a man asked.

"The year 1800." Geb gestured toward the temple to his right. "My ancestors constructed the temple, then the mortuary for embalming. After death, all priests are mummified to give the *ka*—what you would call the soul—a place to dwell. Great Ptah breathes life into the ka of mortal men."

"What about animals? I've heard you offer animal mummification," said a woman. "And do you mummify humans who weren't priests?"

"Recently, we discovered that outsiders wished to preserve beloved pets in this way. As for humans not part of our community, we would need special licenses from the state. We sent one of our own into the wider world to obtain the training and licenses, but he did not return to us. The high priest has been reluctant to risk another departure, though I may be charged with the task.

"And now I must make a rather painful announcement," Geb said with a slight dip of his head. "Our high priest believes the gods are angry at this time. I'm afraid you will not be able to enter the temple." After a buzz of disappointed murmurs, Geb continued. "You are welcome to walk around the building, to view the sacred sycamore tree, the statue of Thoth the Protector visible in the entranceway, and the carvings and inscriptions, but the high priest was quite firm on the point of visiting the interior. I am, however, permitted to tell you what you would see inside.

"There are five gateways before the gathering hall, where an altar stands ready for offerings. Three sanctuaries lie beyond this, the left chapel dedicated to Nefertem, the right, to Sekhmet. In both, there are statues of the gods, who stand ready to defend their lord.

"The central chapel is dedicated to Lord Ptah. He sits on a throne with a round base representing creation. His image is carved from black granite. In his hands are an ankh and a scepter, which should bear the *djed*—"

"What's a djed?" Tink asked.

"A pillar with four crossbars. Ptah's djed was one of the sacred items stolen from our temple."

"Good gracious, those thefts were from the temple itself?" Mayor Marshal looked shocked. "How terrible and sad."

"The djed of Ptah and other symbols in the chapels disappeared last week. For several days, we prayed to prevent plagues from the gods."

"Elvira got the plagues," Josh put in. "Do you think they're over yet?"

"The sacred items are still missing, so I think not, but I don't speak for the gods." Geb wound up his lecture. "If you have questions, I will answer them; otherwise, you may stroll around the temple."

"What would happen if we sneaked in?" a man asked.

"Thoth would devour you."

Josh checked out the temple, which had to be a good hundred and fifty feet long. When he'd made his way around the whole thing, he went back to the gift shop, thanked Geb and Mayor Marshal, then climbed into the Hummer where Archie waited.

"I bought the necklace," Archie told him. "It's in the glove box."

"Must be love."

"Yeah, well, we'll see about that," Archie hedged, "but I sure got Bobbi one helluva gift. Maybe I'll get laid." He laughed, and started the engine.

They drove out of the compound and over the bridge. Archie pulled to the side of the road. "Need to take a leak," he said. "Spending money always makes me nervous."

"Bus is coming. Make it quick."

"I'll go under the bridge." Archie climbed down the riverbank.

Josh drummed his fingers on the window post until he heard the deep, thrumming sound like a huge fan turning on. Startled, he looked toward the bridge, where the noise seemed to be loudest. Monster wings emerged from beneath, each downbeat sending long ripples toward shore. As the piasa gained height, Josh's jaw dropped. Archie dangled butt naked, pants yanked toward his belt in the talon of the gigantic bird. As Josh watched, Archie did a jackknife sit up to catch the piasa's leg. The bird flew away with Archie mooning the world below.

CHAPTER EIGHTEEN

Josh scrambled into the driver's seat, gunning the engine to send the Hummer roaring over the scrubby terrain along the cliff. He kept the bird in sight as best he could while running down brush and rebounding from potholes in the soil.

The piasa banked into a wide turn, heading toward the cliff, with Archie swinging out like a pendulum. Josh tugged the steering wheel and braked hard to skid the Hummer into a head-on position toward the river.

Wait for it, he told himself. *Wait...*

When the piasa began to backwing for a landing, Josh pounded on the horn while twisting and punching the radio button at the same time. The sound blast made him jump in his seat. Startled, the bird fluttered wildly, then dropped below eye level.

"Dammit!" Josh yelled, slapping off the radio. He leapt out of the Hummer to rush to the cliff's edge, looking for a rock, a dead branch—anything to throw down on the bird to stop it from tearing Archie to pieces.

But the piasa rose in front of Josh, blotting out the sky, looking down a hooked beak long as his forearm. It let out a blood-chilling cry and beat its massive wings, sending Josh into a crouched backward stagger. When the gust let up, Josh lifted his head to see the bird step onto the cliff ledge. Its talons were empty. Josh's stomach twisted when he realized Archie was gone.

Furious now, Josh glared at the black, unblinking eyes of the terrible bird. "All right," he growled. "Let's dance."

He backed toward the Hummer's open door, slid inside and threw the truck into reverse. Around fifty yards away, he stopped, slammed the door, clipped on his seatbelt and gripped the wheel until his knuckles went white. Endangered species or not, that piasa was his. Josh wanted vengeance for Archie.

The monster raised its wings. Josh revved the motor. *Come for me, you bastard.*

When it lifted off, Josh swore. He couldn't ram the bird in the air, but it didn't make open sky. Its tail snagged on something. With an immense down stroke, the bird got airborne though its body hung so low, it wouldn't clear the Hummer's roof.

Hand on the door latch, preparing to ditch, Josh saw Archie fly into view, both fists clamped around a piasa tail feather. Just when the bird looked like it was heading straight into the driver's seat, the feather pulled loose, and the piasa shot up. Archie spun, back and shoulder cracking the windshield into a spider web bowl. Still clutching the feather, Archie slid off, hit the ground, then picked himself up to wrench open the passenger door. "Floor it!" he shouted as he threw the feather in back.

But Josh saw in the side mirror the bird was circling. "Cover your ears," he warned before sounding the horn and amping the tunes to the max again. As the Hummer throbbed with noise, the piasa veered left, stroking hard toward the river. Josh cut off the radio.

"Arch, are you all right?" He pounded Archie's arm with joy.

"Yeah…yeah, guess so," he answered uncertainly, feeling around. "Right shoulder's sore. Did a number on the windshield, I see." Pale and panting, Archie managed half a grin. "Huge adrenaline rush…thought I'd have a heart attack," he choked out before slumping in the seat, hand over heart.

"I figured you were a goner when the bird showed up with empty claws…thought you'd taken a dive or been chomped."

Archie shook his head. "She dropped me on the ledge by her cave when you scared her with the horn. I pulled up my pants and climbed partway up the cliff before she remembered me."

"She?"

"Has to be a female. There's a nest in the cave. When her tail hung down, I saw my chance to get over the cliff top where I could hide in brush."

"Welcome back, man," Josh husked, clamping Archie's hand in his. "Welcome the hell back."

The Goreton bus had stopped on the road, passengers standing outside frankly gawking as Josh and Archie approached them. Acknowledging their cheers with a lift of his hand, Archie spoke to Mayor Marshal, assuring her he'd be fine. She thanked God and smiled, told her flock to get back on the bus, and both vehicles headed home.

Josh spent the rest of the day with Archie, only too glad to be with his best friend who might have died that day. They didn't talk about what happened; it was still too fresh in their minds, too real to think about. They watched baseball and action flicks, grilled brats and drank beer until both collapsed on their beds, dead to the world.

Monday brought sober reality, not just for Josh and Archie, who were chewed out by the mayor for the Hummer's new damage, but for everyone in Elvira. The village looked like pillaging hordes sacked the place. Though the public works people tried their best to keep up with overflowing trash cans, lots of tourists didn't use them. Litter lined the gutters along Main Street, adding to the brittle brown lotus petals clogging drains. The village square lay trampled flat and peppered with animal droppings. 'The Little Town of Wonders" had a lot of work to do.

Josh watched Elvirans pitching in—literally. Shopkeepers, scout troops, even ladies' auxiliaries did their share to return the town to its normal appearance. As he swept up around the garage, Josh felt glad to do his bit, but he knew civic spirit wouldn't last through the tourist season. Elvira needed a regular mop-up crew.

Once again, Stedwell was ahead of everyone on this. He posted help wanted info on the village website, inviting Elvira's teens to apply for jobs with his new Team Clean Squad.

Josh found out about this from Archie, who stopped by the garage. The club would be hosting a launch party for Stedwell's cleanup squad, and since Cygnet's official opening was delayed by the restaurant fire, other Elvirans wanted a look at the place, too. "Gonna be busy tonight," Archie predicted. "We need to get there early for Bobbi's birthday."

"We?" Josh inquired.

"You and Georgia, too. We'll double date. It's more fun with a bigger group."

"Any other reason you want us there?"

"Bobbi's leery about vampire clubs because of the vampire ex. She's okay with de Salis, but she's not sure about his people. She'll be happier if we go together. Let's get there by seven."

It was a good plan, so, of course, it didn't work. Josh and Georgia arrived on time, but their friends were late. When Archie and Bobbi appeared, explaining her move to the new place took longer than expected, Bobbi wore the lotus necklace, which Georgia oohed and ahhed over for a bit.

Inside Cygnet, there was nowhere to perch, let alone sit. For Josh, this meant trouble: He'd actually have to dance—and he'd have to do it sober.

"Look," he said desperately to Georgia, "let's get a drink at the Swan. Their bar is open."

"Later." She took his hand, pulling him onto the dance floor. "Don't worry so much. I love the way you move."

Josh made a face. "I'm the world's crappiest dancer, and you know it."

"Who's talking about dancing?" Georgia whispered into his ear.

Josh forgot about feeling dorky, about looking like he was having a seizure, about everything except Georgia's body. Watching her fluid movements with worshipful awe, he found it hard to believe she had any solid parts and equally hard to ignore his own.

Georgia tapped on his arm. "Oh, look! There's Deeble—and he's dancing up a storm. How can he *do* that?"

"Fairy boots." Josh smiled at the old man's obvious exhilaration. Deeble didn't have a partner; he was capering by himself. "Do you want a drink now?" Josh asked Georgia. The club felt hot from body heat and lights.

"Rather have an iced coffee. Let's try the coffee bar."

Their waiter from the Swan manned the counter with fancy desserts. A number of chicks in white Team Clean tee shirts were chatting with him, some giggling, all of them acting like fan girls. Georgia smiled and said, "Hello, Luca" when she ordered her drink. With a slight nod, he returned the greeting, but his manner was distracted, eyes intent on the girls, fingers flexing as he turned to relay the order to the guy behind him, who made the drinks.

When Luca handed her the iced coffee, Georgia yelped, sloshing brown liquid on her skirt. Swiping at the wet spot, she told Josh, "I felt this huge tingling in my fingers and then a shock." She handed him the cup and shook out her hand. "A real zinger."

Quite suddenly, Anton de Salis appeared at the counter, barking something at Luca in the language they used. Luca shot him an angry look. De Salis repeated the words, and Luca turned toward the nearest door, marching out sullenly. There was an audible sigh from the fan girls.

"That was clumsy," Anton fumed. "Unforgivable. Luca may not be ready for this work."

"It's not his fault," Georgia replied. "What can you do about static electricity? I'll go put a little water on the coffee stain."

De Salis wasn't consoled. As Georgia left, he muttered darkly to the remaining counter man, "See there is no more 'static electricity' here," then he looked down at the cup in Josh's hand. "I'll have that replaced and taken to your table. Where are you sitting?"

"We're not. We got here late."

"Perhaps you would join the family in our private area? We have a place to relax when work permits. With a good view of both Cygnet and Swan, we can oversee both rooms. It's there, above the music console, behind the dark glass."

"We don't want to impose," Josh said.

"You'd be doing me a favor. As the Swan's kitchen is closed for repairs, only Ioana at the bar has work tonight. Nina, Tru and I find ourselves at loose ends. The ladies have been pestering me to dance, and I confess I do not know how to dance this way."

"I hear you, but we're doubling with Archie Ferguson and Bobbi Miller."

"Bring them with you. The closing on Ms. Miller's house went well today, but I neglected to obtain from her the key to the hot tub cover. When you're ready, the stairs are right of the console. Ask for help from Fadri, who's handling the music, if you have trouble finding the way."

De Salis looked at the blond guy talking to Megan Shaw. Josh recognized him as the one who attacked Snopes' car. "And there is another problem," de Salis grumbled. "Fadri is quite taken with that girl, whose father opposes our presence in this town. She should not be here. No good can come of it."

Josh said, "Shaw's kind of a temperamental guy. He's an artist and all, but I don't think he's dangerous."

"I hope you're right," De Salis said before he walked off.

Josh snagged Georgia on her way out of the bathroom. They hunted for Archie and Bobbi, found them in line by the coffee bar, and Josh relayed de Salis' invitation. At first, Bobbi hesitated, saying she didn't like to be alone with vampires, but when Josh told her it was only Anton and the two women, she agreed. "If you want to leave, we can always say we're going to dance," Archie reassured her, squeezing her hand.

"I wouldn't mind getting off my feet for a moment," Bobbi confessed. "These shoes are killing me."

Josh looked at Bobbi's stilettos, then at her legs. *Nice legs—very nice legs.* When he looked up, Archie frowned. "Let's get a move on," he said, tipping his head toward the console.

They had no problem finding the stairway; if they had, Fadri wouldn't have been any help. The vampire was involved in some deep conversation with Megan. Georgia said, "Isn't that Vanny's rescuer—the one she's so hot for now?"

"If Vanny wants him, I'd say she's out of luck. Megan's got the inside track."

"Oh, dear," Georgia said pensively. "Vanny and Megan have been friends forever. I hope they don't let a guy come between them."

"Maybe he should take them both on. They'd be like a matched set." Josh waggled his eyebrows and earned a jab to the ribcage from Georgia.

Georgia's eyes went wide when they reached the elegant private area. Upholstered swivel chairs in the Swan colors set around richly gleaming tables overlooked the action below at Cygnet. A couch and more chairs on the other side of the narrow room faced the restaurant, visible through the glass swan decorations set into the ceiling of each booth. Larger panels at both ends of the room gave views of the Swan's bar and entry.

The light was low, the music comfortably muffled. On the table before de Salis, Trulia and Annina sat a bottle of champagne in a glass chiller. "Welcome," said Anton, rising to greet Georgia and Bobbi. He lifted his hand and a waiter came in soundlessly to set champagne flutes on the table. After the waiter uncorked the bottle and poured bubbly into the glasses, de Salis took a taste and said, "It's a good vintage. Enjoy."

"But I thought you guys didn't—" Bobbi stopped herself, looking flustered and embarrassed.

"We don't need to eat or drink," Trulia said, "but we enjoy the flavors."

"I love champagne," Annina declared. When de Salis teased her about liking champagne too much, she brushed away the criticism with an airy wave of her hand. "Sensation is to be relished."

"Your necklace," de Salis remarked to Bobbi, "is quite striking."

"Archie bought it for me at the Egyptian temple," Bobbi said proudly.

"May I have a closer look?"

Bobbi leaned toward him with trepidation, holding out the necklace.

After eyeing the thing for a moment, de Salis said, "Extraordinary. You're aware this is ancient workmanship?"

"They told me at the temple it was one of their best pieces," Archie said. "Didn't say anything about it being old. I got the impression they made it there."

"It appears to have been cut from a larger item. At the edges there's the brightness of recent polishing, as though to remove burring." De Salis sat back in his chair. "Many art works are reused when their original setting is damaged or their purpose changes. After England's Henry VIII broke with the Roman church, priests' vestments with gold and silver embroidery were made into articles of clothing for the wealthy. You were quite fortunate to obtain such a special piece."

"Bobbi's a special woman," Archie gushed, and Josh thought he'd taken a dive over the deep end of stupid with his compliment, but Bobbi ate it up. She beamed at Archie.

De Salis wanted to talk about the club: What did they think of Cygnet? Next, the topic changed to real estate, the house sale and purchase, the hot tub key and Bobbi's new digs. When Georgia started in on a sales pitch about the Katschke house, Josh found his mind wandering. He sipped his champagne, looking through the smoked glass at the dancers below.

Some kind of scuffle began by the entrance, people shoving each other toward the dance floor. Josh wondered who'd be foolish enough to try muscling his way past vampires. A human was as mismatched with a vampire as a kid squaring off with an adult.

To Josh's surprise, the crowd gave way to three guys dressed as mummies. *Ryans*, he thought. They were never short on nerve. Only two of them old enough to get into the club, so they probably cooked up some scheme to gatecrash as entertainers. Josh turned to de Salis, interested in his reaction.

What Josh saw made his mouth go dry. De Salis, who'd never been anything but calm and confident, looked frantic, fearful. He shot to his feet, slammed a hand on an intercom button and commanded his people to leave. The young vampires froze like deer in headlights, then tore out of the club through the back door, not being too picky about collisions with bystanders, plowing through everyone in their path. Josh caught a glimpse of Fadri bounding away, Megan in his arms.

"Anton, they're kids in costume," Josh said.

"No, they're not," he refuted fiercely, keeping his focus on the scene below. "They're quite real and lethal to my kind. One touch would destroy any of us."

He turned to Bobbi, pointing at her necklace. "They're after *that*. Take it off."

Bobbi cupped a protective hand over her necklace.

"OFF!" de Salis roared.

"Now, wait a minute," Archie cut in, rising to his feet. "That's Bobbi's gift. You can't make her—"

Annina snatched the necklace from Bobbi's throat, snapping the cord, scattering beads across the room. She handed the pendant to Anton.

"I'm sorry," he said to Bobbi's shocked face. "There's no time to explain. This must go." He paused, suddenly looking uncertain. "But I can't approach the mummies."

"Give me the thing," Josh said, holding out his hand.

"No, Josh!" Georgia clutched at his arm.

"He will be safe from their deadly touch," Trulia put in. "He is human. But the mummies are very strong. Do not let them take hold of you."

"Throw the pendant to them," Georgia urged.

"Right." Josh took a deep breath. With a quick glance at the mummies, who were moving slowly but steadily across the floor, he scurried down the stairs, burst through the private entrance door, then stopped. The mummies were close, too close. Josh could see writing on their elaborately wrapped bandages. He hurled the pendant over their heads toward the empty center of the room.

CHAPTER NINETEEN

"**F**adri! Why did we run away?" Megan demanded as he set her down inside the village square bandstand. "You can't believe those were real mummies. Mummies always have their arms and feet bound, while that bunch—" She stopped to slap her forehead. "What am I saying? Mummies are *dead*."

"Mummies can be half alive. Fed a drop of vampire blood—not ours, but blood like the Mayans'—guardian mummies stay dormant until needed. Don't ask me how it works; I don't know. When they lose their energy, their keepers look for one of us to feed them, and their touch destroys us."

Megan stood thinking in silence. Then she asked, "How did you guys get mixed up with Egyptians?"

"A group of us traveled to their land long ago, believing Egyptian priests could cure our need for energy—to make us human again." Fadri laughed mirthlessly. "Egyptians were the greatest sorcerers in the world at the time. We knew they tolerated sanguinarians—"

"Sangwe what?" Megan asked.

"Blood drinkers. Goddess Sekhmet was one, and so sanguinarians were accepted. But the Egyptians condemned us for stealing the *ka*—the spirit in the body during life—which should go to the gods when a person dies.

"Their priests refused to help us, and did something much worse: They used us to reanimate mummies. When we tried to escape the priests, they threw up the water curse to keep us within Egypt."

"Huh. I thought they wanted to keep you *out*." Megan leaned pensively against a bandstand post. "What's ancient history got to do with mummies in Elvira?"

"This is puzzling." Fadri shoved his hair off his forehead. "When guardian mummies are sapped of energy, they cannot move, yet those were active."

"Why do Egyptians need guardian mummies?" Megan asked. "What's their purpose?"

"To protect the property of the gods—statues, talismans, things of that nature—through which the gods can act. When such items aren't available, the gods must use other agents, like the mummies."

"Wait, wait," Megan said, holding up a hand. "I'm onto something. Those rats and cats might have been 'other agents'. Maybe they were looking for something rather than punishing us." She began to pace, ticking off points on her fingers. "First, the rats crashed the graduation party, then they came down Main Street and piled up by the salon window. Next, the cats appeared in the square, and lotus petals fell. Finally, there were mummies. What's the connection?"

"You observed all those things."

"Yes. The rats followed me when I ran from Krueger's field—can't complain about that. I met you." Megan flashed a smile at Fadri. "The cats ignored me when the priests called on Sekhmet from the Village Hall steps. That was like special orders or something. But then the cats came back to stare at me, and the lotus petals fell on me first. Tonight, we got mummies. So...so...what does all this mean?"

"Megan," Fadri said, turning her shoulders so she faced away. "Your hair decoration—where did you get it?"

"At the spa." Megan's hands went up to finger the back of her head. Undoing the barrette's clip, she turned and handed the piece to Fadri.

"I know nothing about art," he told her, "but my uncle is an expert. We should show this to him."

"Is it safe for you at the club with those mummies still wandering around?" When Fadri shrugged, Megan decided, "Let's go to the temple, put this thing there, and see what happens."

"Too much danger for you."

"Why? If this is the real deal and I give it back, the gods should be happy. If the Egyptians catch me, what are they gonna do? Shake my hand and say, 'Thank you'. I—"

"We," Fadri said firmly.

"No, *I*," Megan insisted. "They might want you for mummy food. You should stay as far away as possible. Oh, I wish Vanny were here. Even though she's partial to the Mayans because she works at their club, she'd help."

"She works at The Feathered Serpent?" Fadri asked with an odd tone to his voice.

Megan nodded. "Yes, but don't hold it against her. Vanny's my best friend. She was sick over the weekend, so we need to catch up, but she did tell me she met one of your people—blond guy, she didn't know his name. Thinks he's hot. Who could that be?"

"Luca is blond," Fadri said slowly, "and women consider him handsome."

"Well, it'd be sweet if something worked out for the two of them. We could hang together. Why don't I call Vanny?"

Fadri put his hand over Megan's phone. "With more people, there's a greater chance of detection. The fewer of us involved in this scheme, the better."

"Cool car," Megan said of the black Ferrari as they drove toward the Egyptian compound. "Whose is it?"

"Mine. Shipped it to New York, where it waited until our plane with the cousins arrived. Two of them drove it here."

"It must be nice to have money," Megan mused.

"There's no trick to it. After many years, money accumulates."

"I still can't believe you're as old as you say. Do you remember all that time?"

"Most memories are unimportant, so I tend to forget them. What matters, in the end, is now." Fadri pulled over to the edge of the road. "I can drive no farther. The moving water of the river lies ahead. Do you know how to drive?"

"Well, yes, but not stick."

Fadri rubbed his face. "Try not to grind the gears."

Megan's first attempt at clutching resulted in several lurches, then a stall. She tried again and got the car rolling, only to hear the engine scream. "What do I do now?"

"Shift to second. Pull down. No! Depress the clutch first."

Megan hit the brake. The Ferrari whined and died. She stared morosely at the bridge.

"This is not the easiest car to drive," Fadri soothed. He gave Megan more instructions until she said between clenched teeth, "Those Egyptians better be grateful. All I wanted to do tonight was visit your hot tub." Grinning at Fadri's startled but pleased expression, she said, "I'm ready. Are you?"

"I will pass out."

Megan turned to him.

"Don't be concerned. I'll revive once we're past the water."

But Megan *was* concerned when Fadri slumped in his seat, head falling against his shoulder belt as they crossed the bridge. She forced herself to focus on the difficult task of driving his car, succeeding more or less until she turned the corner, where the engine threatened to die again. Megan pushed on the gas and the Ferrari shot forward.

Fadri awoke. "We're clear?"

"Yes, but I'm stopping. You drive."

"Clutch," Fadri told her, shifting into neutral and pulling the hand brake before he switched seats with her. Thankful to be a passenger again, Megan relaxed until Fadri found a hidden spot along the river inlet where they could leave the car. "From here, we walk," he said. "Let's see what's beyond the brick wall."

He leapt up, grabbed hold, and peered over the top. "It's open pasture. There's no cover."

"So we sneak along the wall," Megan said, watching him drop down and dust off his hands. "Or I do, anyway. I wish you'd stay here."

Fadri set his jaw. "We will stay together."

When they reached the section of wall in front of the temple, Fadri listened for any sounds of sentries but reported he heard none. He checked the view from the top of the wall before reaching down for Megan. Over that hurdle, they dashed the few steps to the temple's back, where Fadri took Megan in his arms and jumped to the roof.

"Down," he hissed, crouching, then sprawling on his stomach.

Megan followed his example. "What are we doing here?"

"Looking for the safest way in."

"The light wells." She pointed to the largest of three square openings. "The middle one is biggest. Help me into it."

"I should go first," Fadri said.

"You won't fit. I'll barely make it."

Even for Megan, the space was tight. She wriggled her hips and shoulders to squeeze through the gap. As she dangled from the edge by her fingertips, she felt something solid beneath her left foot. She let go.

It took all of her self-control not to squeal, but the drop wasn't far. When her foot slid from under her, she flung her hands out, grabbed smooth stone, and stopped her fall. She clung there a moment to collect herself.

Eyes adjusting to the darkness, Megan found herself hugging a granite head. "I'm sorry for stepping on you," Megan apologized to the statue of Ptah. "I wouldn't have done it if there were any other way in." She slid down his broad, black arm. "I'm here to return something important to Sekhmet." Standing before the god's seated figure, Megan added, "I'll just be running along. Sorry, again, to trouble you."

She edged backward toward the deeper darkness of the chapel's door, then pondered which way to go in the corridor. Feeling her way along the nearest wall, she found another chapel with a male statue. Megan reversed direction, passed Ptah, and crossed a gateway to a larger room with an altar but no statue. She went on to find a third chapel. Inside, Megan saw the lion-headed goddess.

"Oh," Megan breathed. "You are *so* beautiful." The hole in the chapel's ceiling let in enough light for her to see Sekhmet's regal leonine head above a slim, dainty body. "Great figure, too," Megan said enviously before bending to lay her barrette beside the statue's bare feet. "I hope you're happy to get your symbol back. I didn't steal it," she put in quickly, "so don't get mad at me, okay?"

"You're taking too big a risk," Megan heard a female voice say. She started, staring wide-eyed at Sekhmet. When the voice continued, asking, "Why bring us into the temple?" Megan realized the statue wasn't talking to her. The sound came from the corridor or the altar room. Megan hid behind Sekhmet.

"There's no risk," a male voice replied. "I'm on guard duty tonight. No one else will come here."

"We should have met in the woods like always," a second male voice argued. "Do you have the stuff?"

"It's in the usual place. Do you have the money?" said first guy.

"Yeah."

During the pause that followed, Megan's mind churned. She *knew* that second voice. So, when the female spoke again, Megan listened closely. "Oh, hurry it up, Shane. This place is seriously weird. I feel like Thoth's statue by the front gate is watching, waiting to pounce or something."

Shane. And was that...?

"Nefer, a statue is a statue," said first male voice.

"Maybe it's the darkness or the atmosphere. I don't like it."

Bitter laughter. "I don't either. That's why I want to leave."

"I keep telling you to talk to Dad. He'd understand. You could work for him in the business."

"He would insist I become a mortician as the high priest does. That's not what I want. I have other plans."

"Well, whatever," Nefer said irritably. "Just don't mess up what we've got going. Mummies invaded Elvira tonight. Things are off the chain."

"It's creepy here," said Shane. "Let's go."

Megan heard footsteps moving away. After counting to twenty, she left Sekhmet's chapel to return to Ptah's. Climbing his statue in silence, she reached a hand through the skylight to Fadri, who pulled her up. "You'll never believe—" Megan began.

Fadri silenced her with a finger to her lips. He pointed toward the ground and mouthed 'mummies.'

Megan whispered into his ear, "Can you jump us away from them?"

Fadri whispered back, "I could get us to the wall, but if the mummies gave chase, I could not outrun them. My energy is low; I did too much this weekend and tonight. I feel no stronger than a mortal."

Megan grimaced wryly. "You're like a phone battery. They always lose it at the wrong time. If you need a recharge, kiss me."

Drawing back, Fadri refused, adding, "There are men with torches approaching. Use your phone. Call the Elvira police."

"Aw, jeez, this is getting ridiculous," Chief Brown said to Fadri. "Can't you stay out of trouble, even for one, lousy night?"

"We were trying to do a good deed, to return an object dedicated to the goddess," Fadri said in his own defense.

"I'm getting really tired of your good deeds," Brown grumbled.

They were in the high priest's office, a small space adjacent to his living quarters in the dormitory building. Candles in tall sconces lit the room. The elderly priest, wearing a black robe, sat in a green armchair. Two younger men in black shirts and trousers stood.

The high priest whispered to the middle-aged one, who said aloud, "Our *wr khrp hmw* asks why we should believe you were returning a sacred object and not stealing?"

"I didn't see anything to steal," Megan answered before she realized how bad that sounded. "I hadn't *come* to steal," she corrected herself. "I came to return Sekhmet's symbol."

"The priests couldn't find it. Isn't that right?" Brown asked the Egyptians, who nodded.

The middle-aged priest turned to the younger one, "Geb, you searched thoroughly?"

"I did."

Megan stared at the young priest. "You're the one who met with Shane and Nefer. I heard your voice. If the symbol's missing again, you took it."

"The girl," said Geb, "is either lying or confused."

"*I'm* confused," Brown admitted to the priests. "Alls I know for sure is you found these two on your temple roof after they put in a call to the station. Now, most folks who take up thieving don't call the cops for help.

"*They* say they were here to return something. *You* say you didn't find it, and nothing is missing from the temple other than items we already know about. Megan and Fadri were clean—Sorry, Megan. I really hated to pat you down, but it's the job. And so...." Brown paused. "Other than trespassing, these two are in the clear."

"Chief Brown, I heard that man" Megan pointed at Geb "asking for money from Shane Ryan for 'stuff in the usual place.'"

"What kind of stuff would that be, Mr. Geb?"

"I have no idea," Geb said flatly. "As I said, the girl is—"

"Crooked or nuts," Brown cut in. "I got that. Problem is I've known Megan all her life. She babysat my kids for a while there. Never seemed shifty or flighty to me, so I'm having some trouble seein' her that way."

"You might ask why she and her companion chose to 'return' goods secretly after dark," Geb countered.

Fadri held up a hand. "I'm nocturnal."

"Well, we all have our little problems," Brown allowed. "Megan could have made the trip during the day. Why didn't you?"

"Because of the mummies. They're dangerous to Fadri's people. I realized they were after my barrette. If I brought it back here, I hoped they'd leave Elvira, and I wanted them gone right away."

Brown pursed his lips. "Walking mummies. I heard about those. Way I see it, they were jokers dressed up in rags. Even so, a lot of people got scared, and I suppose you could be one of them. What made you think your hair doodad was special?"

"The plague animals followed me. And another thing: My hair didn't turn red like everyone else's in town." She faced Fadri with an enlightened smile. "I somehow passed as Egyptian."

"The fairies' magic didn't affect us either," Fadri said, "possibly for the same reason. We are different from Elvirans."

Megan held both hands to her head. "Oh! I remember something. Vanny's hair stayed black, too. Chief Brown," she announced, "I know where another Egyptian object is."

CHAPTER TWENTY

Lunch bag in hand, Josh joined Georgia in the park on Tuesday. They sat on the slide and watched Benji work at his solo swinging. Benji would lean forward and tuck up his heels, then lay back and shoot out his legs. He didn't get very far that way, but he didn't give up.

"Benji's growing so fast," Georgia said wistfully. "I need to make the most of this time when he's little. At least I have him all to myself today. Mom's at the office, so I gave Vanny the day off. Poor thing was rousted out of bed by Tom at 7 a.m."

"Why?"

"Official business. The barrette Megan lent Vanny turned out to be an Egyptian treasure. Megan's hair clip was, too. Megan got suspicious about the jewelry after the rats and cats kept following her. She told Vanny the animals were hunting for things belonging to the Egyptian gods." Georgia chuckled. "Kind of a crazy theory, but this is Elvira, after all."

Josh said, "De Salis knew right away the mummies were after Bobbi's necklace. Somebody at the temple is passing off valuables as costume jewelry."

"That's what it sounds like to me. I suppose it's the only way to get the goods away from the temple. Later, a thief could steal them back from the people who bought them."

Benji vaulted off the swing. Alarmed, Georgia stood up. Running toward Village Hall, Benji called, "Daddy!"

Tom looked down as Benji glommed onto his leg, ordering him to "Do the monster!" He staggered toward the slide, swinging his right leg in a wide arc with Benji aboard, whooping gleefully. Tom stopped when he reached Georgia and Josh, saying to Benji, "Frankenstein has to talk to your ma. She knows stuff the monster needs to learn."

Benji nodded. "Mama knows everything." Climbing off his father, he announced, "I'm going swinging now. *Watch* me."

"I'll do that." Tom kept his eyes on Benji for a moment, then turned to Josh and Georgia, saying, "Red, Seldom," by way of greeting.

"If you're going to ask me about the Egyptians, I don't know anything Vanny hasn't told you," Georgia said.

"I have questions for Seldom. When I went to the temple with that thingamajig of Vanny's, the Egyptians reported they'd located two other stolen items. One fit the description Megan Shaw gave Ed. They said they'd finally found it behind a statue. Another piece looked like a gold flower. I lifted prints and found yours, Seldom. Got an explanation?"

"I handled a lotus pendant before I threw it to the mummies at Cygnet last night."

"Living mummies, riiight," Tom jeered. "I say your 'mummies' were Egyptians hoping to scare people into giving up the thieves. They struck pay dirt when they landed the flower. I tried to interview de Salis about these bogus mummies, but I couldn't raise him."

"Understandable," Josh observed. "You can't walk on water, either."

The Bible reference soared past Tom and sailed away. Tom frowned, and went on, "Who gave you the jewelry?"

Josh told Tom the story behind the necklace. Tom noted, "Your account dovetails with Ferguson's and the shop girl's. Too bad she lost her job over this."

"Paige Marshal is the mayor of Goreton's niece. Since the Egyptians were cozying up to the Goreton village council when Archie and I were there, I'd think they'd want to keep Paige around."

"The priests closed the shop for a while so they didn't need her, but I'm guessing they suspect her of helping a priest called Geb, who lit out early this morning. He stole a farm truck, then abandoned it in Goreton. The Goreton cops are searching for him, but chances are he's long gone.

Probably has the last stolen item with him."

"Megan told Vanny Shane and Nefer were involved," Georgia said.

"I checked them out this morning. Their prints weren't on the objects, so there's nothing to tie them to the thefts. They only admit to buying blue lotus from Geb, which isn't illegal, though the Egyptians frown on selling it. Geb turns out to be Nefer's half-brother, Kem Wati's son. We're keeping an eye on Wati's funeral home in case Geb shows up.

"If you run across any more Egyptian treasures, let Ed or me know." Tom checked his watch. "I'm late."

"For a very important date?" asked Josh.

Tom missed that one, too. "Yeah," he drawled, "I'm having lunch with Cissy Rettger at the café. Be nice to see her again; we used to be real close. Had a thing going for a while there."

"Didn't everyone?" Georgia muttered.

"What?" Tom asked.

"Nothing. Enjoy your lunch."

"I didn't," Josh said after Tom walked off.

"Didn't what?"

"Have a thing going with Cissy. I struck out," Josh said.

"Well, now's your second chance." Georgia crumpled her lunch bag. "She's back in town, so you can try again. 'Course, you'll have to compete with Tom, but that should only make things more interesting. I'm sure Cissy would love to have two guys chasing after her." Georgia stood and strode to the swings, saying, "Benji, time to go."

Josh stared after her, dumbfounded. "Georgia?" he called. She gave him a backhanded wave off.

"Bye, Joswa," Benji said when Georgia took his hand. "Mama, you didn't say bye. Has Joswa been bad?" As Georgia led him away, Benji took a long look over his shoulder at Josh.

Women! Josh fumed on the way back to work. *Why did they have to be so touchy?* One little comment about Cissy got Georgia all bent out of shape. She was mad about nothing, nothing at all! Why the hell should he feel guilty for *nothing*?

Scowling, Josh took out his frustration on the dents in the Hummer, which he tried vainly to pull back into shape. Despite his best efforts, the Hummer looked battle worn, which, Josh realized, wasn't too far from the truth. When he'd done what he could, he went into the office to tackle the call he dreaded.

Humph Thoon didn't answer, so Josh redialed, and Chris Thoon did. "I have the right part for your truck," Josh told him.

"Bring it out and put it on," said Chris.

"Not without a police escort."

Chris laughed. Josh held the phone at arm's length until he heard, "You think we're still pissed at you. Nah. Best thing you ever did was lead us to the naiads. After you cleared out, we got a foursome going."

"You, Humph and who else?"

"Me, Polyxo, Anippe and Memphis. Great chicks. Humph paired up with Argiope and Chione. Our buddies picked the pink and green nymphs."

"And Grid?"

"She's not talking to any of us, but that's cool. There are other fish in the sea."

Chris laughed again. Josh put his ear to the phone when the decibel level dropped and said honestly, "I'm sorry my screw-up made you miss competing last weekend."

"No sweat. The naiads kept us busy, you know what I mean?"

Josh did. In a contest between Georgia and a truck race, the race would lose, hands down. And Georgia was only one-sixteenth naiad; taking on three full-blooded nymphs was a staggering thought. It was a miracle Chris hadn't died of exhaustion—maybe that's how the predatory Rusalka story started. "Okay, so I'll see you this afternoon."

"Promise?"

"You got it." Josh clicked off with sigh of relief.

He'd put four quarters in the candy machine when he saw the cats.

There were six, all black, trotting across the garage lot, heading purposefully for the alley between Main and Second. Cats, in Elvira these days, meant something. Josh slipped out the door to follow them.

When he reached the alley, he saw the cats slow their pace. They skulked along in the shadows behind Cygnet. Josh curled his lip, deciding he'd been paranoid. There were probably rats left for cats to hunt.

About to return to the garage, Josh saw Cissy Rettger step out from the Swan's back door. The red hair came as a shock; she'd always been blonde, but otherwise, she looked the same as Josh remembered. *Cissy Rettger, object of a whole year's sweaty fantasies...*

And quite suddenly, Josh was back in high school, watching her from the last row in math class, helplessly hoping some magic would make her sidle up to him after the bell rang, the look in her eye promising "any time, any place."

Cissy hadn't given him that look then, and she wasn't doing it now. She was taking out the trash.

As soon as she opened the dumpster's lid, cats surged from the shadows and jumped her, clawing their way up her clothes until the white jacket disappeared beneath black fur. They went for her hands, paws lashing out to rake the palms she threw up to protect her face. Cissy shrieked, beating frantically at the writhing mass of fur. Fingers closing on a tail, she flung one cat against the wall before Josh moved in and started pulling animals off her.

He struggled with the cats until they retracted their claws and dropped to the ground, racing away to disappear around the corner. While he stared after them, Cissy sagged against his chest. "I hate cats," she moaned. "They're filthy and evil, tools of the Devil." She shuddered, swaying, until he wrapped steadying arms around her. Cissy looked up at him, saying, "Josh Seldom?" Her deep blue eyes caught him somewhere between fantasy-Cissy and the woman in white standing in the alley.

He said, "You should get those scratches looked at."

She shook her head. "Don't believe in doctors. Faith will heal me."

Megan and Vanny burst out the back door of the salon. "We heard a cry," Megan said before stopping to gape with her mouth open. Vanny took in the scene, and then crossed her arms.

"Cats," Josh responded to the girls' accusing eyes. He pulled away from Cissy to hold out one of her scratched hands as proof. "They attacked her."

"Why her?" Vanny asked.

"She has an Egyptian object," Megan concluded. "She must have bought their jewelry."

Cissy frowned and shook her head vehemently. "Never. Wearing heathen trinkets would be a sin."

Josh stared at her. When he'd known Cissy, she wasn't particularly worried about sin.

"The cats do Sekhmet's bidding," Megan informed her. "If she's marked you, there's a reason. Fadri and I figured that out last night. If you don't believe me, ask him."

"Can't," Cissy replied. "Fadri...well, he's gone."

"Gone where?" Megan asked.

"Wherever it is they come from. They took him early this morning."

"*Who* took him? Why?"

"He left on the family's plane with Trulia, Ioana and Annina. I guess they couldn't do anything for him here. He had to go home."

"What," Megan said sharply, striding over to shove her face at Cissy, "are you talking about?"

The door to the Swan opened and filled with the form of Anton de Salis, who blinked, shielded his eyes, then told Cissy, "I am expecting the mayors of Elvira and Goreton. Please prepare appropriate refreshments." Focusing on Megan, de Salis said, "Before they arrive, we should speak." He held the door open for her.

Megan felt frightened. Something bad happened to Fadri. She wanted Vanny with her when she heard what it was.

The two of them crept into the club, where Megan introduced Vanny.

De Salis looked uncertain about including Megan's friend, but he welcomed her graciously. He led them through the kitchen to an upstairs room between the Swan and Cygnet. Megan looked down through smoked-glass windows at the empty dance floor before taking a chair and lacing her fingers together tightly. "Tell me," she said.

"Someone waylaid Fadri on his way home last night—early this morning, rather. He was overcome and bound to a tree. When the sun rose, he suffered burns on the left side of his body. His face, neck and hand were severely damaged. When the police found him, he had retreated into what you would call a coma, though it is different for us."

Megan gasped. She tried to speak, but no words came out. Finally, she managed, "Will he get better?"

Looking away, de Salis reflected in silence. When he spoke, he said only, "His existence continues, and yet this might not be for the best. He may never recover fully. We heal from most injuries, but burns from the sun are very difficult, nearly impossible to cure."

"Oh my God," Megan moaned, no longer bothering to pretend she wasn't crying. "Can't you do something to help him?"

"The only place where he can regain strength is at home, on native soil. I have sent him there with my ladies. He will have the best care."

An evil thought crossed Megan's mind as she imagined those beautiful women lovingly tending Fadri. If he woke, wouldn't he be drawn to them?

As though he'd read her mind, de Salis said, "They are *my* ladies, so you have nothing to worry about." Quite suddenly, he frowned, saying slowly, "Or, perhaps, we both do." But then de Salis laid a reassuring hand on Megan's shoulder. "We are being churlish to entertain such doubts." He turned to Vanny. "You have questions?"

"Like a thousand of them. First off, I should tell you I work for the Mayans. I'm the cashier at The Feathered Serpent."

De Salis' left eyebrow went up, but he didn't comment. He listened attentively to Vanny. "From what I've seen there, you guys are much stronger than humans. How could anyone get the jump on one of you?"

"Near Fadri's car, there were tread marks from another vehicle. Three of the tire prints were deep, while one was faint. Next to that mark was the impression of a square shape. I suspect the other car had one wheel elevated."

"It'd been jacked up," Vanny summarized, "for changing a tire."

"Yes. We're assuming Fadri stopped to offer assistance only to fall into a trap."

"But still," Vanny went on, "why couldn't he fight his way out of there?"

"I know why," Megan said bitterly. "He told me at the temple he felt low on energy. I offered a recharge, but he refused. Oooh, if I'd only known."

"*Recharge.*" De Salis produced the tiniest flicker of a smile. "An interesting term. Fadri used too much of his reserve in too short a time— the fight with the Mayans, and that business on Friday about a girl near their club."

"Friday night?" Vanny leaned forward.

"He took a break, midway through the evening. He wished to visit you, Megan, but decided against it, given your father's feelings toward us."

"So he walked the street instead, and saw Snopes pick me up," Vanny put in. She turned to Megan, who returned her look of shock. They said together, "*He's* the one you crave?"

A moment later, Megan asked de Salis, "How long will Fadri have to be away?"

"He may never return if he cannot heal, unless...."

"What?" Megan asked, despair making her voice ragged.

De Salis shifted in his seat, looking uncomfortable. "There is a legend about a powerful healing device the Egyptians once had. No one has found any evidence this artifact really existed, but the story always comes to mind when we are faced with losing one of our own."

Megan whimpered. Vanny said, "We're slogging through Egyptians in Elvira, and that's part of the reason why you came here, isn't it?"

De Salis nodded. "Irrational as it may seem to you, some of us believe in the tale. Fadri, in particular, wanted to learn what the Egyptians here might know about the legend."

"That reminds me," said Megan. "Cats attacked your chef. Fadri and I thought—*think*—the animals are sent to hunt for sacred things. The chef may have stolen Egyptian objects."

"No." De Salis shook his head. "She did something else to merit punishment from a feline goddess. Cecily Rettger killed the cat left on our doorstep."

"You *know* that, and you're letting her work here?" Megan rasped.

De Salis tapped his fingers on the table. "For a short time. I must wait until she reveals all she knows. I want the one who trapped Fadri," de Salis said with blazing eyes. "That one, I will kill."

CHAPTER TWENTY-ONE

De Salis' phone buzzed. He answered, listened, and then clicked off. "That was Mayor Stedwell. He and the Goreton mayor will be arriving shortly."

Taking this statement as their cue to leave, Vanny and Megan stood, but de Salis wanted a further word with Megan. "Fadri's car—you should drive it."

"No, I couldn't," Megan said. "My father would never let me keep it."

"I am proposing a temporary arrangement only. I still haven't abandoned hope for Fadri's recovery."

"Oh, neither have I," Megan said fervently. She shut her eyes and concentrated on breathing, just breathing. Still, the tears leaked from her eyes. As she swiped them away angrily, de Salis handed her a linen handkerchief.

"I can look after Fadri's horse, but his car is a problem. It is not made to sit idle, and I can't let the cousins use it. They are too brash, too reckless." De Salis shook his head. "You would be a better guardian of Fadri's property." He pulled a set of keys from his pocket, saying, "Keep these for now."

"Only until he's better," Megan agreed.

De Salis turned his attention to Luca, who entered the room to whisper in his ear. Whatever Luca confided made de Salis agitated. He stood and began pacing. Megan nudged Vanny, who was gawking at Luca, and jerked her head toward the stairs. They said hasty good byes and would have left, but de Salis told them, "Wait."

He turned, focused on Vanny. "Mr. Fernando Suarez has called. He wishes to speak to me. He is on his way here. It seems there was an incident at his club on Thursday. You are aware of this?"

"Yeah," Vanny replied. "Someone spilled blood all over the women's john. Scared hell out of the Elvirans who were there, and made the Mayans hopping mad because they hadn't done anything, but it looked bad for them."

"Suarez is a brave man to come to my door," de Salis mused, "for it was a Mayan who attacked Fadri."

Megan sat down. "You're sure?"

"Without question." De Salis tapped his nose. "The Mayan scent is unmistakable. You may wish to remain to hear his explanation."

Fernando Suarez arrived. He wore an ordinary business suit, a choice that surprised Megan when she remembered how Fadri bundled up against the sun. Another man with him, a small guy with light-brown hair, prompted a happy greeting of "Paco!" from Vanny. Suarez gave Vanny a long look when de Salis introduced her and Megan as "friends of Fadri, my nephew, who has been injured."

"I have heard about your nephew, and you have my sympathy," said Suarez. "Such a pity your skins are so pale. The sun is no enemy to Mayans. We can go where we please."

"So I see," de Salis replied. "What brings you here?"

"We are businessmen. It is time we talk business, you and I. You may dismiss your guards; we will not harm you." Suarez waved at Luca and another cousin standing near the rear of the room. Next, he regarded Vanny and Megan. "As for the young ladies, they would be bored with business talk, I think."

"Vanny told me of the trouble at your club," de Salis said, calmly ignoring Suarez' suggestions. "A matter of blood spilled on the floor?"

"A problem for us, yes. Many Elvirans thought there had been violence done, but it was nothing more than a cheap trick—animal blood, stolen from the local motel." Eying de Salis, Suarez waited.

"And you think my people were behind this trick? I assure you, we were not. The same night, we, too, were sabotaged."

"Do not be so quick to be caught in a lie," Suarez cautioned, "for Paco here reported that the woman who entered my club to play her trick on us operated your booth in the village square this weekend."

De Salis' phone buzzed again. "Forgive me," he said, checking a text message. "The mayors are here." He turned, signaling Luca with a lifted finger. "Tell the chef to serve coffee now."

"This is no time for interruptions and pretty manners!" Suarez objected. "We have important matters to discuss."

"Have patience but a moment, Mr. Suarez. I believe you'll agree I'm not wasting your time. Mayor Marshal has a plan to resolve disputes between our groups. Mayor Stedwell disagrees with it. They intended to approach each of us separately with their ideas, but since you are here, they can tell us both at once."

Footsteps on the stairs sent the men to their feet. Vanny and Megan looked at each other, then rose. When Mayor Marshal entered, she said, "Goodness! I didn't expect a group." Megan turned questioning eyes to de Salis, wondering if he wanted her to leave, but he lifted one hand, extending the fingers flatly, gesturing for her to stay. While Mayor Marshal took the empty seat between Suarez and de Salis, Mayor Stedwell sat by Megan and Vanny. De Salis made the introductions.

Mayor Stedwell opened with, "Laura believes the way to eliminate conflict between newcomers is to put distance between you. She's here to urge one group to move to Goreton. That would require relocating a business, which would be costly and unnecessary. I firmly believe we can work things out here in Elvira. We've welcomed you, and proven our commitment to accommodating your needs. We want both of you to stay."

"I'll admit," said Mayor Marshal, "Elvira has tried to be accommodating, but you have limited resources, Mo. Our village is five times larger. When the tourists are gone, we can support a nightclub with local patrons. Our police and fire departments are better staffed and equipped, our—"

"Relocation is out of the question," said de Salis.

"Mayans do not run from anyone," Suarez said.

The chef came in with coffee. Paco muttered something in Spanish to Suarez, who watched the chef set cups on the table. "This is the woman," Suarez told de Salis.

"I know." Turning to Rettger, he asked, "Why did you attack Ruthanne Quinn in the ladies' room here, and why did you then go to The Feathered Serpent to damage that place?"

"Why did you kill the cat?" Megan added.

While everybody stared at Megan, she watched the chef clutch her serving tray with trembling hands. "I…I...didn't."

"Liar!" de Salis shouted. He turned to Suarez. "Is the stench of deceit as strong to you as it is to me?"

Suarez nodded. Paco said, "*Ah mi Dios*," and held his nose.

The chef dropped the tray and made for the rear door, but Luca barred her way. She turned back to the group saying, "Okay, okay. I poured blood on the bathroom floor. It was a joke."

"Sending Ruthanne to the hospital was no joke," de Salis said.

"I didn't mean to hit her so hard."

"And the marks on her neck?"

"Two baby teeth glued to a piece of wood. So what? No harm done."

De Salis said, "Battery is no small matter. Neither is breaking into a motel to steal. Add in vandalism, animal cruelty, and arson."

"*I* didn't steal the blood. Someone else did. I reached through the bathroom window for bags of the stuff and spread it around. I don't even know who was outside the window."

The mayors, who looked confused throughout this exchange, were starting to catch on. "You were part of an organized attempt to discredit the newcomers and force them to leave town?" Stedwell asked.

"They're demons!" Rettger shouted. "Abomination. They don't belong here."

"Who were you working with?" Stedwell demanded.

"People fighting the evil destroying Elvira." The chef lifted her chin.

"We're doing what has to be done."

"And did your noble work include torturing my nephew?" de Salis asked in a deadly quiet voice.

"That wasn't us. I don't know what happened to him."

De Salis shot to his feet and gripped the chef's arms. Turning her to face Suarez, he said, "*Which* of the Mayans did it?"

"I don't know. I don't know!" Rettger wailed as Suarez rose from his seat to scowl into her face. Caught between the two vampires, she looked like she was trying to melt. Her head leaned away from Suarez' glare while her body shrank from de Salis' hands. She struggled to shake herself free, but de Salis' hold was firm.

Suarez sat down, looking disgusted. "She is telling the truth about your nephew. I wanted to be sure the one who did it was acting alone."

De Salis released Rettger, who backed toward the wall above the Swan. Eyes narrowed, he focused on Suarez. "What are you saying?"

"One of my people broke our most important rule: There is only one *jefe*, one chief. In this town, I am jefe. No one does anything behind my back.

"This man was angry with your nephew," Suarez went on. "They fought in the street and he lost. To prove he was a man, he acted the coward, and set a trap."

"Give him to me," de Salis hissed.

"No. This I cannot do. I would lose the respect of my people."

"Let us take him into custody," Stedwell urged.

Suarez snorted. "And how would you hold him? Which of your laws did he break by binding a vampire to a tree? This is not for you humans. This is a matter for us."

De Salis looked at Suarez. "So, it's war."

"Not this day, not if you listen to what I say. The Mayans in Elvira are mine to protect and to punish. I will punish him."

"A wrist slap? No blood for a long weekend?" de Salis sneered.

Suarez shook his head. "We have a place for the ones who break our rule, who think they are above their jefe. With stone walls and silver bars around them and nothing to feed on but the bats and rats they catch, they have much time to think about what they did wrong. Enrique will stay in that place until your nephew returns."

"Enrique...Ricky!" Vanny gasped.

"And if Fadri does not return? What then?" de Salis challenged.

"Then Enrique will learn to be a *great* rat catcher. You have the word of Fernando Suarez." He stuck out his hand.

De Salis studied the hand for a moment before he took it. He said over his shoulder to Luca, "Make certain Miss Rettger remains on the premises until the police collect her."

Luca approached the chef, who yelped from a sharp electric shock, and rubbed the shoulder he gripped. When she yelped again, de Salis caught Luca's eye. The left corner of his mouth turned up when he said, "*Bun appetito.*"

Stedwell stood. "I'd say we know how to solve our own problems in Elvira, Laura. I'll be leaving now, gentlemen, ladies. I have work to do before our next tourist weekend."

An hour later, Megan sat behind the wheel of Fadri's Ferrari at the overlook, hands behind her head, gazing sadly at the sky above Fern Cliffe. "I miss him so much," she told Vanny.

"What a guy," Vanny said wistfully. "So brave."

"So sexy." Megan sighed. "The way his hair falls across his face...."

"Those blue, blue eyes."

"Mmm. And his lips look like they're chiseled out of marble."

"Awesome lips. How about his intense expression when he's punching something?"

Megan sighed again. Then she sat straight, rounding on Vanny. "Wait a minute. He's *my* boyfriend, not yours."

"I know. I just like thinking about him. Is that bad?"

"Well..." Megan tilted her head, considering. "At least, you understand."

"Oh, I do, I do."

Megan rubbed her forehead. "Something his uncle said made me think: What if the Egyptians have a special gizmo to cure Fadri? I mean if they can make mummies walk, they know things science doesn't."

Vanny tossed her head. "I'm not ready to believe in walking mummies, even if you say you saw some. There are easier ways to explain the guys who showed up at Cygnet. But still, the Egyptians have been around a long time. They could have some old thing stashed away where everyone's forgotten about it. What if we make it our goal to find out what the Egyptians know about vampires?"

"How?"

"We have all summer to work on the problem. First thing to do is make some Egyptian friends, figure out who knows about the oldest stuff they have. We need a reason to hang around the temple. You could get a job at the spa braiding hair, or maybe snag the gift shop gig, now Paige has been kicked out."

"They're going to welcome me with open arms after I sneaked into their temple?"

"Just need to spin it. You proved you were honest. You could have kept their sacred object, but you gave it back. And you told them about the one I had, too. I'd say they owe you, big time. The point is if we put our heads together, we'll think of something. We always do."

"You're right." Megan felt a surge of hope. "The two of us—we can do anything."

"Even save Fadri," Vanny said.

"But he's still mine," Megan reminded her.

Vanny smiled. "If I get to stare at him once in a while, that'll be cool. He doesn't have a brother, does he?"

"No, but there's Luca, who looks a lot like him."

"Luca…" Vanny brushed her lips with a finger. "He just might do."

CHAPTER TWENTY-TWO

"This isn't going to work." Josh stabbed his spade into grass beside Georgia's farmhouse. "I'm digging myself in deeper. Literally."

Archie said, "Give me a hand here."

Josh stepped into the hole they'd dug and pulled on the burlap-covered root ball of the young mountain ash tree while Archie pushed from the other side. The tree angled into the depression. Josh climbed out of the hole to tug on the root ball again, and the trunk swung upright.

"Georgia is *not* going to like us putting a tree on her property without asking her," Josh insisted. "She's territorial."

"The one I planted at Bobbi's house charmed the pants off her."

"Yeah?"

Archie grinned. "Life's looking up."

Josh scratched his head. "Women. Who can figure them out? Why'd Bobbi want a tree, anyway?"

"For protection against werewolves. Bobbi didn't trust wolfsbane, felt a flower was too puny. After she found a tip on the Internet saying rowan trees would keep werewolves away, I went to the tree farm in Giantville looking for one. They had a two-fer sale. This peace offering isn't even costing you anything, so stop bitching."

"Thought your wallet was tapped out."

"It was," Archie admitted. "The necklace set me back, but de Salis slipped me a few bucks at the club. Even though he offered to have the blue beads restrung, I guess he knew Bobbi was disappointed. I told her about the money—didn't want her thinking he was a dick like her vampire ex. De Salis is all right."

Josh nodded, looking again at the tree. "Mountain ash is rowan?"

"Yup, and Louies don't want to be anywhere near it."

"Not good when Tom comes by to give Georgia a check," Josh observed.

"It only bothers them when they're wolves. Rest of the time, they react the way we do, seeing a nice little tree with flowers in spring, pretty leaves all summer, and red berries in the fall. Who could ask for more?"

"I still say Georgia won't go for it. She—"

"Can speak for herself," Georgia cut in, sitting on Harley, not ten feet away, with Benji beside her on Hank.

"Joswa, get me down!" Benji cried.

Josh went to lift Benji from the saddle, but kept his eyes on Georgia, who kept her eyes on the tree. Setting Benji on his feet, Josh took Hank's reins, and Benji went to run a hand along the rowan's smooth trunk.

"What do you think, big guy?" Archie asked.

"It's *cool*," Benji said reverently.

"The fairies say it's the tree for the month you were born, February. Rowan means *L* in their language," Josh told him.

"*L*," Georgia said slowly, "as in loyalty."

"And love," Archie added helpfully.

"Look," Josh said to Georgia's unreadable expression, "if you don't want it, we can put it somewhere else."

"No, it's nice." Georgia dismounted and walked Harley closer to the little tree. "I suppose a girl can't have too many *L*s in her life. Thanks, Archie."

"It was Josh's idea," Archie lied.

"Benji, go inside and wash up for supper," Georgia said.

"But I want to look at the tree."

"It isn't going anywhere. It'll be here after we've eaten. Archie and Josh still have to finish the planting and watering."

"I can help," Benji persisted.

"You'll help by setting the table for supper. These two have a ghost hunt this evening. They need to get ready."

"We have a ghost hunt?" Josh asked, surprised.

"Did you have something else planned for tonight?" Georgia inquired with an edge to her voice.

"No," Josh said quickly. He looked at Archie, who shook his head, saying, "Bobbi has to work."

"Then the Katschke house needs an investigation," Georgia told them. "With taxes coming up, Emil's daughter has to fish or cut bait on the museum thing. She doesn't feel right about ignoring her father's wishes, but she can't keep paying bills on an empty house. The de Salis cousins are interested in renting the place. One way or another, a ghost hunt will settle the matter."

"I'll go get our equipment," Josh volunteered.

"You don't want supper?" Georgia asked. "It'd be a long night on an empty stomach for you two. Finish up, and come on inside."

"Oh, uh, yes. Thank you," Josh said formally. "Need help with the horses?"

"I can manage. Benji, in the house." Georgia took Hank's reins and led both horses away.

"See? I told you a tree would melt her heart," Archie crowed. "Planting a tree means you're thinking about the future. Women like that."

Josh eyed Archie with awe. Maybe his knack with women wasn't all about his looks.

Just as Georgia served strawberry-rhubarb pie, Ruthanne showed up. She wore a khaki jumpsuit.

"We're not doing *Ghost Busters* tonight," Archie told her, "or *Thirteen Ghosts*, either." He pointed at the cardboard 3-D movie glasses in her front pocket. "What are those for?"

"Scoff if you want," Ruthanne said loftily, accepting a piece of pie from Georgia, "but *I'm* not having spiders crawling up *my* spine. Thought I'd try the glasses on the off-chance they'd help me see what I normally only hear."

"Normally," Archie said under his breath.

"Aren't you scared of ghosts?" Benji asked.

"I'm only scared of spiders." Ruthanne paused. "And snakes…oh, and critics." She answered his unspoken question. "Those are people who don't like the stories I write."

"I'm scared of the Big Bad Wolf," Benji confided.

"Don't have to be anymore," Josh told him. "The new tree will keep big bad wolves away."

"Really?" Benji's eyes lit up.

"No doubt about it. My friend Bobbi told me so," said Archie, "and she's really smart."

"Bobby's a girl?"

"Oh, yeah," Archie confirmed. "She's a girl, all right."

"This is great," Ruthanne said of the pie. "Will you give me the recipe? I'd like to use it at The Black Swan." To the astonished faces around her, she explained, "I'm the new pastry chef. The old one moved up to *sous-chef* when the *sous-chef* became chef."

"What happened to Cissy?" Archie and Josh asked together.

"Far as I know, she's rotting in the county jail. She was the b—" Ruthanne looked at Benji. "Uh, the one who clobbered me at the restaurant. De Salis called to tell me what happened. He said she smelled of…well, the wrong scent that night, but he couldn't be sure since she'd done the cooking. On Saturday afternoon when she came in to work, he knew she'd been up to no good."

"Saturday?" Georgia asked.

"There'd been vandalism at the club, quite nasty."

"What happened?" Benji asked.

"Your father arrested her," Ruthanne said smoothly. "Turned her over to the sheriff's department. They have detectives to find out who else worked with her."

"Poor Tom," Georgia said without a hint of regret in her voice. "He seemed so eager to recapture old times." She smirked as she cleared the table.

"I'd make that 'poor Anton'." Ruthanne told the story of Fadri's injury and departure as well as Enrique Molinero's guilt, keeping the report detail-lite for Benji's sake.

When she finished, Archie said, "Molinero is Bobbi's ex-husband."

"Hope she's not fond of him. His leader promised Anton he'd be punished. Molinero's gone from Elvira," Ruthanne said. "Are we ready for ghost hunting yet?"

The Katschke house started out as a two-floor, red brick square with a steep roof. Somebody connected a boxy frame addition to the original core then added a back wing crosswise. There was a barnyard to the west, and an oversized garage to the east. Pulling in the driveway next to Archie's van, Josh could see Georgia's farm across the untilled field behind the house.

Archie had gone with Ruthanne to get the ghost hunting equipment, leaving Josh to suffer Georgia's cool politeness until she decided to give Benji a bath. Josh felt indignation: Georgia wasn't being fair. She was unreasonable. She—

"Planning to sit there all night?" Ruthanne demanded, pulling open his truck door.

"No. And I hope you aren't going to make a lot of noise and wisecracks."

Ruthanne clucked her tongue. "Someone's feeling grumpy..."

"Let's get this done."

After collecting their gear from the van, they entered the Katschke house through the side door. This opened into a mud room and then a huge kitchen/laundry, both spaces looking unchanged since 1940. A back stairway led up to an empty, cavernous room with gray-flowered wallpaper. "A dance studio?" Archie suggested.

Ruthanne shook her head. "A dormitory. I did some research on the house. The family who lived here before the Katschkes had twenty-one children."

"Jeez," Archie said. "What happened to them?"

"The children grew up and moved away. The parents lived into their eighties."

A tour of the older section revealed another big bedroom upstairs and two smaller ones plus a bath. On the main floor, a living room and a dining room faced a hall leading to a screen porch. Standing in the hallway, Josh said, "One bathroom for all these rooms."

"Plus an outhouse," Archie concluded. "You know, it wouldn't be hard to put in more bathrooms, and those big rooms could be subdivided."

"If the de Salis cousins move in, you might pick up some work," Josh said.

A loud thump from the living room sent the ghost hunters rushing in to look for the source. Ruthanne spotted a glass paperweight on the floor. While she inspected it, Archie reached into his duffle to unload equipment, handing Josh an EMF detector and an IR thermometer. He set a recorder on the end table by the couch, then pulled out the camera for himself.

"Don't I get anything?" Ruthanne asked.

"You can get the lights," Archie said.

Ruthanne flounced toward the wall switch. Josh told Archie, "Give her the K-II. If she hears anything, we might get visual confirmation."

While they waited for their eyes to adjust to the darkness, Archie coached Ruthanne on the meter used to detect magnetic fields. "If the lights turn on in response to questions, a spirit could be answering. Keep your finger on the power button. Oh, and make sure your cell phone's off."

Ruthanne stood by the couch next to Josh, while Archie settled into one of two armchairs across the coffee table. Josh switched on the audio recorder. He said, "Mr. Katschke, if you're here, please make your presence known."

They waited.

Archie whispered to Ruthanne, "Hearing anything?" She shook her head and shoved the K-II at Josh. "It hurts my thumb to keep it switched on, and it's distracting. Think I'll try my 3-D glasses."

Ruthanne circled the room, looking at things but not touching them. She wrinkled her nose at the dust on the furniture. "Place needs cleaning." Whirling suddenly, she exclaimed, "In your *dreams*."

"What?" Josh and Archie said together.

"He told me he'd like a French maid—someone with a cute ass." Ruthanne made a face.

Archie whispered, "Where did you hear the voice?"

"There—opposite you." Ruthanne felt around the other armchair. "Oh, the air here is chilly, like opening the door to a fridge."

Josh stood and reached across the table with the IR thermometer to probe at the chair seat. "Huh. Three degrees colder than the room."

Ruthanne giggled. "He said, 'Watch it, sonny. You're getting personal with that thing.'"

Josh drew back. Ruthanne spoke to the ghost. "Mr. Katschke, we've come to talk about your house and about what you might have seen last week. We're not here to make you go away." She filled him in on the situation since his death, then proposed he take on vampire roommates.

In the silence following, Archie said, "We need to get something recorded. From here, it looks like you're talking to an empty chair."

"Oh, right," Ruthanne said. "Josh, hand me the colored-light thingy."

He gave her the meter and spoke to the unseen spirit. "Wave your hand twice for yes, once for no." Josh cleared his throat, then asked, "Are you Emil Katschke?" The K-II flashed twice.

"Sweet," said Archie. "Could you do that again?"

Two more flashes. A pause. Two more flashes.

"Lower the temperature by the chair," Josh said. He gave the thermometer to Archie, who announced, "Temperature dropped another two degrees."

Ruthanne sat on the couch, leaning forward toward the chair. "About these vampires," she continued, "they're pranics, who feed on life energy. Since you're dead, they wouldn't be a problem for you. They're all young men, so you'd have kind of a fraternity house going." She paused, listening. "Oh, sex is their preferred feeding method." With a smirk, she faced Josh and Archie. "*Now*, we have his attention."

The K-II meter flashed and kept flashing. "So, how about you meet the guys and decide if they're okay?" Two flashes. Ruthanne sat back, looking satisfied.

Josh said, "Ask him about the fairy murder."

"Ask him yourself," Ruthanne countered, taking off her silly glasses to rub the bridge of her nose. "He can hear you."

Josh related what he knew about Sedge's death, then waited for Ruthanne to interpret. She reported Katschke didn't know anything. Disappointed, Josh pursed his lips.

"But he thinks Carl Beckett might," Ruthanne added.

"*Carl Beckett*?" Josh squeaked. "Georgia's father?"

"Mmm. He likes to toss a few horseshoes in the backyard at the farm now and again, Emil says. Emil's gone to get him."

"Temperature's normal in the chair," Archie observed. "Hand me the EMF meter."

Josh did, watching Archie count off the needle's steady rise. "Okay," Archie said eagerly, "looks like we've got another customer."

Ruthanne nodded. "It's Mr. Beckett. He said, 'Tell Josh he'd better treat my little girl right'—big exclamation point after the *right*, Joshie."

"I am, sir." Josh pulled his shoulders back. "Leastways, I'm trying to. She's mad at me just now, and she's so stubborn."

"Because she loves you," Ruthanne translated.

"You're making that up. Carl Beckett wouldn't say that."

"Oh, no? Mr. Beckett, wave your hand at this box I'm holding, two times, please."

Two flashes. Josh sagged against the couch, stunned.

After Ruthanne asked about Sedge, she listened for a long time, then her mouth dropped open. Archie tried to get her to answer his questions, but she waved him off with a "Shush!" Finally, she said to the chair, "Thank you. I guess you've given us what we need to know. I'll pass on your messages to your family. Take care.

"He's gone," she told Josh and Archie.

"And…?" Archie asked.

Ruthanne went to the wall to turn on the lights. She blinked and said, "Tink Withers killed the Red fairy."

CHAPTER TWENTY-THREE

"**I** can't arrest Tink Withers on some lame-ass tip from a ghost," Ed Brown said flatly.

"Look, Ed," Josh said, "Tink's dangerous. She tortured and beat Sedge to death. She can't be allowed to run around loose."

"We don't know that for sure, and she's not exactly runnin' around loose," Ed replied. "She's bein', uh, supervised."

"How?"

"Tom's with her. She asked him to dinner in Goreton."

Josh leaned back against his truck's seat. "Old Tom has the worst luck with women," he choked out. "First, he goes after Cissy, now Tink." He started to chuckle, and then burst into laughter.

Ruthanne reached in through the window to take the phone from Josh's hand. "Ed, it's me. Carl Beckett saw the fairy murder. He—" Ruthanne paused to listen, frown lines deepening at the corners of her mouth. "Yes, of course, I know Carl died, and no, I don't still have a grudge against Tom."

Josh reclaimed his phone. "At least, search Tink's house," he argued. "Look for evidence."

Ed told him, "To get a search warrant, I gotta call a judge in Goreton. It's pushing on eleven. He'll think I'm nuts, and cuss me out for disturbing him. What's the probable cause? There's nothing on the books about fairies. Like I said before, they ain't people."

"Vandalism and property destruction," Josh suggested. "Georgia's electric fence was cut."

"Even if I believed you—and that's saying a lot—there's no reason to go after vandalism evidence in the middle of the night."

"You know we're talking about more than vandalism. The murder was gruesome, sick. And even if you don't care about Sedge, the fairies do. Without his shirt, his spear and his wing, he can't go on to the, uh, the Happy Hunting Grounds—"

"That's the Otherworld," Ruthanne corrected.

"Whatever," Josh said, scowling at her. "The fairies won't forgive us if we don't find Sedge's personal effects. Who knows what they'll do? Elvirans might be redheads forever or the fairies could stonewall the mayor's tourist plan and make a lot of *people* unhappy."

Silence. Ed exhaled heavily, then said, "All right. I s'pose I can give Tom a call, tell him something's not on the up and up. I'll see if he can find out where Tink was on the night the old Red guy died. I'll get back to you." He clicked off.

"You hit a hot button when you reminded him about the red hair," Ruthanne told Josh. "Ed's so proud he married a natural blonde."

"He's not going to help us much, though," Josh concluded sourly. He opened his door, swiveling to face Archie and Ruthanne so he could bring them up to speed. After the recap, he asked, "So...so what do we do?"

"I say we break into the Withers' house and search Tink's bedroom," said Archie.

"The stuff's not there," Josh realized, shaking his head. "Have you ever tried to hide anything in your bedroom that your mother *didn't* find?"

Archie grinned sheepishly. "My mother found weed in my closet, porn under my bed, and condoms in my underwear drawer when she wasn't even looking for those things. She decided to clean the closet, shampoo the carpet, and put away laundry."

"What's wrong with condoms?" Ruthanne asked.

"I was thirteen."

"Oh. Well, you've made Josh's case. Now, if I were Tink, I'd have a hidey hole in the garage. Two women living together never clean their garage. I should know. I have to muscle junk out of the way every fall when I want to make space for my car before the snow flies."

"Have we all taken stupid pills? We're not burglars," Josh said. "And even if rifling through a garage in the dark weren't the dumbest plan in the universe, we'd never pull it off with Mrs. Withers in the house."

"Wait—let me see if she's there." Ruthanne closed her eyes. Seconds later, she squeezed them tighter. She stayed that way for a good minute before looking at Josh and Archie. "I can't find her," Ruthanne confessed. "I don't know why, unless she's outside Elvira. Even farther away, I usually get *something*, if only a close-up of the person's face. I never tried looking in on Mrs. Withers before, but she shouldn't be different from everyone else."

"Check on Tink," Archie said.

Ruthanne had no luck finding Tink, either. "I don't understand it! She's supposed to be in Goreton, only ten miles away. I draw a blank when I try to see her."

"Get in." Josh reached for the handle of his passenger door. "Arch, follow in the van. We're going to the Withers' house."

"We need reinforcements," Ruthanne said. "There's something altogether too weird about those women. I'm calling Anton."

Ruthanne was baffled when de Salis politely but firmly declined her invitation to burglary. "I can't understand it. It'd do him good to get out. He closed the clubs until the weekend. All he's doing is brooding in his house. And besides, this would be an opportunity for us to know each other better. He's attracted to me," she confided to Josh.

He pulled the truck to a stop at the corner of the dead-end street. "Ruthie, mosquitoes are attracted to you pretty much for the same reason."

"A lot you know," she huffed. "I've had *scores* of men after me."

"Yeah, the grocery checkout line gets kinda long before holidays."

"You have no eye for beauty," Ruthanne declared, "except for Georgia. I don't know what she sees in you." Ruthanne looked over her shoulder toward Archie's van pulling up behind them, and then threw open her door.

Josh caught her arm. "There are lights at the Withers' house. I'll cruise the street, see what's up. You two go around the block to park by the grade school. If Tink's Jeep is in the driveway, or if it looks like Mrs. Withers went to bed, I'll join you."

"What if she's awake and she sees you?"

"Then I'll stop to talk with her. I want to ask her a question."

Freed from Ruthanne, Josh crept down the street with his headlights off. The porch light was on at the Withers' house, and so was a lamp in the living room. Josh scanned the driveway, spotting only a Toyota parked in front of the detached garage. When he looked back at the house, he saw Mrs. Withers peering out the window.

All right. Josh steeled himself, parked, and left the truck. He picked his way over the uneven stone walkway, then stood on the step and rang the bell. Mrs. Withers answered in an instant.

"Joshua?" she said cautiously. "It's a bit late for a visit. Silverbelle's gone out for the evening."

"I know it's late, ma'am, and I'm sorry. I wouldn't have bothered you if I your lights were off."

"I'm a night owl," Mrs. Withers said. "Do my best work around midnight, but I usually don't entertain at this hour." She drew back and waited.

Josh took a deep breath. "I'm betting you know how Sedge's wing got to my place."

Mrs. Withers lowered her eyelids. "Come in." As Josh did, she muttered, "You always were a clever boy, Joshua."

She didn't ask him to sit, so Josh stood facing her, saying, "You put it there. Anyone else would have thrown the wing away. You knew it was important, but you didn't give it to the police. Why?"

Mrs. Withers held out her hands. "I couldn't think of what else to do. You told me of Sedge's murder. I knew the Red fairies would be furious, and I didn't want them turning against me. I've always been closer to the

Greens. I feared the Reds would suspect I'd been involved in his death."

"You weren't?"

"No! How could you even think that? The fairies are treasures. They're...they're my life."

Josh let out the breath he hadn't realized he'd been holding. "Okay. I'm really glad to hear it," he said honestly, "but tell me how you came by the wing."

Rubbing her forehead, Mrs. Withers recalled, "I found it lying on my driveway. After getting over the shock, I decided someone wanted to incriminate or to taunt me. Everyone knows how attached to the fairies I am."

"Did you check around for Sedge's copper shirt and spear?"

She nodded. "I went over every inch of the yard."

"How about the garage?"

"It's crammed with Silverbelle's boxes from college. I never go in there."

Josh was about to suggest a search when he jumped, startled by a crash and the sound of glass breaking. Mrs. Withers shot into the kitchen, pulled a flashlight from a drawer, and flipped on the light switch by the side door. "Come with me," she called over her shoulder. "We'll catch them this time. Damned kids keep trying to steal beer from my garage fridge."

Outside, Josh's heart sank. There stood Archie, hunched like a stage villain, fumbling with something on the ground. Under the glare of Mrs. Withers' flashlight, he straightened his body but grinned crookedly.

"Archibald Ferguson!" Mrs. Withers cried in her schoolteacher's voice. "You are too old to be stealing beer. You can buy your own."

"Uh, yeah, uh," was Archie's eloquent response.

"And who's that?" Mrs. Withers aimed the beam toward the ground to reveal Ruthanne, tangled in electric cord, smashed Christmas lights littering the grass around her. "*Ruthanne Quinn*?" Mrs. Withers marched over to where Ruthanne worked herself loose from the cord. "Goodness, are you all right?"

"Guess so," Ruthanne mumbled, standing and brushing bits of colored glass from her clothing.

"Well, then, you should be ashamed of yourself. Stealing! I don't know what your poor grandmother will say."

"Mrs. Withers, I'm twenty-nine years old, so my grandmother isn't responsible for me. I'm sorry I pulled down the Christmas lights on your garage. I can pay for new ones and someone to hang them."

"What on earth were you thinking?" Mrs. Withers' gaze swept from Ruthanne to Archie.

"It's not the way it looks," Archie began, flashing his winning smile, the one that always made girls wriggle and shove out their chests. "It's...well, we're, uh..." He looked at Josh.

So did Mrs. Withers. "There's something more going on here," she accused as she strode toward him. "First, you stop by so late, then these two clumsy burglars turn up. What are you really after?" Whirling, she pointed a finger at Archie.

White roots burst from Archie's shoelaces to snake toward the ground. From the neck and sleeves of his tee shirt, slender stalks emerged and sprouted leaves. The stalks thickened, twining around his neck and arms, then branched and flowered before the petals dropped away, leaving oblong bolls that darkened until they burst into white puffs. In less than a minute, Archie's head and upper body were covered in cotton. Only his terrified eyes and mouth were clear of it.

"Speak truth!" Mrs. Withers commanded.

"We're looking for Sedge's stuff," Archie choked out before sneezing fluff away from his nose. His shoulders thrashed helplessly.

Turning to Josh, Mrs. Withers hissed, "You knew. You were *certain* I'd found the wing before you came here. This has all been a setup."

"Yes, ma'am," Josh admitted. "We did know."

"But *how*?"

"A ghost gave us the heads up. Could you let Archie go, please?"

With an open-handed wave across her body, Mrs. Withers made the cotton plant disappear. "I don't believe in ghosts," she told Josh.

"Most people don't believe in fairy magic, but we just saw you do some. I'm impressed."

"Why? You could call fairies when you were a grade schooler."

"It was just coincidence fairies showed up to stop Tommy from pounding me that day," Josh said. "And speak of the devil...."

Crammed inside his mother's red Beetle, Tom pulled into the driveway. He got out slowly, extracting his bulk like a contortionist unwinding from a cage. He said, "Mrs. Withers, is Tink, I mean Silverbelle, here?"

"No. Isn't she with you?"

"We had a...a misunderstanding. She left. I thought she'd go home." Eyeing the others, Tom frowned, asking, "Are you having a party?"

"Joshua and his friends believe Sedge's belongings might be in my garage."

"Sedge?"

"The murdered Red fairy."

"Why do you think his stuff would be here?" Tom asked Josh.

"Mrs. Withers found Sedge's wing on her driveway. The murderer might have stashed other trophies nearby. Didn't Ed call you?"

"My phone battery's dead. Mind if I have a look?"

Mrs. Withers led him to the garage. Tom heaved up the door so hard the springs thrummed.

An old refrigerator stood against the right-hand wall. The rest of the space was filled with boxes, furniture, tools and whatnot. "Silverbelle rented an apartment in Providence," Mrs. Withers explained. "She had a complete household. She hasn't sorted through everything yet."

"Man!" Tom complained, wrinkling his nose, "What *is* that smell? It's like something died in here."

"That's possible," Mrs. Withers said. "I suppose animals get in from time to time."

Along with the others, she stepped forward to watch Tom wedge his huge body into the narrow aisle between containers. About midway, he could go no further. With a frustrated scowl, Tom said, "Look, I'll have to move some of these things to get past this point."

"Back up and let me by," Ruthanne said. "I'm small enough. You'll have to guide me, though. I don't smell anything."

"You're not a wolf," Tom said.

"True. Say, there aren't any female wolves. That's discrimination."

"It keeps things simple. Let a bunch of women into the lodge, and they'd hang lacy curtains in the windows."

Ruthanne sputtered, "That is the most insulting—"

"And it rules out mating," Tom interrupted, silencing her. He pointed toward the back left corner of the garage. "Check there."

For once, Ruthanne did as told without quibbling. "Yeah, I'm starting to smell it now," she reported after some forward progress. She slipped between an armchair and an ironing board. "Must be near here. Phew! Really stinks." Disappearing from view when she bent to inspect something, a minute later, her head shot up and she wailed, "Oooh, yuck, eww!" and bolted. Scrambling through the chaos, she fled the garage to stand outside sucking in long breaths, ignoring the chorus of questions around her until she pulled herself together and announced, "There's a little *arm* in there—an arm, a wing, and part of a shoulder. It's...oh, ick," she moaned, grimacing horribly. "It's all rotting."

Tom, Josh and Archie shoved Tink's goods aside, carving a wider path for themselves. Josh reached the spot where Ruthanne freaked out. On the floor, he saw a tarp lying in a heap. Near it stood an open-topped cardboard box lined with plastic. The plastic covered a crumpled wing and the miniature arm and shoulder, now bloated, discolored, ghastly. The edge of the shoulder was green, but not from decay. A scrap of cloth clung to the flesh. The wing pattern was undoubtedly Reed's.

Fighting the urge to vomit, Josh forced his eyes past the arm, reaching for the plastic layer, wondering if more lay beneath.

Tom was tall enough to peer over the back row of cartons. "Don't handle anything inside the box," he warned. "Bring the whole thing out so we can get a good look at it under the light. Then, we phone Ed."

Mrs. Withers turned so pale when she saw the carnage that Ruthanne took her inside the house. Ruthanne returned with a pair of rubber gloves and gave them to Tom, who inspected the contents of the box. There was nothing below the visible layer.

Tom seemed to be struggling with the fact he'd found part of the fairy who wounded him. "I don't get it," he said, stripping off the gloves to rub his gray forearm. "How can the Green fairy who, uh, got bit, be here?"

Headlights flashed up the driveway. Josh expected to see Archie in the van, which he'd gone to the school lot to get, but it was Ed's cruiser. Striding toward the box, Ed stared inside, curled his lip, and stood back. He said to Tom, "Nothin's right about this. At the station, Bucky— Bucky Niemayer's been doing night dispatch," Ed informed the others, "reminded me of things that don't make sense. Since the ruckus at the compound, he's been mulling over how a fairy could tangle with a wolf.

"First off, says Bucky, no wolf could catch a fairy who wanted to escape. It's like dogs and squirrels. They chase 'em, but they never catch 'em.

"To his way of thinking, the fairy had to be laying for a wolf, but he'd be crazy to take on the whole pack; he'd need to get one alone. That wouldn't be likely on cub initiation night, so why pick that moon? With all the hoopla, it'd be a piss-poor time for an ambush."

"I had a flat. That slowed me down," Tom recalled. "I was last to arrive."

"So, let's say the fairy saw his chance. Now, you had to be human to drive. Alls the fairy need do is nick you with the sword when you was gettin' out of the car, but no, he waits till you're shaggy, then faces you down, slicing your paw instead of your throat. That's nuts. Whether he was scared or set on taking you out, he'd aim for those jaws, I reckon."

"It could have been something about honor," Josh put in. "There's no glory in stabbing a man's back. Could be he didn't want a man—it had to be a wolf. Slashing the arm might have been mistake or panic."

"Maybe," Ed allowed, "but there's more that don't add up. The fairy lost a lot of his body including one wing. On top of that, his neck was broke, but he somehow flew all the way from where he attacked Tom to the road. How'd he do that?"

"Don't forget the sword," Josh said. "We never did find it. Even a dying fairy would hang onto his sword; their weapons are that important to them."

"But the corker is this," Ed continued, "Tom was a man when we found him. When Bucky was run over by the truck, he stayed a wolf till morning. He's said time and again that if he'd been human, someone might have stopped and called for an ambulance, but an animal got passed by. My brother Earl stayed a wolf even when the hunters skinned him. A wolf stays a wolf until the moon's set."

Everyone looked at Tom. "There's a way to turn back for one night," he said. "Only the Alphas know the secret. It's complicated, so a human has to do it. Hurts the wolf like hell, can even kill him if it goes wrong."

"Well?" Ruthanne said.

"I'm not telling you how!" Tom said. "You're a blabbermouth."

"Fine, then. Keep your little secret." Ruthanne tugged on Tom's sleeve, leading him away from the house, whispering, "Just answer this: Does Tink know how do to it?"

"Tink?" Tom squinted at Ruthanne.

"Yes, you blockhead! *You* didn't kill the fairy because the part you supposedly munched is here—at her house, with her things. She killed him, left the rest of his body by the road, and then called the police."

"Tink didn't put Reed by the road," Josh said slowly, as the puzzle came together in his mind. "She had his body in a bag before Ed and I showed up. Tink didn't even have to wait until Tom turned wolf and face that danger. She stood by the tree where we found him, flagging him down before he reached the wolves' parking area. When he started to change, she used the sword on him, and he collapsed. She got scared he'd die, so she turned him human, knowing Goreton Hospital wouldn't treat a wolf, but they would treat a man. Finally, she parked his car with the others. Huh." Josh paused to reflect on what he'd said. "Some plan."

Tom looked thunderstruck. "I don't remember seeing Tink that night, but things get kind of fuzzy right before the moon rises. It's for sure I never told her the secret. How would she know what to do?"

"She's smart, really smart," Ruthanne reminded everyone. "She found a charm in a book to lure fairies to her. Why couldn't she find a way to make werewolves human? She knows how to do research—to *learn*." Ruthanne said to Josh, "We thought S. Withers on the library checkout slip meant Sylvia, her mother, but the *S* stands for Tink's real name—Silverbelle."

Turning to Tom, Ruthanne asked, "Why did you quarrel tonight?"

"None of your business."

"Look, I could give a damn about whatever you have going with Tink, but if she's angry, someone might get hurt. How did you piss her off?"

Tom scratched his head, looked down, and then turned up his palms. "I don't know. We talked about the old days, how we'd been close as kids. Then she told me she had a crush on me in middle school and high school. I kinda knew that, but I acted surprised.

"She said she hated being in Elvira, back where people made fun of her and her mother." Tom took a quick look at the open kitchen door. He lowered his voice. "She liked living in New England, and asked if I'd ever leave Elvira. I said no, I have a son. I won't abandon him. I'm here to stay, at least until Benji grows up."

Ruthanne closed her eyes. When she opened them, she reached out to grip both of Tom's arms, saying, "Benji's not with Georgia, and Georgia's in trouble. You've got to do something—fast!"

CHAPTER TWENTY-FOUR

Josh and Ruthanne reached Georgia's farmhouse with Tom only seconds behind, having mowed down half a dozen statues on Mrs. Withers' front lawn to get past Ed's cruiser. They found the back door standing open, and the house dark except for one light over the stairs leading up to the bedrooms.

The staircase looked like a huge, fuzzy snake had slithered toward the landing but stopped to digest an enormous meal. There was a lump in the middle of the coiling cotton plants grown from the stairway runner. The lump moved.

Josh and Tom collided, their shoulders too wide for the narrow staircase. Tom's football shove missed Josh, who'd already slipped past him to tear at twined stems over the lump. After three yanks, Josh spotted a pink nightgown. "It's Georgia."

"Get the crap off her face," Tom said, thundering toward Benji's bedroom.

As Josh worked frantically to uncover Georgia's head, Josh heard Tom bellow Benji's name, throw things around, and bellow again. He returned to stand over Josh, who stared at Georgia's closed eyes. Tom announced, "He's not there."

"Hiding," Josh said instantly. "Tell him it's okay to come out." Turning his head, Josh yelled to Ruthanne at the base of the stairs, "Call 911, then search the rest of the house for Benji."

Tom shouted, "Benji! It's Dad. You're safe." Only silence answered him. He rummaged through the other bedrooms before he inspected Georgia. "Shallow breathing. Irregular. Clear out," he ordered Josh.

"No!"

"Dammit, I know CPR. Lift her chest."

Josh shifted his legs to make room for Tom to kneel beside Georgia and tug on the fibers still binding her ribcage so he could slide one hand beneath her back. Tom tilted her head and pinched her nostrils. He covered Georgia's mouth with his, the movement smooth, practiced—*intimate*, to Josh's eyes. Tom laid his hand between Georgia's breasts.

A stab of primal outrage lanced through Josh, piercing his gut. Georgia wasn't Tom's anymore. "*I'll* do that," Josh husked, pushing a palm heel against Tom's shoulder.

He glanced up, shaking his head, and taking a breath. "Gotta get this right—Benji needs his ma. Come on, Red, *breathe*."

Josh's anger dissolved. Tom wasn't focused on Georgia; he was thinking about his son. The hand on her breasts rose. He pulled it away as Georgia gasped, then coughed.

Her eyelids flickered open. Confused, she looked from Josh to Tom. Remembrance flooded her eyes and she said, "Tink Withers took Benji. *Why?* What does she want with him?"

Tom looked like he'd been hit in the face with a baseball bat. He muttered, "I told her Benji kept me in Elvira."

"Oh, shit," Georgia moaned, struggling to sit up. "She always was jealous you married me instead of her. Maybe she never gave up hoping she'd win you in the end, but she forgot about Benji."

"This is my fault," Tom said. Guilt and fear warred for control of his features.

"This is *Tink's* fault," Josh said firmly. He supported Georgia's back as she sat up. "Tell us what happened."

"I heard noise downstairs, jumped out of bed, and saw her at the bottom of the stairs. She pointed, and the carpet *attacked* me. While I fought it, she came up the steps and said, 'Serves you right, you conniving bitch.' Then she went into Benji's room and...." Georgia squeezed her eyes shut.

She inhaled deeply, let the air out, opened her eyes and went on.

"Benji screamed for me. I could hear him fighting her—then she slapped him. She *slapped* my baby." Georgia's features twisted with rage, then settled into anguished pride. "Benji didn't give up. He must have slipped away from her because she started swearing at him. Next, she told him she'd kill me if he didn't go with her, and it was silent in his bedroom.

"I didn't see them leave. This stuff covered my face by then. But I could hear Benji cry, 'Mama! Mama!' His voice got fainter, and then I couldn't hear him." Tears pouring down her cheeks, Georgia hissed, "Get this mess off me. I'm going to find that monster and deck her—*kill* her if she harms my boy."

Tom stood up. "I'll find her. I'll go to every place we ever went as kids, every place she ever mentioned. I'll—" He didn't finish the sentence, but dashed down the stairs and out the door.

Josh tore away the last of the cotton cocoon. "There's an ambulance coming."

"I don't need an ambulance," Georgia snarled, rising to her feet. Josh steadied her when she wobbled. "I need Benji. We have to find him."

Find him… Josh remembered Ruthanne. *Where the hell was she?*

In the kitchen, Ruthann greeted the paramedic, who reached the foot of the stairs, looked up, and gaped. Georgia said, "I'm okay. Don't need you. Sorry," then she slipped into her bedroom and shut the door.

"What happened here?" Tony Benetto asked.

Josh descended the stairs to tell his former classmate, "Fairy magic."

"*Fairies* did this?"

"No, Tink Withers. She has the Gift."

"Always believed the Gift was a story," Tony said.

"It's not. Tink used magic to trap Georgia and kidnap Benji."

Josh pulled out his phone to call Ed but put the phone away when Ed came through the door.

Eying the stairs, Ed whistled, then said, "That's a piece of work." He turned to Josh. "Ruthanne filled me in over the phone. Bucky put out a BOLO on Tink and an Amber Alert on Benji. Got the judge working on warrants for battery, kidnapping, and attempted murder. The sheriff's department, the state police, the Goreton force plus all the rent-a-cops I have on file for weekend work have been called in. Your pal Archie's volunteered, too. If you're sure Georgia's okay, I need to get those guys organized." Ed turned to leave. Tony Benetto followed him through the door.

Georgia came out of her room dressed in jeans and a flannel shirt, curling her lip as she skirted the debris on the stairs. "Let's go," she said. Then her face fell. "I don't know *where* to go, where to start looking for Benji."

"I've been trying to picture him in my mind," said Ruthanne, "trying to get a fix on his location, but all I see is darkness."

"Oh, no!" Georgia moaned. "Benji's afraid of the dark. He's—" She turned away, swiping at her eyes. Then she whirled to face Josh and Ruthanne. "What if she's put him under ground, in some hole or grave, like those people who were buried in coffins with only an air hose? *My God.*"

"Tink hasn't had time to do anything elaborate," Josh reassured her, praying he was right. "I don't think she intended to kidnap Benji before tonight. She got mad at Tom, and acted on impulse. She'll have to figure out what to do.

"Ruthie, I have an idea of how you can see more." Josh pulled out his phone, pressed a key, and waited. He said, "Uh, hey. It's Josh Seldom. Benji Hanrahan's been kidnapped, and we need your help to find him." He listened. "Great. We'll be there in a few minutes."

Anton greeted them at the door of what had been Bobbi Miller's house. He wore a thick, white terry robe, a monogrammed dS on the pocket. He looked weary.

"I was soaking in the hot tub," Anton said as he invited them in.

Josh felt a twinge of dread, not about Anton, but about the house. He shrugged off the feeling; there were more important things to worry about than a nasty spirit in the basement.

The last time Josh entered the living room, he saw flowery couches and gingham armchairs. Anton's taste ran to antiques, not the heavily carved Victorian stuff that still cluttered a lot of old Elviran houses, but lighter woods with slimmer proportions. The chair Josh chose was upholstered in pale blue silk.

"How can I help you?" Anton asked, taking a place on the facing loveseat.

"We need help finding Georgia's son. Ruthanne's psychic abilities can't pin him down. I'm thinking you could get more if you tasted a drop of Ruthanne's blood—you could read it or something, like you did mine when the fairies thought I'd killed Sedge."

Anton rubbed his mouth. "Unwise."

"Please," Georgia begged, "if there's anything you can do to save my baby, please, *please* do it."

"It would mean harming Ruthanne," Anton said slowly. "I don't want to do that, and I can't, according to my agreement with the authorities here."

"A drop of blood? No biggie," Ruthanne scoffed.

"Blood only tells me about a person's emotions. To connect with your mind, I'd have to take some of your life essence, and this is not a good time. I'm...fighting hunger." Looking at Josh, Anton said, "I didn't shake hands when you entered my home for a reason: After centuries of managing hunger, it can still get the best of me." Anton dropped both hands to his knees, tapping the fingers against them, his body rocking restlessly.

"You're afraid you might not be able to stop," Josh concluded. "What if I agreed to clobber you if you didn't?"

Anton shook his head. "I'd retaliate by reflex, use too much force." He wrapped his arms across his chest, hands clutching forearms as though he need to hang onto something. "This is embarrassing. I know better than to let myself get this way, but with all that's happened...."

"How much?" Ruthanne asked. "How much of this life force would you take?"

"Minutes, hours, even days of your life."

Ruthanne raised an eyebrow and ran her fingers across her forehead. She asked, "Would I get vamped?"

"No, though you'd absorb some of my memories. There is reciprocity, up to a point."

"And if you didn't stop?"

"You'd shrivel and die."

The room went silent as everyone but Anton traded looks, then Georgia said, "If it'll help, take my energy, then, uh, mind-meld with Ruthanne."

"This isn't *Star Trek*. This is for real," Anton warned.

"Nothing is more real to me than rescuing my son. I'd die for him."

"You can tap me, too," Josh offered. "In fact, tap me first. Leave Georgia be."

Ruthanne stood, saying firmly, "We're wasting time, and this is *my* vampire experience. Nobody's going to spoil it." She went to the love seat, shooing Anton over with an impatient flick of the wrist. "I trust you," she said to his worried eyes, "but just in case, Josh, get ready to pick up the chair you're sitting on."

"Careful! That's a Louis Quinze," Anton said.

"If you turn beast, Josh will hit you with your lovely Louie Cans chair, then use it like a lion tamer. Now, get to it." She lifted her braid off her neck, closed her eyes, and leaned against the loveseat's backrest.

"All I have to do is touch your hand," Anton said.

Ruthanne opened one eye. "No way. It's got to be a fabulously sensual kiss to the neck so I can write this up in my next book. I can't have the sexy vampire hold the heroine's *hand*."

Anton looked amused. "You want a love scene?"

"Hell, yes." Ruthanne tapped the place where her neck and shoulder met. "Lay one on me, just here. That's a sweet spot."

Anton rubbed his mouth, and then reached tentative fingers toward Ruthanne, turning her head toward him. "Open your eyes," he murmured, his voice sounding different, deeper. He held her gaze for a long moment before he leaned across her and lowered his dark head into the curve of her throat.

Ruthanne's eyes closed and her shoulder twitched. Her body went rigid before it started into something like pole-dancer's shimmy. As she writhed, one of her legs rode against Anton's calf. She moaned.

Josh stood, ready to heave the chair at Anton, but he looked toward Georgia for confirmation. Georgia's face was flushed. Her glazed eyes were riveted on Anton. "Omygod," she breathed. "The man has *great* hands."

Josh sat down and studied exactly what Anton did. His left hand stroked Ruthanne's hair or cupped her face while his right caressed her shoulder, then moved down her arm, stroking, circling, gripping the flesh eagerly yet gently, as though it were a precious discovery. His fingers followed the curve of her hip, the arc of her thigh. He didn't raise his head from the side of her throat, although he turned his face, lips savoring cheek and earlobe. The movements were subtle, confident, and erotic as hell, though nothing he did would have made the cut in a porno flick. There was a sort of elegant choreography to it all, as though he'd done this a thousand times.

He probably *had* done this a thousand times, Josh realized, but the night was getting away from them. Anton must stop, and it looked like no one but Josh could stop him.

He didn't really want to use the chair, didn't think he'd need it. Instead, Josh jumped to his feet and clapped his hands sharply, shouting, "Time out. Stop!"

Anton turned his head, eyes flashing fury, eyes gone black. His body tensed. He snarled—and Josh seized the chair.

Then, in a heartbeat, it was over. Anton shut his eyelids and held them closed. Ruthanne whimpered. Anton rose from the loveseat to stride toward the window where he stood, hands clasped behind his back.

Ruthanne stirred. She opened her eyes languidly, catlike. She whispered, "Wow. Just...wow."

"Hope you don't write those words in your book, Ruthie," Josh said.

As he expected, a wisecrack brought back the everyday Ruthanne.

She felt around her face. "Do I look different? Is there a white streak in my hair?"

"You look fine," Georgia said. "In fact, you've never looked better. Your skin...it has this pearly glow."

Ruthanne shook out her wrists and wiggled her feet. "I'm kind of pins-and-needley, and my heart's going a mile a minute. Where's Anton?" Josh pointed toward the window. "Come back," Ruthanne called.

He did, sitting apart from her, saying, "That went better than I expected."

Ruthanne looked indignant. "What do you mean?"

Anton smiled, turning to face her. "It means I didn't take much from you. You have an incredible richness of energy. It's—" He shook his head, looking like he wanted to lick his lips but was too refined to do it. "There's no way to describe how you taste."

"Cheesecake," Josh suggested. "A little bit goes a long way."

"What did you sense from Ruthanne?" Georgia asked urgently.

"Dampness. She—"

"Hey! You don't have to talk about that," Ruthanne objected.

Anton laughed. "I refer to your vision of Benji. You sensed darkness as well as dampness of two sorts: fresh water and a mustier smell, as though water passed through earth or..." He fingered his chin. "Or rock. Yes, rock. Also the scent of dry wood. The boy is near those elements."

Georgia shot to her feet. "The waterfall cave at Fern Cliffe. Josh, you know it."

"The one the fairies don't want us to visit because it's special to them?"

"Yes. Tink would figure none of us could go there, and since she can control fairies, she'd get no trouble from them. Come on, come on. Let's go." Georgia gripped Josh's arm.

"Wait. There are other caves along the river both north and south of the Egyptian complex. They fit the description, too."

"The *piasa caves*?" Georgia choked out.

Josh asked Anton, "Can you and your people search the river areas?"

"I can't leave the house. It's started to rain."

Everyone stared at Anton. "Moving water paralyzes my kind, but the Mayans are unaffected by the curse," Anton explained. "I'll call Suarez at his club." He plucked his phone from his pocket.

"Remind Mr. Suarez my sister, Vanny Beckett, works for him," Georgia put in.

"Indeed? I met her today." Anton held up a hand. He said to the phone, "Suarez, there's a problem in Elvira. A boy's been kidnapped. He's the nephew of your employee, Vanny Beckett. We think the child's in a cave, but there are many caves around Elvira. None of my people can function in the rain. If you sent a man to hunt along the river—"

"South of the Egyptians," Josh prompted.

"South of the Egyptian temple, that would be most helpful. Send someone reliable and well-fed."

Georgia's face went grim. "Vanny must go to make sure Benji doesn't end up a vampire nibble."

Anton looked pained by what he heard on the phone. "Let's skip on past the insults about pranic weakness, shall we?" He rolled his eyes. "The boy's in danger. Vanny's friend, Megan Shaw, has my nephew's car. They could use its speed to shorten the drive time." He waited, nodded, and clicked off. "He's arranging things now."

"I should call my mother," Georgia said.

"She can't help, and she'd worry herself sick," Josh said. "Call Ed, instead, once we get on the road. He'll tell Tom and the others to concentrate on the river caves north of the Egyptians. Anton, thank you. Ruthanne, are you ready?"

"I think I'll stay here. With Anton's help," she gazed at *him* like a nibble, "I might see more."

"No. You're not safe alone with me, not tonight, at any rate. You must go."

"Sheesh," Ruthanne said as she climbed into Josh's truck. "Vampires are so fickle. One minute, they can't get enough of you—"

"And the next," Josh cut in, "they're fed up."

Ruthanne grimaced. "At least you didn't have to destroy Anton's precious Louis Quinze fauteuil chair." Her hand flew up to her mouth. "Did I say that? I did! All of a sudden, I know a lot more about history." She rubbed her hands together. "Regency romances, here I come."

CHAPTER TWENTY-FIVE

Vanny texted Megan to come right away. She took the passenger seat in Fadri's Ferrari after Paco crammed himself into the back.

"Why would that bitch Tink Withers do something like this?" Vanny raged. "I mean is she so hard up for guys she has to obsess over *Tom*?"

Making a U-turn, Megan concluded, "Some people don't know when to quit. It's the fatal attraction thing."

"God," Vanny prayed, "please, please don't let this come out like the movie, don't anything really bad happen to Benji. He's just a little kid, a sweet, adorable, little kid. Please...."

Paco reached forward to pat Vanny's shoulder. "We will find the *niño*. Do not fear, *hermanita*. There is no nose better than Paco's."

"What else did Georgia say to look for?" Megan asked.

"Um, fresh water, musty water, rock, dry wood. Omygod!" Vanny cried. "You don't think she's going to start a fire someplace?"

"It means...it could mean many things," Paco said. "The wood is a good clue. Along the river, there is much fresh water and wet rock in this rain. Dry wood will be a rarer scent."

Megan drove away from the town and turned west onto Ryker Road, a dead-flat stretch between farms. "I've been practicing with this thing. Think I have the hang of it now. All right," she said with gritted teeth, "get ready for light speed to the river."

The Ferrari did what it was born to do. Vanny shut her eyes when the scenery blurred. Paco whooped. Megan concentrated on driving, gripping the wheel with white-knuckled hands. She didn't let up on the gas until they'd streaked over the crest of the hill leading down to the south bridge across the river. At that point, she clutched to coast, braking in time to make the turn onto the cliffside road. Pulling to the shoulder, she let the engine idle to cool and asked Paco, "Where to?"

"I must take the air outside." Vanny made way for him and stood watching Paco lift his head only to flinch as raindrops splashed his eyelashes. Shading his brow with a hand, he sniffed the wind until he pointed and said, "Over there, by the other bridge."

Going around to the driver's side, Paco said through Megan's window, "Leave the car here. We should make no more noise."

"Did you smell dried wood?" Megan asked after she parked.

"No. I smelled fear—and blood." Vanny whimpered and clutched Paco's arm. He squeezed her hand, telling her, "There is more fear than blood, a good sign. The child is alive."

"We should call the police," Megan said.

"Not yet. If the *puta* is there and feels trapped, she may think to throw the boy into the river so police look for him and let her get away. That is what I would do."

Vanny gasped. "Paco!"

He shrugged. "I am a vampire. We are very good at surviving. But," he said gravely, "I have taken no child for his blood. May that night never come."

They crept along, trying as best they could to stay in the moon shadows, but too often the rocks leaned away from the road, leaving them exposed to the view from above. The rain stopped, making the going easier. Vanny complained about their slow pace until Paco reminded her of dangers beyond the crazed kidnapper. Several times, he threw out a warning arm, halting the girls while he smelled the air. With a raised finger, he mouthed 'big birds' and then pointed upward.

Across the river, the Egyptian temple grew larger as they approached the bridge nearest to it. Paco thrust out his arm once more, jerking his chin toward yet another cave, but this time when he sampled the air, he said, "There is the place with the blood. A bird is in there, too."

Vanny couldn't help it; the horrified words burst from her lips, "Tink

Withers *fed* Benji to a piasa?"

Megan clapped a hand over Vanny's mouth and dragged her into a cleft in the rock face before Paco explained in a careful whisper, "No, *hermanita*. I am not smelling death, just fear and some blood. Both bird and human are in that cave. How this can be, I do not know."

"Could you handle a piasa?" Megan asked.

"I have never seen one. I cannot say."

"Vanny and I'd be no help. Piasas are too much for us." Megan's eyes went wide when she said, "Giants aren't afraid of them. Vanny, do you know any giants?"

"No, but Georgia does, sort of. She met some when she went to Giantville with Josh. He fixed a giant's monster truck. I'm calling him."

Vanny watched two giants cross the river in a speed boat. Livid with fury and terrified a piasa would attack or that Tink Withers, if she were in the cave, would panic and harm Benji, Vanny wanted to slug the guys when they tied off on a rock and hopped onto shore, casual as you please, like they were heading for a party.

She wagged a finger in their faces—or would have, if she could have reached higher—and sputtered, "Quiet! We're *sneaking up* on the cave."

"Giants don't sneak," said the taller of the two, who boomed at her in his normal voice, "and we don't have to be quiet. Nothing'll make a piasa leave her nest at night during hatching season." He stuck out a huge hand. "I'm Humph Thoon. This is my brother, Chris."

"Vanny, Megan and Paco," she returned, latching onto his fingertips, which were all that would fit in her hand. "We're not only worried about the birds. There could be a dangerous psycho in there. Didn't Josh explain this to you?"

The giants looked at each other and laughed. Humph said, "Any human in the cave would be warming the piasa's belly."

Vanny hissed, "My *nephew* could be in there."

Humph put his other foot in his mouth. "Not much chance he's alive, then."

"He's alive—someone's alive," said Paco.

"And how do you know that?" Humph challenged.

"I am a vampire."

Before he could go into his signature fang-display pose, Vanny elbowed Paco's ribs. "Not now." She asked the giants, "What are you here to do?"

"Chase off the piasa," said Chris.

"But your brother said—"

"They won't leave on their own," Humph cut in. "That doesn't mean we can't force 'em out. Chris, get the stuff."

While Chris returned to the boat, Humph peered up at the cave. "Nice ledge in front." He waved a hand at the others. "You little folks climb up the rock a ways so you can get in the cave after we say it's safe, but stay out of sight. When mama piasa comes out, she'll be angry.

"Oh, and you're not going to tell anybody about what we do. We don't want humans messing with the birds. We leave them alone unless it's an emergency like this." He muttered, "I hope the kid's okay. Sorry about what I said," and he strode off to take a giant's armload of dried branches from his brother, leaving Chris to climb the cliff behind him, lugging a gas can and a knapsack. Vanny, Megan and Paco found a spot on a sheltered slab of rock.

Ignoring a wuffing sound coming from the cave mouth, the giants went about setting wood on the ledge. As they worked, the noise from the cave grew louder, and gusts of air blew their hair back. While Humph put the last branches in place, Chris opened his knapsack to pull out a wad of cloth, which he wrapped around two long sticks. He poured liquid from a plastic bottle on these while Humph splashed gas on the firewood.

They separated, Chris going to the right side of the cave mouth, Humph to the left. Chris lit both torches, tossing one to his brother. Then the giants climbed into the cave.

Vanny held her breath. She glanced at Megan, who chewed her thumb. Paco didn't have breath to hold, but his hands were clamped together. They waited.

They heard the giants bellowing at the bird, and the bird's angry shrieks. Claws scraped, wings swished, the piasa's beak clacked. The light flared and dimmed as the giants' torches moved around. There were grunts and surprised yelps from the giants, and more than a little swearing.

Then a roar erupted from the cave. The sound was so loud Vanny jumped. She lost her footing and slid down gravel toward the river.

She didn't slide far. Her heel caught on something softer than rock, and she pitched forward. It took a second before she recognized the face of Shane Ryan scowling up at her.

"Hey! Off the threads," he said, shoving her away from his chest. "This is a new shirt. I just got it from Paige."

"I'll give you *threads*." Vanny grabbed the cloth at his throat. "If you're in this with Tink, I...I'll rip this thing apart and shove it down your throat."

Shane clamped a hand on Vanny's. "Flash," he said, prying her fingers loose. "I don't even know what a tink is." Shane looked down at the rumpled cloth and frowned. "Don't go all postal on me."

"What are you doing here?" Vanny demanded.

"A stakeout—at least, I planned on a stakeout until this cliff turned into Iraq. No chance Geb'll show up now."

"Geb?"

"Nefer's half-brother, the guy who stole from the temple. I remembered him bragging about being in a piasa cave and saying it'd be a great place to stash stuff he didn't want the other priests to find. This cave's closest to the Egyptians. Geb's lazy. I figure this is the one."

"So you've come to nab the goodies."

"Wrong. I plan to wait until Geb comes to nab the goodies. Tom Hanrahan will owe me one, and I'll have an in with the wolves."

Vanny frowned. "I thought you *were* a wolf."

"I lied. Nefer dumped me when she heard I wasn't a Louie, but I still might get in." Shane's face brightened. "Tom said so last weekend."

"Tom's son could be in that cave," Vanny told him. "If you want to make points with Alpha Louie, you should punt the Egyptian bit and help us save Benji."

"Hey, yeah," Shane agreed. "Great idea. What do I do?"

"After the giants evict the piasa, you can search the cave with us."

"Who's *we*?"

"Megan and Paco. Paco's a vampire."

"Cool. I haven't met one of those. I'm in."

Megan minced her way down the slippery rock. She gaped at Shane and asked him the same questions Vanny had. He said, "I'm not doing an instant replay."

"It's okay, Megsy. He's one of the good guys tonight," Vanny summarized.

Another roar from the cave, and this time, Megan stumbled toward Shane. He caught her before she could head-butt him, saying, "Jeez, if you girls are so hot for my body, I'll put you on my list." The smirk left his face when his jaw fell open at the sight of the piasa's head, neck and wings unfolding from the cave, stretching toward the river. The bird beat her wings once, twice, and the downdraft scattered the branches on the ledge. With a squawk exactly like a chicken—a chicken bigger than an SUV—she took off toward the Egyptian temple.

The giants came out of the cave, looking the worse for wear. Humph's shirt dangled from one shoulder. A gash crossed his chest. Chris had lost a hank of hair and his belt. He held up his cargo shorts with a clenched fist. Their faces were smug until they saw the piasa banking into a turn, wheeling toward her nest. Rushing to re-lay their firewood, Humph barely finished before Chris struck a match and tossed it on the pyre, watching it flare into life as fire blazed across the rocky ledge.

The piasa swooped in, then back winged, screeching. She swung left and right, desperate to find a way around the fire. She kept at it until she brushed flame with a wing tip. With a shrill cry, she flew over the top of the cliff.

Vanny scrambled up the rocks toward Chris, who stood in the

narrow space between fire and cave mouth. "Did you find Benji?"

Chris looked at her sadly. "I only saw a nest."

"He *must* be there. Paco said—" She spun around. "Where's Paco?"

Megan and Shane weren't far behind her. Megan said, "Paco took off. He smelled another human and thought it might be Tink. He went hunting for her."

"Well, he was wrong," Vanny said sourly. "It was Shaney here. His body spray smells like a girl's. Let me by," she told Chris. "I have to see for myself."

"Don't take too long. This fire won't last. Humph and I are heading up over the cliff to track the piasa, but we can't keep her out of the cave once the fire dies."

"I'm going in," Vanny called to Megan and Shane.

The interior of the cave was roughly twice the height of a standing piasa, but only a couple feet wider than a bird with its wings tucked in. No wonder the giants were able to keep her from crunching them; she had little room to maneuver. Drops of water rained from the ceiling, falling on Vanny's head, startling her. There were bones on the floor, here and there. She trod on one, and hop-stepped to keep from turning an ankle.

With only the firelight behind her, she couldn't see to the end of the cave. She felt her way along, one hand trailing against the right wall, turning slightly when the cave opened up to a larger space filled with withered tree branches piled about three feet high. Round, wider at the top than the bottom, the nest held two white eggs. The cave's rear wall arced behind it.

Vanny cupped her mouth and called, "Benji! Benji!" She heard a chirp by the nest, but the eggs weren't hatching. "Benji, where are you? It's Aunt Vanny."

Her heart jumped into her throat when she saw a little, blond head peek up over the far rim of the nest. Round eyes studied her. Benji didn't move.

"Benji, it's *me*. Can you come to me? I won't I'll fit back there."

His head disappeared. Vanny heard him working his way through sticks at the base of the nest. Then he stood before her, caked with grime, one knee stained dark red, his face pale and his eyes confused, but he was *alive*. Vanny crossed the distance between them and wrapped him in her arms, kissing his head, his face, hugging him fiercely. "Sweetie," she murmured, "I am so glad—*so* glad—to see you. Why didn't you tell the giants where you were?"

"I don't know the giants," Benji said.

Vanny looked at his knee, a bloody scrape covering most of it. "You're hurt!"

Benji touched the knee. "The big bird went away. I wanted to go home, and I climbed out of my hiding place, but it came back. I hid again. The rocks hurt my knee."

"Should I kiss it to make it better?"

"No," Benji whispered. "I wet my pants. I'm stinky."

"It's okay to wet your pants when you're really, really scared."

Benji pulled away muttering, "I couldn't help it. I had to *go*."

Vanny lifted his chin. "Of course, you did, and the silly, old bird forgot to put a bathroom in here."

Benji let out a tiny giggle. Vanny kissed his cheek. "I want my mommy," he said. "Where's my mommy?"

Vanny whipped out her phone and handed it to Benji. "She's looking for you. Soon as we get outside, we're going to call her to say hello. Then I'll take you home to her."

"Okay. Aunt Vanny, I'm hungry."

As she picked him up, Vanny knew Benji would be all right.

Standing by the cave entrance, Megan saw Vanny emerge from the darkness carrying Benji. "Hey! You found him. Woohoo!"

Benji waved at her. Megan heard a phone clatter to the floor and Benji say, "Oops."

"Don't worry," Vanny soothed. "I'll look for it later."

"Let me," Megan offered. "You two get going. The fire's losing it."

As Megan passed her, Vanny asked, "Where's Shane?"

"Somewhere inside. He's hunting for Egyptian objects. Didn't you see him?" Megan tousled Benji's hair. "Hey, tough stuff, glad to have you back."

"Shane better get his ass moving, or he'll be trapped—not that he'd be a big loss," Vanny tossed out as she stepped onto the ledge.

Shane's voice came out of the north wall. "*Thanks.*"

"What the hell are you doing?" Megan inquired. "Where are you?"

"Searching. There's a split in the rock. It's tight, but—sonuvabitch! I found something. I'll hand it to you. I'm wedged in here. Need my arms down to get out."

Megan followed Shane's voice toward the wall. She saw a hand holding a metal bar. Taking Shane's find, she brought it closer to the firelight. The piece was shaped something like a Christian cross, but the four arms were too short, too thin. "Wonder what this is?"

"It's a djed, symbol of Ptah. It's gold—and it's mine," a man's voice said from the darkness.

Megan knew that voice. "Where did you come from, Geb?"

"Give it to me."

"I don't *think* so." Megan shoved the djed into her waistband and bent her arms, making boxer fists she hoped looked convincing. "I know karate."

Geb stepped into the light. He was dressed in ordinary clothes and carried a long staff held across his body with two hands. "*I* know staff fighting. Been training at it all my life. How do you think we protect ourselves from piasas? Throw me the djed."

As Megan considered hurling it at Geb's face, Shane made his move. He squeezed through the crevice, but too slowly. Geb's staff whacked his arm. Shane screamed and sank to the floor.

The other end of Geb's stick whipped around to lie against Megan's neck. Geb stopped short of a blow, holding the staff like a knife against her throat, showing her what he could do. "Next time," he said, "I crack your skull. Now give me the damned djed."

Shane tackled Geb's knees, and Geb went down. Megan sprang out of the way as the two of them tussled on the floor. She searched for a long bone to club Geb. Shane held his own despite favoring the arm Geb smacked. By the time Megan found a usable bone, the tide had turned against Shane.

A movement at the corner of her eye caught Megan's attention. Paco sailed down from above to land on the ledge. Megan said, "Help Shane. He's the one getting pounded."

Paco strode in, snarled, and Geb looked up, his fist drawn back for another strike to Shane's mouth. Geb wasn't impressed by the small intruder. He said haughtily, "I'll get to you next."

Instead, Paco got to him. Seizing the upraised arm, Paco dragged Geb away from Shane, lifted him up by the hips, and held him over the fire embers. Geb shrieked, dancing on air to keep his sandled toes from roasting. "This is a bad guy, *chica*?" Paco asked Megan.

"Yes!"

"Can I have him?"

"Not for a snack, not now," Megan said. "The police want him."

"But I can play a little, no?" Paco walked to the rim of the ledge and let Geb fall. Geb howled as he skitter-skied down loose gravel, collided with a rock, flipped, and sat down hard. Paco bounded after him, but Geb wasn't easy prey. He picked himself up and dashed to the river, where he dove in. Seconds later, his head popped up and he shouted, "You'll never catch me. I'm half naiad," and he laughed before he disappeared under water.

Paco ran along the river's edge until Megan lost sight of him. Whether he caught Geb or not didn't matter. She had the djed. The Egyptians would be thrilled to get it back.

Shane groaned. Megan went to him, reaching out to help him stand. "How much are you hurt?" she asked, looking at his face. He'd have a shiner tomorrow.

"I'm okay," he lied, rubbing his shoulder. His voice sank. "But I messed up. I didn't stop him. I—"

"Tried. That's what matters." Megan pulled him along toward the cave's mouth. "Now, let's go! We gotta get out of here before Big Mama comes back."

"One sec." Shane shook free of Megan's grip, took a step, and leaned toward the floor. "There. I found the phone."

"And the djed," Megan reminded him. "Not bad work, Shane Ryan. Not bad at all."

CHAPTER TWENTY-SIX

Josh listened to Georgia chat on the phone with Benji. She sounded loving and strong, soothing. There wasn't a trace of the half-mad creature she'd been since they started their search of Fern Cliffe. She'd been on a rollercoaster of emotion for the last hour, chomping at the bit to reach the waterfall cave, raging when they reached it and found nothing, weeping on his shoulder until the call came in from Vanny asking for a giant's phone number. Then Georgia flared again, frustrated the short beam of the flashlight wouldn't let her run full out toward the truck. She tripped on roots, swore, and fretted her way back to the overlook, finally slumping in her seat, exhausted. But when Vanny's next call came and Georgia heard Benji's voice, the calm mother took over.

Until she clicked off. "Hurry! Hurry! They're taking him home. I have to be there."

Ruthanne, who'd stayed in the truck, demanded a full explanation of what happened. Georgia talked non-stop all the way into town. Josh ignored the speed limits, flooring the gas pedal, unable to speak. Throughout the whole ordeal, he'd been terrified they'd find Benji dead, that Georgia's world would collapse, and his, with it. It had been too hard to think about Benji himself, too hard to imagine his little life snuffed out. It was like picturing the world after nuclear war. When he tried to do it, his mind shut down.

He found his tongue once they reached Mike's garage. Making a sharp left turn into the lot, Josh jammed the shift into park, then told Georgia to move over and take the wheel. "I'll drive the Hummer to the river. I want to see for myself what went down."

"But why? Benji's safe," Georgia argued. "It's over."

"Nobody's found Tink."

"Let it go. I don't want anything happening to you. There are cops from everywhere looking for Tink. Tom—" She stopped. "Oh, I guess he'll be at the farm. He'll want to see Benji." Georgia's eyes narrowed. "Don't you?"

"I'll see him tomorrow. Give him a hug for me. Now, go," he said, shutting the truck's door. Georgia caught his sleeve, planted a quick kiss on his lips, and drove off.

Josh let himself into the station and pulled the Hummer key from the pegboard. Mike had put in the new windshield and replaced the back quarter panel today, crowing about finding replacement parts so easily. The Hummer looked good, and it handled well on the drive out of town.

Along Ryker, Josh passed half a dozen cop cars going the other way. A lone cruiser blocked the cliff road. Josh talked to the state trooper, but learned nothing. The guy wasn't Elviran.

"Where's Ed Brown?" Josh asked.

"Searching for the kidnapper." When Josh glanced toward the far bridge, spotting an Elviran cruiser, the trooper added, "Don't even think of going there. Road's closed, too."

Cops, Josh reflected as he took the Hummer up the hill and turned inland, *lost the knack for breaking rules*. He lumbered over the scrub on the plateau, glad the first section was fairly smooth. When his spine started to complain about the bouncing and jouncing, he'd reached the place where he'd fought the piasa. Ed Brown stood there, holding a flashlight aimed at the ground. Josh parked and went over to him.

"I should cite you for that off-road stunt," Ed noted.

"Are you going to?"

"Nah. Other fish to fry." He waved his flashlight toward a hole in the rock. "That there's the start of a tunnel. I sent a man down it. Couldn't make it myself—shoulders too broad."

"Shoulders," Josh said.

Ed sucked in his beer gut. "Yeah, so he got to the bird's nest, saw her there, and crawled out backwards. That Tink Withers is one crazy broad. It was plain stupid to put Benji in with a piasa. The whole thing makes no sense." He shook his head. "Anyways, the trail's grown cold. I'm heading back to town. Maybe somebody else turned up a lead on her whereabouts."

"I'll stay here a while. If I find anything, I'll give you a call."

"Suit yourself. We've gone over the area with a fine-toothed comb." Ed hiked toward his car, then stopped and turned toward Josh. "Don't drive on this ground anymore. It's fragile. Tearing it up isn't eco-friendly." Josh stared, astonished, at Ed's departing back. Moments later, the cruiser drove off.

Josh stood in the darkness, thinking about Tink. Ed was right to call her crazy, but stupid? No. She'd aced every class in school. She found ways to capture fairies and to turn werewolves human. What was her connection with piasas?

He remembered the conversation between Goreton's mayor and Tink on the steps of Village Hall. Mayor Marshal said, "An egg would be worth a fortune." Tink mentioned doing research, interviewing giants, writing a paper about the birds.

"Damn. Piasa eggs," he said aloud.

"So, you figured it out."

Josh spun around to find Tink coming through the tall grass behind him, holding her index finger pointed like a gun. Waggling her other hand, she said, "Crawl down the tunnel and bring me an egg. Just one. We wouldn't want to deplete an endangered species, would we?" She chuckled, but her eyes weren't laughing.

"And if I don't?"

"I'll root you, shove you into the tunnel, and seal the exit. The police cleared the area. They've no reason to come back tonight. So, unless you want to spend your last hours suffocating in a hole, you'll do what I say."

"Someone will spot the Hummer."

"I'll take it. The police are looking for my Jeep. Toss me the key—

and your phone." She widened her stance to sight down her finger.

Josh pulled his phone out, pitching it to her. He fished in his pocket for the key but flung it into the weeds.

"Asshole," Tink hissed, stomping on his phone. She didn't take the bait and go searching for the key. She shrugged. "I can bury a vehicle in brush. No big deal."

"What am I supposed to do about the piasa?" Josh asked, playing for time.

"Improvise. I planned to take the egg in the morning after the bird went hunting. You could wait it out, hoping she doesn't notice you, but you're bound to move and give yourself away. The space behind the nest is too small for you."

"But not for a child. Why'd you put Benji down there?"

"Thought he'd be a handy hostage. Stupid brat. I could have had a good life with Tom if it weren't for the bitch's kid."

"Why'd you try to kill Tom if you crave him so much?"

"I didn't. I wanted him sick so I could comfort him. Spent hours in that damned hospital getting him used to the new me—the *beautiful*, new me." Tink's eyes narrowed. "You're stalling. Move!" She slipped a vinyl cooler bag from her shoulder and threw it at him. "Use this for the egg."

Josh still hadn't come up with any way to escape. Maybe he'd think of something in the tunnel. He hung the bag around his neck, swung it over his back, and lay down to pull himself into the hole.

The tunnel wasn't too tight. For once, Josh appreciated his light build. He smirked at the image of Amazon Tink making the same journey until he thought of little Benji with her in the darkness. *Poor kid.*

And poor me. Josh approached the opening into the cave. He knew he'd arrived when he sensed warmer air, the smell of wood and *bird*. The piasa was way overdue for a bath. Josh peeked into the cave, found a wall of branches before him and smelly tail feathers overhead, pressed against the wall. The bird faced the cave's mouth.

Squeezing his head and chest into the space beneath the nest's rim, Josh pulled his knees through, remembering how his last encounter with the bird ended when Archie plucked a tail feather. Would the same thing work twice?

Josh never found out. His left knee knocked into the nest, shaking it. The bird stood up, her back claw raking Josh's scalp. His arms jerked up to protect his head and connected with bird rump, goosing her. She hopped forward, squawking her alarm.

With adrenaline-supercharged speed, Josh jumped to his feet, leaned over the nest, and groped for an egg. He found two, grabbed one, fumbled it, and then grabbed it again. The bird turned slowly in the tight confines of the space. Josh ducked; the beak missed him. He shoved his legs into the tunnel and wriggled backward.

The piasa roared, a deafening sound in the narrow tunnel. Josh didn't stop until he was sure she couldn't get to him. He paused to put the egg into the bag. Hands freed, he could crawl more easily, but what should he do when he reached the tunnel's end? If he gave Tink the egg, she'd seal him in, just for spite.

Then it came to him—a flash memory. Bully Tink on the playground. Her signature move...

He heard her snarl, "What's taking so long?"

Josh rubbed blood from the cut on his head over his face and hands. He smeared his shirt with it. As soon as his feet found the tunnel opening, he moaned, "I'm hurt. It's bad..." and then he shut his mouth, afraid he'd overact, and she'd catch him at it.

"Oh, for God's sake, Seldom. Get out here and give me the egg."

He heard her snort as he pulled free, clutched the bag, and then twisted to sprawl on his back. Through blood-caked lashes, he watched her come for him, eager for the egg. She couldn't root him until she had it. *Wait for it. Wait for it....*

Her foot swung back for the kick to his ribs as he'd known it would. On the playground, Tink never missed an opportunity to kick him when he was down. But he wasn't a scrawny kid anymore. A man's hands seized Tink's honking great foot, wrenching it sideways, making her screech and topple.

Josh flung himself at the Hummer and tossed the egg bag onto the passenger seat. He yanked the spare key from the visor and shoved it into the ignition, jamming the shift into gear as his foot stomped on the gas. He'd made it!

Not quite. His shirt started to squirm, the neckline sprouting tendrils that snaked around his throat. He needed to tear them away, but he had to watch the ground. If he broke an axle in a pothole or smashed the driveshaft against a rock, he was done.

By the time he reached the road, the stems were choking him—and so was rage. He was *sick* of plants, Tink and fear! Slowing to stab the A/C button and whip the dial to max cool, he aimed the vents at his face. As the arctic blizzard hit, he felt the tension on his throat give way. Plants wilted in the cold. The vent fans were blasting the seat beside him, too, and Josh thought about the egg. Cold might hurt the chick inside, so he stuffed the bag into the Hummer's huge armrest bin.

Josh jerked his head around, spotting Tink's Jeep wrestling its way out of tall grass. He started to pull the Hummer's wheel around to ram her, but he stopped himself. He didn't need to chase Tink—she'd chase him. He had the egg.

Leading her to Elvira wouldn't work. Tink would know his plan. But in open country, she might think she could root him, force him to pull over or be strangled by her damned plants.

Josh had a different idea. He headed for the highway north to Goreton with Tink's lighter Jeep gaining on him until the Hummer reached cruising speed and its V8 outpaced her Straight-6.

Approaching the bridge across Wolf Creek, Josh felt his stomach twist, but he told himself, *Sometimes a man's gotta do what a man's gotta do.* He was betting a woman with a "beautiful, new" face wouldn't want to eat three and half tons of steel.

Slamming on the brakes, Josh felt the ABS kick in, and fought it, clamping down on the wheel, sending the Hummer into a drift. He caught a glimpse of Tink's Jeep veering left toward the river before his rear end clipped the bridge and the Hummer's back wheels swung over the embankment, spinning on air, until a tire snagged against pavement, snapping the nose around. Josh's head smacked the side window. Dazed, he felt, rather than saw, the front end drop, and the Hummer roll downhill. For a second there was nothing, then branches slapped windows, mud sucked at tires, and a giant splash of river water went up when the right front wheel sank in. Josh's neck whipped forward. The seatbelt bit his chest. He gasped for breath.

Josh sat stunned when Tink appeared at his window. With a smile, she held a miniature sword tip to his throat. Head swaying left and right, she rebuked him like a child. "Joshie Seldom —tsk, tsk. You are such a *loser*. You can't even pull off a simple drift. There's barely a scratch on my Jeep. How could you think you were a match for me?"

"No one's a match for you, Tink," Josh muttered. He rejected the idea of pushing away the sword faster than she could impale his throat. His arms were shaky, his fingers numb. He wasn't ready.

"Flattery, Seldom?"

"Not what I meant. You're a head case—always were, always will be. You'll never change."

"Now there, you're wrong. I'm going to be a *rich* head case, while you, pathetic worm, will spend your life in the muck of Elvira, among all those dirty, little minds, thrilled to have Tom's leavings." Tink sighed. "It's almost a shame to force such a life on you, almost a favor to end the pointlessness—and I owe you one for hurting me by the cliff."

Josh felt the sword prick his skin. To distract Tink, he asked, "Is that why you killed the fairies—to do them a favor?"

"No! I *hate* fairies. They're like cockroaches; they should all be exterminated."

"I don't understand," Josh said, flexing his fingers in the deep shadows by his knees. "What did fairies ever do to you?"

"Chased off my father, for one. When he told my mother, 'It's me or the fairies,' she chose the stupid *fairies*. I have a fairy name, a fairy nickname. Fairy books, fairy bedroom, fairy clothes—fairy *underwear*. It's disgusting," Tink seethed. "Revolting." She tossed her head.

"Anyway, I'm bored with you. Hand over the egg."

He started to unlatch his seatbelt. Tink laid the edge of the blade across his jugular. "Uh uh-uh," she warned.

"I put the egg on the other seat. I can't reach it with my belt on."

Tink peered into the Hummer's cab. "There's nothing on the seat."

"It must have been thrown in back," Josh lied, "when I was slamming around on the road. Check it out."

"*You* check it out. I won't let you trap me. Get out and open the rear doors. Don't try anything because I take the sword away. I can still root you."

Josh cut the engine and extracted himself from the driver's seat, taking his time, testing his muscles. They were steady now. He was ready. Tink stood behind him.

He back-elbowed her ribs, swiveling to follow up with a left hook. That was a mistake. Body bent over, Tink's head was down. Instead of striking her windpipe, all Josh's fist met was her neck, but he'd staggered her, pushed her into the Hummer's side. He went for an uppercut.

Tink went for his groin. Twisting her hips, Tink's shin came up between his legs and connected. She didn't drop him, but tears sprang to his eyes and Tink gained the time it took to raise her hand and point her finger. "I have had ENOUGH of you!" she seethed. "You're dead."

For a second, Josh thought she'd moved him—lifted him into the willow shrubs, but instead, stems came up around him, shooting out of the ground to pen him in. He could barely see the Hummer, and still more pencil-sized sticks were rising, hardening into leafy branches higher than his head, thickening, and filling the gaps. Arms pinned to his sides, Josh felt pressure all around his body as the stems squeezed together. They closed over his face, flattening his nose, cutting off his air, burying him in a living coffin.

He would die here—in the dark, alone. As he sucked in a desperate breath, he remembered…

"I'm afraid of the dark," six-year-old Joshie confessed to his fairy after telling Sedge about a nightmare. "I'm afraid to be alone in the dark."

"Ye're never alone, laddie, when fairies are about. If ye're set upon, ye've only to make the Call. Here, now, I'll show ye again what's to be done."

Adult Josh made the Call, a silent summons from the depth of his heart.

A babble of voices—young and old, male and female—flooded his brain. He couldn't understand the words, but the meaning was clear: *We're coming.*

Josh bit into the branches, gnawing until his breath gave out, but he made enough room for his mouth and chin. He let his weight sag, and his nose slipped into the space. Josh took in air, precious air, and waited.

Tink's voice cried, "What do you want?"

"Ye've a man trapped in yon shrubbery," said a female fairy voice. "We'll have him. Give him up or fight. Ye'll not best us all."

Josh shouted. His voice didn't penetrate the willow shroud.

"I'd never fight you. I'm Silverbelle Withers. My mother's a great friend of yours. She has the Gift, of course. So do I."

A male voice said slowly, "Ye've a fairy blade in yer hand."

"I found this by the road over there," Tink lied silkily. "Does it belong to one of you?"

"It be Reed's!" cried the female. There was a rustling of wings and clatter of metal.

"Is he here?"

"Our Reed is dead, slain by a wolf," the female spat out.

"How sad. You'll want his sword. You must have it."

After a pause, the warrior asked, "And what of the man ye've caged?"

"Seldom? Well," Tink said in a low, confidential tone, "he got pushy with me. Wouldn't take no for an answer. First, he asked me to meet him by the river, then he wouldn't let me leave. He forced me off the road. I had to defend myself."

Josh heard a general murmur of agreement before Tink finished with, "Please don't let him follow me. Keep him here until I drive away?"

"Aye, that we will, lass," the female fairy agreed. "He'll not be troublin' ye more this night."

"I'm very grateful," Tink's voice said humbly. "Thank you."

Josh could hear the fairies circling his willowy prison, but they did nothing to free him until the sound of Tink's Jeep faded in the distance. By the time they dissolved the willows, he could only groan and tell them, "Tink Withers tricked you. She killed Reed, but she made it look like a wolf did. Now you've let her go."

"Lies," a Green warrior said.

"Truth. The authorities in Elvira found Reed's wing at her home. Tink hid his sword in her car. *Look* at it. It's clean. It wasn't lying on the ground all these days since Reed's death."

A blonde Josh recognized as Arrowroot from Mrs. Withers' drawing studied the sword in her hand. "This blade has seen neither rain nor dew. 'Twas the woman who lied."

"After her!" a warrior shouted, and all the fairies except Arrowroot flew off. She said, "I be needin' to know why my Reed met his end. What injury did he do the woman?"

"None. Her mind," Josh said, tapping his temple, "isn't right. She's screwed up—insane. I'm sorry for your loss."

"With blade and wing found, Reed will no longer wander the path of lost spirits, comfortless and alone. For that," said Arrowroot, "I thank ye."

"Back at ya. I'd have been done for if you Greens hadn't rescued me from Tink's trap."

"'Tis the least we could do for a man with the Gift," said Arrowroot. "How is't we don't know ye? Art from afar?"

"Nope. Elvira born and bred. I'm just a late bloomer, I guess."

"An' one who's seen hard use this day. Here," she said, pointing to his head, "is a troublesome wound. Shall I heal ye?"

"Please." When the cool hand touched his scalp, Josh felt tingling, either from the healing or from staring at a really great body, even if it was tiny.

"There. Ye're hale once more." Arrowroot turned toward the bridge, but reversed herself and hovered before him. "I'll be tellin' the folk in Elvira ye're here so they can help ye make fer home," she said before she flew away.

As it turned out, Josh didn't need a lift back to Elvira. He coaxed the Hummer from the river and climbed to the road by the time Archie arrived. Archie parked, took a long look around him, and walked over to lean into Josh's passenger window saying, "Yo. You're a mess. The Hummer's a mess. The bridge is a mess."

"I've kept busy."

"So I see. I still don't understand why Tink hung around when she should have cleared out."

"She wanted the piasa egg." As Archie tilted his head curiously, Josh remembered no one else knew about the egg. "Unless Tink found it, there's a piasa egg in the armrest box."

"I'll check." Archie climbed into the passenger seat, opened the bin and squawked. His wasn't the only squawk. Josh watched a chick hop out onto Archie's lap. Its *cheep* sounded like a question.

"No!" he yelled, recoiling. He held the chick at arm's length, telling Josh, "Piasas imprint on the first thing they see. This one thinks I'm its mother."

Josh grinned. Archie scowled. He peered into the mini-piasa's enormous, woeful eyes. "Aw, hell." Then he breathed, "Aw, hell..." in a resigned whisper when the chick flopped onto his chest and lay its sleepy head against his neck.

CHAPTER TWENTY-SEVEN

An anxious group waited by Fern Cliffe's overlook at twilight on Thursday evening. The mood of somber expectation kept voices low. No one knew what was coming; no Elviran had ever been invited to a fairy funeral before, and there'd be two tonight, for Sedge and for Reed.

Mayor Stedwell said to Josh, "After Tom found Sedge's belongings in the Withers' garage, I brought the items here and turned them over to Moss, telling her we'd identified the murderer but Miss Withers escaped. Moss took the news well, I thought.

"So, I was surprised when Reds and Greens showed up at Village Hall yesterday. I expected a fight, but warriors of both clans were only escorting Moss and a Green called Arrowroot. Arrowroot was Reed's mate, I learned. She wanted his remains and personal items. Then they invited me to the funerals and told me to bring 'elders, and any other long legs who should come.' I said yes, of course. Now, I'm wondering if I misunderstood. We've been here at least forty-five minutes."

"Fairies don't stress about time the way we do," Josh told him, "and their day starts at sundown. They should be along soon." As Stedwell returned to where his wife talked with Mayor Marshal and Ed Brown, Josh looked over the rest of the crowd. The Watis and the Seagrams were quietly contemplating the valley below. Mrs. Withers, positioned slightly apart from the couples, seemed stiff and uncomfortable, clearly uncertain of whether or not she was welcome until Mrs. Wati went to stand by her, pointing out something in the distance that made them both smile.

It was funny to watch Mr. Benton trying to talk with the two giants in attendance. The giants resembled the Thoon brothers and were probably their parents. The old man stood tall as he could despite his rheumatism while the giantess was bent nearly in half. Near them, Mr. Deeble looked at his feet, studying the fairy boots he said he'd worn so he could make the trek to the funeral site.

"Too bad Archie couldn't be here," Josh remarked.

"Well, he's a mother now," Georgia said with a wry smile. "Big responsibility. I'm glad Bobbi's giving him a hand with the chick. Nice of her to let him set up the coop in her backyard."

"*I'm* glad he has an excuse to spend most of his time at her house," Josh said, putting his arm around Georgia's shoulders to give her a little squeeze. "More privacy for us at the loft." Feeling tension in her shoulders, he looked closely at her face. "You all right?"

"Mmm," she said with a tight-lipped smile. "I'm worried about Benji. I keep thinking Tink will try something else."

"Tink's long gone, and besides, Benji has the best protection Elvira can offer. Mrs. Withers taught him the countercharm to rooting today, remember? And Tom's doing a stake-out at your mother's house, with Anton as backup. Tink wouldn't stand a chance."

Georgia nodded. "That is reassuring. I suppose I should be more trusting, but it's hard, you know?"

Josh hugged her again. "Benji will be safe."

"I expected Ruthanne to be here. She's always curious about things, and she did so much to find out what happened to the fairies."

"She's with Anton, supposedly using her psychic abilities to scan for Tink, though that didn't work the other night. I'm guessing Ruthanne's hoping she's got a shot at Anton with his ladies are gone."

"Heartless hussy," Georgia said lightly.

"Big-headed, heartless hussy," Josh added. "I mean compared to those gorgeous women, Ruthanne's chopped liver."

"I dunno…. She's nothing if not persistent, and Anton seems to like her. Anyway, I'm grateful she's helping to protect Benji."

"Yeah." Josh jerked his chin toward Vanny and Megan, who chatted with Paco and Luca, representatives of the vampires. Near them stood

Shane, dark shiner a contrast to the bright, new wolf key dangling from his shirt pocket. "The girls look cheerful."

"After Megan returned their treasure, the Egyptians were forced into giving her the job she wanted at the gift shop. She's happy about that. Vanny...she's like Dad. Nothing keeps her down too long." Georgia sighed. "I can't believe Ruthanne talked with my father. I miss him so much. Wish I could have been there."

"He said you, um..." Josh hesitated. Carl Beckett said Georgia loved him. He was dying to know the truth, but terrified to ask.

"Oh, look! The fairies are here." Georgia pointed toward the cliff's edge, where a crimson glow appeared along with the sunset. A troop of fairies, all haloed in red light, flew into view, circled the humans, beckoned, and then swirled away to the west.

Stedwell said, "It appears they want us to follow them. Everyone have flashlights?"

Everyone but the vampires did. They smirked at each other; they didn't need no stinking flashlights. Stedwell led off. When he passed the still-unused fairy tour gift shop, he cast a wistful glance at it but continued along the path illuminated at intervals by fairies.

Josh expected a storm of mosquitoes, but there were none. Only fireflies flickered along the cliff face, never crossing the path or escaping to the trees. He suspected they were confined by magic.

As he trudged along with Georgia, Josh walked slowly, purposely lagging behind the rest of the party. He wanted to get back to their unfinished conversation. When he thought they were far enough away from the others, he told her, "So, your father said I should take good care of you, and he also said—"

"I know what he said," Georgia cut in. "Ruthanne told me."

"Did he get it right?" Josh ventured.

"He always believed a woman couldn't be happy without a man."

"That's not an answer." Josh stopped to face Georgia.

"Look, when you started talking about Cissy...."

Josh rolled his eyes. "You're *not* going there again, are you?"

"No." Georgia dipped her head, muttering, "I overreacted, and I'm sorry." She looked up, an earnest expression on her face. "But I can't help thinking you're feeling restless, and maybe I'm becoming too dependent on you—gotten used to having you around. The other day, I was thinking about Christmas presents for Benji, and I started wondering what I should get you."

"What's wrong with presents?"

"It's the idea we'll still be together by then."

Confused, Josh's brow furrowed. "After our dinner at the Swan, you liked the idea. You said, 'I think I'll keep you a while longer.' "

"I know. That was probably a mistake."

Josh put down his flashlight and took Georgia's shoulders in hand. "Are you breaking up with me?"

She shook her head but didn't look at him. "I just believe we...we need more space."

Josh let go of her. "Space usually means there's someone else in the picture."

"Not this time, well, not in the way you mean. It might be better for you to be with someone who has less baggage."

Josh lifted her chin with a finger. "If you're talking about Benji, you're way off base. He's smart, brave, funny, and if Elvira had a contest for cute kids, he'd mop the floor with the other contestants."

Georgia smiled. "He is rather special."

"Like his ma. Listen, babe, back in high school, I was a dumbass. I'm still a dumbass most of the time, but I know one thing: I want you. I'm so damned proud to be in your life and Benji's. Forget buying me stuff for Christmas. You two are the best presents I could ever have."

Josh knew if he kissed her the way he wanted to kiss her, she'd cry. Then she'd get embarrassed because she'd have to explain to the others why her face was red and blotchy. So he wrapped an arm around her, kissed the top of her head and said, "We'll talk about this more if you want, but later, all right?"

"Yes." Swiping at her eyes, Georgia sniffled, then bent to retrieve

Josh's flashlight before tucking back under his arm.

Something moved in the trees. Josh gripped the flashlight and aimed it into the forest.

"What?"

"Nothing." Josh released her shoulder and took her hand. "Looks like we lost the fairy guides. Let's see if we can spot one."

They found a fairy waiting where the path turned away from the rocks. The warrior waved them toward the funeral party assembled on the east bank of Willow River where it merged with the two parts of Wolf Creek. Overhead, Red fairies flew a circle above the intersection of the three streams. To the south lay the western tip of the wolves' island.

"Wait a minute," Josh objected. "This is the border between Red and Green territory, miles away from the overlook, but we've only been walking a few minutes, and we should have crossed the highway."

"I guess fairy paths don't conform to our ideas of distance. Why are there rock piles on both sides of the river?"

Moss hovered by Stedwell's ear, telling him something. He turned to the others, saying, "We're each to put a stone on the mounds, which Moss calls 'cairns'. They're memorials. The materials for this one are there." He pointed to a loose heap of large, smooth river stones. Selecting one, Stedwell stepped up to the cairn, closing his eyes for a moment before he placed his offering near the top. "For Sedge," he said, "the warrior." One by one, each person followed suit.

Josh went last, and took the longest time to say goodbye. "You saved my life, old friend," he whispered. "You never gave up trying to teach me fairy magic when I was a kid, and you were right: I can do some. I hope you find everything you want in the Otherworld. Look in on Elvira once in a while, okay? We'll miss you."

When all the stones for Sedge were laid, the Red fairies flew to perches in the trees, and the Greens, who'd been waiting there, took to the air. Arrowroot pointed her finger at each bank in turn. Morning glory vines spilling down the west bank lifted, stretched, thickened and spanned the gap, forming a bridge.

Stedwell went for it. Reaching a tentative foot toward the vine bridge, he took a deep breath, and then put weight on the foot. He stepped forward, nodded, and began to turn his body toward the crowd. His hip stopped midway through the action. Looking down, he felt around with his hands. Surprise on his face, he announced, "There are invisible handrails here. I can't see them, but I can feel them. The footing's fine. Don't be afraid."

Encouraged, the humans formed a line, but the giants shook their heads. "We'll meet you on the other side," the man said, and he reached for the woman's hand. Together, they climbed down the bank to wade the river, which came up only to mid-calf on them.

When Mr. Benton's turn at the bridge came, he looked stricken. "I don't think I can do this."

"I'll help." Mrs. Withers placed her hands on his waist. "Take it one step at a time. There's no rush."

The old man made it across with Mrs. Withers' assistance, and then Megan strode forward. From the center of the bridge, she called up to Arrowroot, "Luca over there…" she pointed toward the young vampire, "can't cross moving water. Please don't be offended. He's asked me to put a stone for him on the cairn." When Arrowroot nodded, Megan moved on.

Georgia had no trouble with the bridge, her swaying hips reminding Josh again of her dancing. And that reminded him of other things she did so well. Determined to get his mind back on track, he crossed the bridge without thinking about it.

Reed's cairn rose as everyone placed one stone—or two, if you counted Megan's contribution. Stedwell stepped forward, calling to Arrowroot, "Would it be appropriate for me to say a few words for both fairies?"

Arrowroot must have known about human politicians and speeches, or maybe fairies were just as long-winded when they had an audience, but she rejected Stedwell's offer with a shake of her head and a smile. Shooing the other Greens back to the trees, Arrowroot landed on the bridge's invisible handrail and waited until a Green female brought her a basket made of flowers. From the other bank, Moss flew in with a copper cup. The fairy women looked at each other, then overturned their urns to pour ashes into the river, releasing the empty vessels afterward.

Two young warriors joined the women on the bridge. The Green held Reed's armor and sword; the Red, Sedge's chain maille shirt and spear. The warriors dropped the dead fairies' possessions into the river.

Georgia frowned. "Someone could step on those weapons."

"No, they'll seek their owners," Mrs. Withers assured her. "They'll never be found in this world."

A cheer rose up from the fairies, who took to the air and flew in two lines toward the bridge. When Reds met Greens, the lines curved. Arrowroot, Moss and the warriors joined in, forming the third arm of a spiral that soared ever higher until it disappeared beyond the trees.

After moments of silence Stedwell said, "I guess the ceremony's over. We should leave." He swept an arm toward the bridge.

Georgia and Josh found themselves in line behind Shane. Josh said, "So you got into the wolves after all."

"I'm provisional," Shane admitted. "This time it's for real. Tom said I'd have a whole year's probation, but if I kept my nose clean, I'd be in."

"Congrats," said Josh.

"Are you sure you want to be a wolf?" Georgia asked. "There are a lot of problems involved."

"It's what I want for now," Shane told her. "We'll see how it goes. In the meantime, I'm supposed to work with the other wolves—in human form, of course—to plant rowan trees around the Green village. That's the deal we cut with the fairies so we could keep the wolf compound."

"How'd you learn about rowans?" Josh asked.

"A Bobbi Miller posted a comment on Elvira's website. Pretty smart chick, whoever she is."

"We'll tell her you said so," Georgia put in, and then it was Shane's turn for the bridge.

Watching Shane, Stedwell observed, "His hair's dark." The mayor surveyed the others standing on the opposite bank, and grinned. "Everyone's back to normal. Every*thing's* back to normal." Stedwell exhaled a deep sigh.

"You think so?" Josh watched Georgia make her way across the river.

"No doubt about it. We've sorted out the problems—and I'm grateful, very grateful for your help with all this, Josh. I can't thank you enough." Stedwell grasped his hand. "But now we've been through our shakedown cruise, it'll be smooth sailing. We're all set for a good tourist season." With a jaunty step, Stedwell moved toward the waiting crowd.

Josh smiled. He crossed the fairy bridge hastily because the vines were starting to unravel. He didn't tell Stedwell about the eyes he'd seen from the forest path—big ones, golden, framed by leaves. In time, Stedwell would learn no one could be certain of anything about Elvira.

Elvira had a mind of her own.

ABOUT THE AUTHOR

"Reality can be beaten with enough imagination."—Mark Twain

Sanna Hines never got the memo requiring imagination to end with childhood. She kept exploring astonishing worlds, discovering Elvira during some dark days in her life. Sanna found enjoyment and laughter in that place, and hopes you did, too.

Like her vampire characters, she knows martial arts, having earned two black belts in Tae Kwon Do. Sanna and her family live in Maine.

Sanna Hines' Worlds http://sannahines.wixsite.com/sanna-hines-worlds
Another World https://sannahines.wordpress.com/
Amazon https://www.amazon.com/Sanna-Hines/e/B011HCBJPE
Facebook https://www.facebook.com/sanna.hines.author
Goodreads
https://www.goodreads.com/author/show/14050716.Sanna_Hines
Twitter @sannahines1

All reviews are greatly appreciated.

ALSO BY SANNA HINES

STEALTH MOVES
Young Adult Thriller

"I love a good suspenseful book with twists, turns, and surprise conclusions. The title alone would draw any mystery lover to read this psychologically chilling tale."—*Readers Review Room, Gold Bookworm Award*

Three daring, daylight kidnappings stun Boston. When Beacon Hill preppie Liv Smallwood sees her extraordinary classmate taken, she launches a campaign to draw all of Boston into the search. Two obstacles stand in her way: bodyguard and kidnapper. Holly Glasscock wins the role of Liv's bodyguard with bold moves of her own. She'll need wit, courage, and heart to keep Liv from the man who calls himself "Stealth," a man tormented by the death of his twin brother, Brandon. One person with two souls, Stealth will do anything to appease Brandon, even risk a final, desperate capture.

Shining Ones: Legacy of the Sidhe
Irish Fantasy Adventure

"An entertaining, well-crafted story with unusually complex and entrancing characters."—Kirkus *Reviews*

Police officer Tessa Holly can change her body any way she chooses. She will never grow sick or old. Born a descendant of Ireland's magical *Tuatha dé Danann*, Tessa expects to follow her clan's Rules in all things. But when her brother and a human girl are seized by enemies, the Rules don't help. To rescue the captives, Tessa must rely on a man no one trusts as her guide through cairns, castles and cathedrals of Ireland and Britain in search of her people's greatest treasures.